I0629234

PERCHANCE

Borgo Press Books by MICHAEL KURLAND

Perchance: A Tale of the Paraverse
The Princes of Earth: A Science Fiction Novel
A Study in Sorcery: A Lord Darcy Novel
Ten Little Wizards: A Lord Darcy Novel
The Trials of Quintilian: Three Stories of Rome's Greatest Detective
The Unicorn Girl: An Entertainment
Victorian Villainy: A Collection of Moriarty Stories

PERCHANCE

A TALE OF THE PARAVERSE

MICHAEL KURLAND

THE BORGO PRESS

MMXII

PERCHANCE

Copyright © 1988, 2012 by Michael Kurland

FIRST BORGO PRESS EDITION

Published by Wildside Press LLC

www.wildsidebooks.com

DEDICATION

For Linda...

CONTENTS

PROLOGUE

The Princess of the Golden Orb paused at the edge of the clearing. Panting for breath, she crouched under the fallen statue of an antique hero and peered fearfully up at the pink-streaked yellow sky. Sharp-eyed calla birds circled somewhere above; she sensed the malignant touch of their aura. Behind her croaked the six-legged scouts of the Nimber Horde as they crashed through the forest following her scent. They drew ever nearer.

She had one slim chance. Before her in the clearing stood the long-unused temple consecrated to Loth, God of Visions, God of Vengeance, God of Last Resorts. Once carefully tended by dozens of acolytes as an act of holy devotion, the temple, the clearing, and all that had been the work of humans in and about it were long fallen into disuse and decay. She must cross the overgrown clearing to the ancient alabaster temple and gain access through the long-unused priestess door. If she could remember the words of power. If the door had not been permanently frozen shut by the dead hand of time. And she must act before she was attacked from either above or behind by the minions of those who would displace the few remaining humans from all that had been theirs.

Long moments passed.

Despite the danger, despite the waves of fear that coursed through her body, leaving her weak and nauseated, she felt a curious sense of detachment from the awful scene. It was as though part of her were somewhere else, watching with interest as she performed this intricate ballet of fear and death.

She crawled cautiously around the massive bronze thighs of the fallen god and then, gathering what reremained of her flimsy skirts about her, raced toward the temple.

From above came the high-pitched shreee of a calla bird, and then another, and a third, as they prepared to dive. She looked behind her, and saw the first of the six-legged Nimber scouts reach the clearing. There was no turning back. She ran on.

The flapping of great leather wings sounded overhead, drawing closer. Talons raked across her back. She screamed.

Still screaming, she woke.

PART ONE
WHAT DREAMS MAY COME

CHAPTER ONE

The morning commuter from Philadelphia crossed the Hudson a scant five hundred feet above the Schuylkill Palisades. Like an airborne chain of silver sausage links, the segmented craft bobbled along, slowly losing altitude as it approached its mooring on the west side of Manhattan's Great Central Park.

Delbit Quint stared out the tiny porthole of the third-rater cabin, watching the ground rise up to meet the air-train. As he watched, the mooring lines were cast out, and the ground crew rushed to catch them and secure them to the landing winches. The engines stopped, and a new silence enveloped the cabin. Slowly the winchmen reeled the lines in, and the string of silver balloons was made fast to the earth.

A double honk sounded over the loudspeaker. "Attention third-rater passengers! If you are detraining in New York, please gather your belongings and prepare to exit the rear door of your cabin," came the flat, nasal voice. "You will have ten minutes. Exiting the forward door will not be permitted."

Delbit put on his jacket and took his brown-paper-wrapped bundle of clothes from the overhead. Quietly he joined the line of passengers threading their way toward the rear of the long, skinny left aisle of the great, fat third-rater cabin.

Delbit followed the crowd of passengers across the hard-packed dirt field to the large third-rater exit gate at the far end. The second-raters headed toward their own gate. Private carriages met the first-raters, pulling up to the egress as they detrained.

Outside the third-rater gate, among a small group of greeters, stood a tall, bewhiskered man in a brown dress suit with a gold insignia on the breast pocket. In the man's left hand, held before him like an amulet, was a small, discreetly lettered paper sign reading Delbit Quint.

Delbit surrendered his ticket at the gate and walked over to the man. "Sir?" he said, taking his cap off. "I'm Delbit Quint."

"Don't call me sir," the man said sharply, folding the sign in quarters and putting it in his pocket. "I'm no better than yourself. Quint, eh? Is that all of your luggage? Good, then come along."

The man led Delbit across the road to a high-bodied, angular electric touring landau with a chauffeur in a costume like his own. He held the rear door open for Delbit, who looked the vehicle over curiously before he entered. It was a highly polished deep red color with gleaming brass fittings, fully the equal in elegance to any that had come for the first-rate passengers. Delbit was impressed. The device on the door panel matched the insignia on the man's coat: a pair of birds facing each other and flying upward. Each bird held something in its beak, the one on the left a pen, the one on the right a lightning bolt, pen and bolt crossing each the other in the center of the design. Around the X thus formed were the letters F C A E B, and underneath was the motto, *Learn Ye Inner Truth & Bee Free.* The man slammed Delbit's door and walked around to the other side of the landau, pausing briefly to speak to the driver. He got in the rear next to Delbit and slammed his own door. The electric started its silent way.

"Where are we going?" Delbit asked.

"To the clinic," the man told him.

"What clinic?"

"The Faineworth Clinic."

"What sort of clinic is it?"

The man twisted in his seat to look at Delbit. "Don't you know what you're doing here?"

"No, sir," Delbit told him. "I surely do not."

"I should think," the man told him seriously, "that before becoming involved in an endeavor of this nature, you would ascertain what it is that you're going to be required to do. Well, no matter, you'll know soon enough. And don't call me sir. My name is Bantersea Dobbins, and I am called simply Dobbins."

"My master sent me," Delbit told him. "Master Fessily Branterberger of the Branterberger Top-Lance Gentlemen's and Ladies' Quality Shoe Works. He didn't bother telling me why I was wanted. I don't even know whether I've been loaned, sold, or traded."

"You're indentured?"

"I'm an articled apprentice."

"Comes to the same thing," Dobbins told him. "I may be a servant under the bond, but on my off-times I'm my own man, free to come and go as I choose after reasonable hours; free to give notice if I have cause. I tell you, young Quint, it makes all the difference."

"I'm sure it does," Delbit agreed. "You work for the clinic?"

"I am on the household staff of Dr. Faineworth himself," Dobbins said. "I am his personal man. Most of my duties involve serving him at the clinic in a professional capacity." He tapped himself on the chest and added, "But I sleep in the house."

"I see," Delbit said. Status among upper-level servants was as important as status among the gentry, and sleeping in the house was, for a manservant, high status. The maidservants, of course, all slept in the house, under the watchful eye of the chief housekeeper. If you were an articled apprentice or an indentured servant, it didn't matter where you slept; you had no status.

The electric turned uptown on Broadway and bounced its way north. Delbit pulled aside the curtain and stared out the window at the passing shops. It looked much like Philadelphia except that the buildings averaged a bit taller, some as high as nine stories, and the shops seemed more open to the street than he was used to, and many of the shop signs were not in English.

"Dobbins, what language is that?" Delbit asked, pointing to the blue-and-gold sign swinging above a jewelry store.

Dobbins leaned forward and looked out. "I believe it's Flemish," he said. "We have a big Flemish and Frisian colony here on the West Side. Good citizens, if a bit clannish. Came over after the Walloon Uprisings."

"All the signs are in English in Philadelphia," Delbit said.

"Of course they are," Dobbins told him. "Pennsylvania Commonwealth has restricted immigration. New York State has unrestricted European immigration. Not many Chinamen make it here, but a lot of Flems and Fresses and Armenians and Jews and Hellenes. We got a bunch of Swedes after the Danish occupation, but most of them settled in Boston. All good citizens, for the most part. And we've got the best restaurants in the Constitutionally Confederated States right here in New York. Those Flems really know what to do with a side of beef."

Delbit looked at Dobbins with new interest. A servant who knows about such things, a servant who could afford to eat out, was a superior creature indeed, in Delbit's view. Working for this Dr. Faineworth might prove to be a pleasant and interesting experience. Delbit wondered again what was in store for him. So far in his nineteen years, the only interesting experiences had proved painful.

The Faineworth Clinic was a three-story mostly Georgian building on a couple of acres of land on the east side of Broadway right above 110th Street. It had been added to from time to time, with each of the additions zigzagging off in one direction or another from the main building. Each segment had been treated as a fresh architectural challenge, independent of whatever it abutted. The building appeared to be at war with itself. In the front yard, to the right of the drive, was a large white wooden sign. The emblem on the landau door was duplicated on the sign, with below it the words:

THE FAINEWORTH CLINIC
FOR THE AID AND EXAMINATION
OF THE BEWILDERED
LEARN YE INNER TRUTH & BEE FREE.

The electric pulled around the drive past the front doors and made a sharp right into a narrow brick half-oval tunnel that went through the building. "We enter the back," Dobbins explained.

"Of course," Delbit agreed.

Dobbins brought Delbit in through the back door, which entered on the institution's kitchens, and led him through a series of corridors and passages toward the front. The place was as ornate and eclectic on the inside as the outside. Dark wood paneling gave way to antiseptic painted plaster, which abruptly changed to figured wallpaper. Carpeted hallways intersected tiled lobbies and parquet vestibules. An occasional stripe of colored paint crossed the walls vertically or diagonally for no apparent reason. Delbit examined this passing scene with interest, and concluded that it was designed to create the bewildered people that the clinic then examined.

"Wait here," Dobbins said, taking Delbit through a light-colored door in the painted plaster section of hallway and into what looked like the anteroom to a doctor's office.

Delbit sat himself on the red couch which took up the left-hand wall and waited. After about ten minutes the inner door opened and he was called in. As he had suspected, the inner room was a doctor's office, with a large desk in the middle of the floor, two massive cabinets full of obscure medical instruments looming behind the desk, and a variety of large naturalistic paintings covering the walls. The floor was covered with a dark red carpet which ended precisely a hand's-breadth away from the wall in all directions, revealing six inches of highly polished wood. The man sitting at the desk, who Delbit assumed must be the doctor, nodded and smiled. He was tall and beanpole-thin, and had a large rounded nose and small pointed ears. His teeth also appeared to be pointed. "So this is Delbit Quint," he said, leaning back in his massive wooden chair and smiling a broad smile. "A pleasure, it is."

"Delbit, this is Dr. Faineworth," Dobbins said, gesturing him forward to the front of the desk.

"A pleasure to see you, lad," Dr. Faineworth told him, his

voice thin and reedy. "You are, so to speak, just what the doctor ordered." He chuckled. "I suppose you're wondering just what you're doing here."

Delbit allowed himself a slight smile. "I am a bit bewildered, yes, sir."

"Ah! The lad has a sense of humor. We should have guessed." The doctor leaned forward. "Sit down, Delbit, lad, and let me explain."

Dobbins brought over a straightback chair and placed it in front of the desk, and Delbit sat.

Dr. Faineworth pulled a piece of light blue paper from a stack to his right and placed it below his nose. "These are your Articles of Apprenticeship," he told Delbit, peering down at the paper as though it were a new species of bug. "They give the master the right to sell you, if he so chooses, as you know. Well, I have bought you. You will be delighted to know, I assume, that you are no longer apprenticed to a master shoemaker, but to a medical doctor. I can promise you that you will find it different. More exacting, more demanding, longer hours, but more rewarding, if you do your job well. And more painful, much more painful, if you do not. But, of course, we all assume that you will. Do you understand?"

The doctor paused and stared expectantly at Delbit, waiting for his reaction. Delbit was surprised to discover that he didn't have one. Two days ago he had been peacefully, if not happily, sweeping the floor of a steam-operated shoe factory in Philadelphia; yesterday Master Branterberger had told him he'd be going to New York City; and now he found out that he'd been sold. He would probably have a reaction soon, but at the moment he merely felt as if someone had kicked him in the gut.

"You have five years and two months left under the articles, is that right?" Dr. Faineworth asked, after waiting a minute for Delbit to speak.

"That is so," Delbit said.

"Your father sold you into apprenticeship? I assume things weren't going well with him?"

"My stepfather," Delbit explained. "I think he was tired of feeding me."

"Interesting," Dr. Faineworth said, but he didn't elaborate. Delbit waited silently. Sooner or later someone would tell him what was going on.

Dr. Faineworth pushed the blue paper aside and pulled over a pink paper to take its place. He examined it for a moment, then stared up at Delbit. "I have your school records here," he said. "Pennsylvania Commonwealth Free School number 125 thinks highly of you."

"Yes, sir," Delbit said.

"It is that record that has occasioned my interest in you," Dr. Faineworth explained. "It includes your test results from the alpha-battery and the omicron-battery of tests you took in the first and sixth grades. You remember?"

"Yes, sir," Delbit replied. What on earth did his sixth-grade tests have to do with anything?

"You're fairly bright, you know that?"

"Yes, sir." Delbit was actually very bright, a fact which he had learned to conceal, as it had never done him one bit of good. Intelligence was of small comfort while sweeping the factory floor. The master and the other 'prentices tended to resent it when his intelligence showed in any form whatever. "If you were so smart, you wouldn't be a 'prentice" was one of the milder comments. Which was grossly unfair, as his opinion had never been asked in the matter.

"Well, I can see you're not modest either. That's fine, lad. Modesty never won a war." Dr. Faineworth leaned back in his chair and put his hands behind his head, his black-sleeved elbows sticking out like wings on either side. "Would you like to know what you're doing here?"

"Yes, sir." There was no doubt about that.

"You remember a bunch of tests you took on a big machine, where they pasted electrodes all over you?"

"Yes, sir, I remember." Painful, irritating, boring, and pointless. The Faineworth Apperception Tests, they were.

Faineworth—well, how do you like that.

"Well, one of the things that test did was to take what I like to call a mental profile of you. One might say that it showed the way your individual mind does its thinking in different situations, based on the way the electrical currents move about in your brain. Do you see what I mean?"

"Yes, sir." Delbit had read up on the theory, as much as was in the school library, and knew about the singleton waves from the top of the brain and the doubleton waves from each side, and the slow rhythm from the back. But he decided to let Dr. Faineworth do the explaining. By now not appearing smart had become a fixed habit.

"Well, I needed a certain type of brain—a certain very specific pattern—to aid me in some work I'm doing. And so I went over school records of all the East Coast schools using the Faineworth Tests for the past ten years. And, Delbit my lad, you have it."

"Yes, sir." Delbit swallowed. This didn't sound too good. He would have to go over the New York State Apprentice Protection statutes, if there were any such and if he could get a copy. He really didn't think he wanted anyone fooling around with his brain. And if he had wanted anyone to do it, he didn't think it would be Dr. Faineworth.

"While I need you for this project your work will be interesting, and not very arduous. I decided to buy your articles from your previous master, as it was simpler than borrowing or, er, renting you. Especially as I have no idea how long the project will last. You will sleep in the servants' quarters of the clinic, and eat at the servants' table, but you are excused from all duties except for this project until further notice. If you have any special needs, you will tell Dobbins, and he will see to it. Do you understand?"

"I think so, sir."

"Good. Now come with me and I will show you the reason for all this." Dr. Faineworth rose from his chair and strode into the hall without pausing or checking to see if he was being followed.

Delbit scurried after him, and Dobbins stalked behind.

Up two flights of stairs the doctor strode, and across into one of the new sections, and through a locked door, which was opened for them by a hefty male nurse on the inside. "Everything quiet today, Fenton?"

The nurse gave a two-fingered salute. "Snug and shipshape, Doctor," he said.

"And our unidentified guest?"

"Quiet as a bunny, sir."

"Very good." The doctor led the way to the end of the corridor, past a double row of white-painted locked doors, to the final door on the right.

"In here, young Delbit, is the object of my interest and the reason you're here," Dr. Faineworth said, tapping lightly on the door. "A nameless young lady of unknown antecedents, who was found by our constabulary wandering about on Lower Broadway about two weeks ago."

"Naked," Dobbins added, some strange emotion crossing his face. "She was naked as a jay."

Faineworth gave his servant a sharp look. "That is neither here nor there," he said. "The young lady is amnesiac, and suffers from strange and terrible nightmares. Of both of these things I rather hope you, young Delbit, can help us cure her."

"Me?"

"All will be explained in due time. For now, let us have you meet the young lady. She may act a little, ah, sedated, but that is the effect of medication we're giving her. She'll be so pleased, I'm sure, to meet you. Don't say anything to get her excited."

Dr. Faineworth pulled a large key ring from under his coat and isolated one large key.

"She's a very interesting case," he said, turning the key in the lock and pulling at the door. "We have every hope that—why, what's this?"

Delbit looked into the small cell. There was a cot on the far wall and a basin and toilet to his right. On the cement floor was a small pile of woman's clothes.

There was nothing else.

"She's gone!" Dr. Faineworth said. "I'll be damned!"

CHAPTER TWO

Delbit spent the next two days adjusting to his new environment. Dobbins found him a bed on the servants' floor of the clinic, sharing a room with three dull teenage boys-of-all-work. After lunch on the third day, Dr. Faineworth called him into the laboratory and explained the techniques of deep breathing, relaxation, and mental disassociation that Delbit would need for his projected job. Of what use this would be when the subject had disappeared from a locked room, leaving only a pile of clothes in her wake, was not discussed. What effect this electrical probing would have on his brain, or the girl's brain, was dismissed by the doctor as beneath consideration.

"You are going to get into this girl's mind, young man," Dr. Faineworth told him. "The similarity of your brain waves to hers will make it possible for us to monitor the girl's dreams while she is asleep. That is why I have purchased you at great expense, and diverted you from an otherwise useful existence as a shoemaker. You will, in effect, be an observer at these dreams. I warn you that, as they seem to be nightmares, the experience may not be the most pleasant you have ever had. Although you will be awake, and therefore not as impressionable, you may be horrified by what you see. This is all very theoretical. I cannot tell you precisely in what form you will experience the young lady's dreams. We are on the frontiers of science, as it were. But the theory is good, and it is worth the risk. The value of these experiments is incalculable."

Worth the risk to whom? Delbit wondered. He tried to

imagine what it would be like to be in someone else's dream, and found that he couldn't, and that the idea bothered him. A dream was surely an extremely personal thing. But he didn't say anything. He had long since learned the futility of protesting the inevitable.

On the fourth day the girl came back, escorted by a constable, who had found her wandering above Lower Broadway naked at four in the morning. He wrapped her in his greatcoat and brought her uptown to the clinic. "I figured that if she weren't a patient of yours, Dr. Faineworth, then she ought to be," he said.

The next day Delbit was up in his room sewing the gold insignia of the Faineworth Clinic on his jacket when Dobbins appeared at the door. "Come," he said, beckoning with a bony hand. "Dr. Faineworth wants to see you."

Delbit followed Dobbins to Dr. Faineworth's office and waited in the anteroom to be called. Faineworth was the sort who liked to keep you waiting a few minutes, just so you wouldn't forget who called whom. Delbit picked up a copy of the *New England Journal of Homeopathetics* and settled down on one corner of the red couch.

Ten minutes later Dobbins ushered him into the inner office. Dr. Faineworth was sitting behind his desk, and a squat, excessively wide man with red mutton chop whiskers sat to one side. "Stand up straight," Dobbins whispered, stopping Delbit squarely in front of the desk.

"Ah, Delbit, here you are," Dr. Faineworth said, glancing up from the folder he was studying. "This is Mr. Edbeck, an associate of mine who is interested in the case at hand. Come along with us. We are going to try once again to introduce you to our mysterious guest. It may aid you in some way in visualization or resonance or something. And since the girl must know what's happening, since we have to wire her to the synapse recorder, she should meet the man who's going to be on the other end. No use in adding unnecessary or preventable stress to the experiment. At last report she was still in her, ah, room." He stood up and strode out of the office, the others following in his wake.

"A very interesting case, as I have explained," Faineworth told his chubby friend Edbeck as they headed toward the young girl locked up in the closed ward. "We are calling her Exxa, the unknown female. We don't know where she came from, and we don't know where she went—or how. It's not everyone who can vanish from a locked cell. A pair of Confederal agents have been around asking about her. And a third man—a tall, hooded chap with the strangest accent. I don't know how they got word; presumably someone on staff here. The concept of loyalty is a dying one in this age, I fear."

"The CDE?" Edbeck twisted his puffy face into a worried grimace. "What did they want?"

"They want to know where the girl came from. I told them I'd have to get back to them on that. They want to know if she can really disappear. I told them not to be ridiculous. Exxa is our property, Edbeck, and the government is going to have to keep its grubby paws off."

"What of the third man?"

"He said he had heard reports that we were holding an amnesiac young woman here, and he wanted to see whether it was his sister, who has been missing for a few weeks. He was obviously lying—and not very well. It was as though he were unused to the necessity of masking his desires beneath untruths as the rest of us do. A very strange and disturbing man. I told him nothing, and sent him on his way."

"You're calling the girl Exxa? Not a very flattering name, surely," Mr. Edbeck commented.

"I didn't want to pick a name that might have some unknown connotation to the young lady."

"Ah," Edbeck said, his puffy cheeks jiggling as he nodded his head, "very wise. Very astute."

"One must be careful," Dr. Faineworth said. "The mind is a delicate battleground. Purely from the scientific standpoint, a lot can be learned from this girl, once we can reunite her with her memories."

"Science is all very well," Edbeck said, puffing to keep up

with the doctor's long strides, "But what of the more practical considerations that we discussed?"

"If my theories are correct...." Letting the unfinished thought reverberate, Faineworth knocked on the locked door to the ward. "Ah, there you are, Fenton. Let us in; I have brought some guests to see our lady friend."

They followed the burly male nurse silently down the ward corridor and stopped before the locked door.

Faineworth took a deep breath and turned the key in the lock, then pulled the door open.

The room was not empty this time. A slight, brown-haired girl stood by the cot, her hospital robe pulled around her. She glared at the group in the doorway. "It's about time you got here, Dr. Faineworth," she said, her voice musical but cold as ice. "The attendant told me I had to wait to talk to you. Now I am talking to you. What have you done with my clothes?"

She's just a girl! Delbit thought, trying to get a look at her from over Edbeck's broad and chubby shoulders.

"Please, I have some people to introduce you to," Faineworth told her. "I will get your clothing for you if you like. There didn't seem much point to it, my dear, with you disappearing all the time and leaving it behind."

"Why, what a charming young thing," Edbeck said, putting his hand to his face in a pudgy gesture of appreciation. "You didn't tell me she was so attractive, Doctor. Shame on you!"

"I don't like being locked up," the girl said, ignoring Edbeck and advancing toward Faineworth until she could poke her finger in his chest, "and I don't like having to wear a shapeless cotton bathrobe which smells of disinfectant!"

Faineworth held up a warding hand. "It's for your own good," he said.

"I choose my own good," she told him, walking back to her cot and sitting on the edge.

"We are trying to help," Faineworth assured her blandly. "Remember, they were our clothes in the first place. The first time you came here, you were wrapped in a horse blanket.

We've clothed you, fed you, and given you a place to sleep. Our intentions are honorable. It is difficult to know what to do, but we're doing our best. We don't have people disappearing from our locked wards every day—or appearing naked on Broadway four days later. And you've done both three times now."

Three times? Delbit wondered why nobody had mentioned that to him. Probably they didn't want to crowd his mind with unimportant facts. Appeared and disappeared three times? Moving to the side of the door so he could see in past Edbeck's bulk, he looked at the girl with some interest.

Her light brown hair fell in soft curls below her shoulders. Her slender body, now tense with anger and frustration, looked to be soft and supple in repose. And her large, wide brown eyes encompassed universes in their depths.

She is younger than a spring day, Delbit thought, *and older than life*. Unaccustomed to such thoughts, he shook his head and stared, unconscious of staring. A long-suppressed emotion stirred deep within him.

"I have not done it with purpose," she said. "I have not willed it to be so. I will repay you for your kindnesses. And what I do against my own will, I do as easily against your locked doors."

"You've stopped taking your medication," Dr. Faineworth said. "Fenton tells me you refuse to do so."

"That is so. Keeping me sedated may make it easier for you to manage me, but it does me no good. I do not choose to be so."

"We will discuss that," Faineworth said.

"Come now, this is very interesting," Edbeck said, waddling farther into the room. "You mean, girl, that you really do what Dr. Faineworth says? That you disappear—poof—and reappear—plop—and don't know where, when, or how?"

The girl looked the chubby man over carefully. "That is so," she said. "What business is it of yours? Are you a doctor?"

"Mr. Edbeck is an associate of mine," Dr. Faineworth said.

"A medical associate? Dr. Faineworth, I am not here to be put on display. I will not have you bringing around casual friends or associates to gawk at me. Next I know you'll be charging admission. I suppose I'm lucky that you left me with a bathrobe. And who is that young man who stares at me as though I were a gazelle?"

"Mr. Edbeck represents the Confederal Government," Dr. Faineworth explained, indicating his fat friend. "The Confederal Department of Examination is interested in your case."

"What case?" the girl demanded.

"And young Delbit here has come all the way from Philadelphia, in the Commonwealth of Pennsylvania, to help diagnose your problem. He will help us monitor your dreams, and with his aid, perhaps we can learn to prevent these nightmares you've been having."

"This is the help you've been promising me? This boy?" She glanced disdainfully at Delbit before fastening her gaze on Dr. Faineworth.

Delbit was not insulted by this reaction. He would have felt the same way himself, he was sure, in her place. But he would help her if he could. He silently promised her that. It seemed clear that Dr. Faineworth had no intention of doing so. Edbeck from the Confederal Government? Ridiculous! He was too short for the CDE. And he wasn't wearing a hat! What the doctor was after was unclear to Delbit, but it clearly was not an unmitigated desire to help this girl.

"I shall help you," Dr. Faineworth assured her, speaking to her slowly and patiently as one would to a balky child. "But first I must know what to do. Remember, a doctor swears to do no harm. I have to better understand your case—your situation—before I can be sure that what I do is for your good. I have only your good in mind. It is clear that your bad dreams are somehow associated with your disappearances. We must study those dreams. This boy Delbit, here, can help us. He is a useful tool, nothing more. You must not get upset at his presence."

Thanks a lot, Delbit thought. But he said nothing.

"No more than at yours," the girl told Faineworth.

"That is not the right attitude to take," Dr. Faineworth told her. "We are here to help you, after all."

"Let me be on my way, if you want to help."

"On what way?" Faineworth asked smoothly. "You don't know who you are, or where you're from, or what you're doing here. You don't even know your right name."

"I know that if you leave me alone, I'll be better off," the girl told him.

Edbeck advanced toward the girl and sat on the edge of the cot next to her. "Tell us where you go when you disappear from here," he said, taking her hand, "and how you do it. The CDE wants to know."

"I've told you before," the girl said in a tired voice. She removed her hand from Edbeck's grasp, but made no attempt to move away. Where was there to go? "I don't know how I do it. And the other place—where I go when I disappear from here—seems to be nothing but a forest in all directions, with a wide river about a mile from where I appear."

"Is it a place you dream about?" Edbeck asked.

The girl shook her head. "No," she said. "My dreams are all—populated. This place is not."

"So," Dr. Faineworth said. "You go to the same place each time?"

"I seem to," the girl agreed.

"We will talk more about this," Faineworth said.

"I want to get out of here," the girl told him.

"Your request will be forwarded to the proper authorities," Faineworth told her. "In the meantime, please bear with me. I am trying to help you regain your memories."

"I haven't much choice, it seems," the girl said. "Please have the guard bring my clothes."

"That I will do," Faineworth agreed.

"Did you notice the girl's reaction when I told her you were from the CDE?" Faineworth asked Edbeck as they walked back to the office.

"I wondered why you did that," Edbeck commented. "But the girl had no reaction that I could see."

"That's it!" Faineworth said. "She seems to have good recall for events and facts outside of her direct life—a common syndrome in amnesia. Yet she reacted to the CDE not at all. Most people react strongly to any mention of our government's most secret police—apparent strong approval masking cringing fear. But our Exxa seems ignorant of the existence of the organization."

"That is so," Edbeck agreed. "What does it mean?"

"That my theory may be correct. That young lady may not be from around here."

"This city?" Edbeck enquired.

"This universe," Faineworth replied.

* * * * * * *

At four o'clock the next morning Dobbins came to Delbit's room and shook him awake. "Come," he said.

Delbit groggily slipped into his pants and shirt and pulled his boots on. "Where?" he asked.

"Downstairs. The doctor wants you."

Dr. Faineworth was waiting impatiently in his office. "Are you fully awake?" he asked Delbit. "Come, sit here. Have a muffin. Prepare to go to work."

Delbit took the plate of muffins and buttered one. "Work?" He looked fuzzily about the room. "I don't think I'm awake. It takes me a while to wake up in the morning. And it's not even morning."

"Have some coffee. Do you drink coffee? It will wake you up. Dobbins, get him some coffee. Here, put a lot of cream in it."

Delbit sipped at the coffee and ate his muffin. "What—?" he said, and then paused, considering what to ask.

"What are we all doing up at this hour?" Dr. Faineworth rubbed his hands together. "This is the true witching hour, my lad—the dreaming hour. For most of the night we sleep soundly, dreamlessly; but during the early-morning hours we begin to dream. You and I are going now to capture one or more of those dreams. Finish your coffee."

"Yes, sir." Delbit drank up his coffee and stared impassively into the immediate future like a man examining the edge of a cliff he is about to leap off.

Dr. Faineworth looked up at the clock on his far wall and strummed his fingers on the desk. "All right. Enough coffee. Enough time wasted," he said a couple of minutes later. He took off his suit jacket and wrapped a white laboratory smock around himself. "Let us see about entering the land of dreams. Come with me."

Delbit was taken to a small, white-painted room down the corridor. "Exxa is asleep in the next room," Faineworth told him. "We call it the sleep research room. She wears a special helmet, with built-in electrodes. You will don a similar one, and lie down here." The doctor indicated a black leather couch in the center of the room. "But you will not sleep. You will receive mental images through this device here"—the doctor pointed to a large black box that was humming ominously in the corner— "and report back to me on them. Is this not quite simple? Good. Now lie down."

With a feeling that might have been shared by St. Barnabas as he prepared to face four hungry lions, Delbit lay down and allowed them to strap the leather helmet to his head.

CHAPTER THREE

She was in a long corridor, an endless corridor, racing past rows of too-solid oaken doors that were barred against her to the left and right. Gas lamps flickered in twisted brackets along the wall, and strange, horrible faces peered out from unexpected corners, their mouths twisted into grotesque greetings, and then disappeared at her approach.

She was searching for something—something—what?—she couldn't quite remember. There was something intangible that she needed desperately, and it was hidden from her behind one of these doors. But which one? The convoluted brass markings on the doors shrieked of hidden knowledge, scribed in a secret but once familiar script. But try as she might, they meant nothing to her, and the knobs shrank from her grasp.

Onward she went, as the corridor widened, and the sky flashed orange from the great globe of a dying sun. She turned and found that the corridor had disappeared.

She turned back.

Wide, empty plains surrounded her now, endless miles of arid desert—dangerous, forbidding, deadly desert. The giant calla plants stood at distant intervals, their crests as high as their taproots were deep, and they whistled softly for her to approach. But she knew it would mean death.

"Hello, " the man's voice said. "Where are we?"

Man's voice?

She spun around. There was a man—no, not more than a boy—sitting—(sitting?)—sitting at a table—(table?)—a few yards from her. It was a round metal table, painted white, with a hole in the center. A white metal pole went through the hole and spread a wide umbrella over the table and the two chairs.

This was somehow wrong. Out of place. Where had she seen the boy before?

Could he be one of the Golden Orb? She looked at him closely, but could not detect the stain.

Was he of Nimber blood? His ears were not pointed.

She closed her eyes and turned around, and turned back and opened her eyes, and he was gone.

Was gone.

—Wasn't gone at all. And neither were the table and chairs.

"Who are you?" she asked. "And what do you here?"

"I've been sent to watch you," he said. "We weren't sure whether you would be aware of me or not. My name is Delbit Quint. This is very strange."

"What is?" she asked.

"I'm on your side, I promise you," the lad said. "Don't worry. But don't trust Dr. Faineworth as far as you can spit."

"You do not speak sense," she said. She sat at the table with him, under the crystal towers, and they sipped tall cups of blue fizz. "Tell me of yourself," she said.

"You're dreaming," he said.

"That is possible," she agreed. "Is not all a dream? And if not mine, then whose?"

"No, no," Delbit said. "I don't mean in general. I mean here. Now. This is a dream."

The girl smiled at him. "Then I am dreaming you?" She reached across the dining-car table and patted his hand as the train entered a tunnel.

"Yes...no." Delbit looked around as the area went dark. "Hello?"

They were standing atop a giant cube of polished metal, which gleamed silver in the bright, though sunless, sky. Around them was a flat, burnished plain, dotted with distant geometric shapes.

"This is very disconcerting," Delbit said.

The girl now wore flowing robes of power, and clutched before her the Golden Orb, as a talisman to protect her from harm.

Delbit was in his coveralls, and barefoot. The surface of the metal cube was cold under his feet.

"You're still here," the girl said.

"I am," Delbit responded. "I feel like an intruder, but I can't get out any more than you can. The doctor said that you probably wouldn't be aware that I was here, but obviously that's not so."

"What doctor?" the girl asked.

The great cube they were standing on rumbled and rolled over, pitching them onto the slippery blue surface below. There was a grinding sound, and a great maw opened beneath them.

"They've found us!" the girl screamed. "The Nimber!"

Blackness surrounded them as they fell into the void.

* * * * * * *

"Transcribe it as accurately as you can," Dr. Faineworth said, tapping the desk with his forefingernail. "Every nuance, every gesture, every word may be important."

"Yes, sir," Delbit said. The doctor had provided him with a small desk, like a schoolboy's, in a corner of his office, a supply of lined paper, and a pen and ink. For three days now, early every morning Delbit had been electrically attached to the mysterious girl's sleeping mind, and had gone along as an uninvited guest into her dreams. It was the strangest experience of his young life: part of him lying on a hard leather couch, staring at the white ceiling, the greater part of him within the strange worlds of the girl's unconscious mind. Then he had been disconnected from the apparatus and given breakfast. Then he had spent the rest of the morning and afternoon hand-printing out (because Dr. Faineworth couldn't read his handwriting) every detail of the girl's dreams.

The job was not to his liking. What could be more personal than a dream? Being in the girl's dreams was bad enough physically—or mentally—or whatever the right word was. It certainly seemed physically real while he was there. And the dreams all ended in sheer terror, a terror that washed over him while it engulfed the girl.

But if it would help the girl get her memory back, it was worthwhile. And Delbit believed that Dr. Faineworth did want the girl to get her memory back. It was what the doctor planned to do after that that worried Delbit.

* * * * * * *

Down in the oppressive depths below the ruby palace of the Calla Host, in an ancient torture chamber whose walls were lined with instruments the use of which could only be dimly remembered but whose very appearance provoked terror, the Princess Whose Name Might Not Be Spoken awaited her fate.

Slender silver chains encircled her body, binding her to the central pillar, and silver wristlets held her arms above her head. Helpless and proud she waited.

Far away in one of the many ancient hewn-stone corridors that passed the chamber, she could hear the footsteps of the Archpriest of Loth, coming to wrest from her the dreadful secret of the Golden Orb. The sound, as steady as the dripping of water, relentlessly neared; now louder than the squeaking of the rats, now louder than the beating of her heart.

"I don't think I like this one," said the boy (the boy?), the boy who—who—who was tied beside her. The serving boy who had been her companion on many a better-fated adventure, and now must share her doom.

"Quiet, Vondar," the princess whispered, "the Archpriest is blind. Do not aid him in finding us."

"Delbit," the boy said. "My name is Delbit. Let's play another game; this one is scary."

"Game?" the princess whispered. "I do not understand."

"You know," Delbit said, "you have an awful lot of nightmares. I'm surprised that you're still willing to go to sleep."

"Nightmares?"

"I'm going to try something, Exxa. I don't know if it will work, but the doctor is going to start some kind of experimenting on you today, and I've got to do something."

"What are you speaking of?" The stone walls of the ancient chamber receded in the distance. "And who is Exxa?"

"Let me take a chance," the boy said. "We're going somewhere else for a while."

The room shifted again, and blackness closed in about them, until only the boy's face remained in front of her. Then, slowly, the universe expanded outward once again and everything had changed.

They were walking down a country path, with a waist-high stone wall on one side and a fenced-in meadow on the other. The sun was high, and the air was still, and somewhere a frog was croaking.

"Where are we?" the girl demanded. "The Calla—"

"There are no Calla anything here," Delbit told her. "And no Nimber, and nary a Golden Orb. This is where I grew up, before my father died, and nobody can hurt us here."

"It's very pretty," the girl said, looking at the pastoral scene about her.

"Tell me about yourself," Delbit said. "What you remember."

"I am the princess of—"

"No, no," Delbit said. "Your waking self. The girl without a name, that Dr. Faineworth is calling Exxa. You can do that without waking up. We will stay here, in this dream, in this pretty place, while you tell me about yourself."

"Dream?" the girl considered.

"Tell me about yourself," Delbit repeated.

The girl looked off into the meadow, and several cows stared back at her. "Yes," she said, "of course. You're the boy at that—hospital—where the doctor—Faineworth—wants to explore my dreams."

"That's right," Delbit told her. "Tell me about that. What do you remember?"

The girl stared straight ahead. "I don't remember much," she said.

"Tell me what you can."

"I was for a long time in a—I guess it was a hospital—another hospital—a big building in the middle of a great city—before I came here," the girl said. "That's the earliest thing I remember."

"A long time?"

"Two years. A little more."

"In a big city? New York?"

"Where is that?"

"Where you are now. But we're pretty far uptown. Downtown, where you, ah, were found when you came back, that's where the big buildings are."

"Oh, yes. Big stone buildings. No, that's not it. The city I was in was much larger. Buildings so tall they were lost in the mist. With more metal and glass. Very shiny."

Delbit shook his head. "I don't know any place like that."

"Well, that's where I was."

"And before that?"

"I have no memory of any time before that."

"Do you know your name?"

"At that hospital they called me Jane. Here they call me Exxa. Neither is my name. What it truly is, I cannot tell you."

"Where is it that you go when you disappear?"

The girl shrugged. "I don't know. A forest."

"How do you do it?"

"I truly wish that I knew. I—twist something. Like turning sideways, but inside my head. And there I am."

"And you come back the same way?"

"That is so."

"Well, I should tell you that the doctor has it figured out, he thinks, and he's going to start experimenting on you sometime soon."

"He has what figured out?" the girl asked.

"I'm not sure," Delbit said. "But I don't think you're going to like it."

The girl nodded. Delbit had the impression that she was quite prepared not to like it. "Thank you for telling me," she said.

The sky darkened. They looked up.

And the girl began to scream, as giant birds with glowing red eyes and cruelly pointed beaks circled overhead, blotting out the sun. First one dived toward them, and then another, and a third.

Delbit covered his head with his hands and jerked from side to side to evade the sharp beaks and claws. One clutched at him, and he screamed as its talons pierced his scalp.

* * * * * *

"You ripped the electrodes out," Dr. Faineworth complained querulously.

"Sorry," Delbit said. He was standing in front of the doctor's desk, the position from which he received criticism and instruction.

"You were supposed to be awake—aware of what was going on."

"It was a very powerful image," Delbit said.

"Do not let it happen again, or I shall supply an even more powerful image." The doctor leaned back in his chair and dismissed Delbit with a gesture. "We are ready to proceed to the next step," he told his stout friend Edbeck, who was filling a chair to the right of the desk.

Delbit retreated to his desk in the corner and bent over it, apparently hard at work transcribing his night's experiences. Sometimes, when they realized he was there, they sent him out of the office. And this time he didn't want to leave. Whatever was being planned for the questioning of the girl, he wanted to know.

"When you say 'the next step,'" Edbeck asked, his eyes half lidded and his hands folded over his belly, "are you referring to one minuscule, mincing step along a long and badly marked trail, or a giant stride along a short, well-lighted path? I only ask to have some frame of reference."

Faineworth chuckled. "Edbeck, my friend, do you have any idea of just what it is we're striving for here?"

"You have told me several times," Edbeck said. "And, obviously, impressed me with the potential that lies within this girl's fair body. Else I would not be here. My fortune is your fortune, Doctor, as soon as I sense a profit to be made. So far it is all guesswork."

"Guesswork?" Dr. Faineworth sat up, and his hand slapped the desktop. "Does the girl not disappear?"

"Yes, but—"

"And where do you suppose she goes—Rhode Island Free State?"

"She goes—somewhere else, Dr. Faineworth, not of this world. That is clear, and I agree with you. The only possible point of dissent is whether we can exploit this—elsewhere—for our own benefit. And on that point I remain unconvinced. The girl goes, yes; but can we follow? You don't know, and I don't know."

"Elsewhen," Dr. Faineworth said.

"Pardon?"

"I rather think it's not 'elsewhere,' Edbeck, but 'elsewhen.'"

Edbeck smiled incredulously. "She travels into the past? Is that what you're saying?"

"Perhaps. But more probably she goes, let us call it, sideways in time."

Delbit's head jerked up at that, but he quickly lowered it again and resumed his carefully edited transcribing of last night's dream.

"Don't have sport with me, Dr. Faineworth. Just because my scientific knowledge is not as strong as yours does not mean I am an innocent gull." Edbeck shook his head. "I do not swallow raw fish, my medical friend."

"Come, come, Edbeck, do not allow your thoroughly admirable skepticism to get in the way of your even more admirable cupidity. There's nothing intrinsically strange about the suggestion, once you accept that she came from somewhere else. And we have empirical evidence of that; we've seen her go back and forth three times. I'm giving you my theory as to where she goes. If I'm wrong, then we'll soon know. But still, as you say, she goes somewhere. And soon we shall find out where that somewhere is."

"A forest," Edbeck commented, looking unconvinced. "Of use to us only if the market for raw lumber were to suddenly increase."

"That is merely a part of her illness," Faineworth said. "This cycling back and forth between here and some primitive forest."

"You believe so?"

"Obviously. The girl does not come from a forest; so much is evident. The same brain damage that gave her amnesia brought her here, and causes her to cycle between this, ah, reality and that forest. And, Edbeck—"

"Umph?"

"—that amnesia, that brain intrusion, is induced."

"You think so?"

"No, no, my petulant friend. I know so. Such is my specialty. Such is my training. It is what I myself have been trying to do for these past twenty years. I can at least recognize an external intrusion, even though I cannot as yet create it. And I'd give a considerable part of my fortune to discover who did create it, how they accomplished it, and where they learned the trick."

Edbeck thought that over for a few seconds, and then suddenly sat up. "The devil you say! You mean someone else did that to her?"

"Just so. The tests show it. Clever, whoever did this. Deucedly clever. Sections of her memory are, effectively, blocked off. And there are now built in, let us call them, signposts warning her not to approach. 'Calla' and 'Nimber,' for example, are two concepts she is not even to explore. So they mean something important to whoever did this to her. And so they will to her when she has her memory. It's a fascinating technique—quite beyond anything we can do. Believe me. If anyone in this country—or this planet—were using such techniques, I would be aware of it." Faineworth slapped his hand firmly on the desk. "One more sign that she's from another, ah, place."

"Well, wherever it came from, if it's beyond our skills—"

Yes, Delbit silently agreed.

"We could not do it, Edbeck, my friend, but we can undo it. That is a different sort of problem."

"We can?"

"Most assuredly. But we are not going to for the moment."

"We're not?"

"No. For then she would fly away, untethered. We must first find a way to tether her to us before we restore her memory."

"Ah. And how do we do that?"

Dr. Faineworth reached over to the floor by the left side of his desk and lifted a cardboard box onto the desktop. "My newly designed cerebral monitor," he said, pulling out a thick leather helmet. It looked much like the one Delbit wore for his dream-interloping, but it was larger and had a great bundle of wires coming from the top instead of the mere twelve that Delbit's carried.

"The helmet connects to a recording device that is being made for me now," Dr. Faineworth said. "Sixty simultaneous outputs. When I get it, sometime tomorrow, the girl gets hooked up and stays hooked up until the next time she disappears. And I think I have determined how to induce her to disappear."

"How?"

Dr. Faineworth separated a white wire and a red wire from the bundle going into the helmet. "These two wires here," he said.

"Ah," Edbeck said, nodding wisely.

Delbit took a deep breath.

"Then, once we have induced her to disappear, we look at the readings. Then we adjust the apparatus to give us more of what seems to be the most interesting."

"Then she comes back, and we do it again!" Edbeck said, clapping his pudgy hands together.

"Precisely. And after the third or fourth time, we should have it pegged. Just what she's doing and how she's doing it."

"It won't damage her, will it?" Edbeck asked.

Faineworth considered. "Not irreparably. Possibly not at all. We can only find out through making the experiment."

"Slipping sideways through time, eh?" Edbeck pursed his lips. "Faineworth, just what does that mean?"

Delbit, feeling as though his ears were burning, got off his stool and walked across the room to the door. He had two excuses ready for leaving, lunchtime and going to the bathroom. Would the doctor stop him? Would the doctor see through his excuse? Delbit felt as though the truth were written on his face.

Dr. Faineworth launched upon an explanation of alternate universes, waving a finger at Edbeck, and Delbit passed unnoted from his sight. Delbit climbed the stairs and, drawn by some unexamined emotion, approached the girl's cell. "Got to ask Exxa some questions," Delbit mumbled to Fenton, when he reached the closed ward. Fenton, unquestioningly, unlocked the girl's door and Delbit passed inside.

"Yes?" The girl was sitting on the side of her cot, and she looked up as Delbit entered. It was the first time he had seen her—outside of her dreams—since the day Dr. Faineworth had introduced them.

Delbit closed the door. "You've got to get out of here," he said urgently, after making sure that Fenton had moved away from the cell.

"You're the boy—" the girl said, pointing a slender finger at him. "And you—" She paused thoughtfully, and then smiled. "My dream partner," she said. "How nice to see you between dreams. This isn't a dream, is it?"

"No," Delbit said "And you've got to get out of here."

"How do you suggest I do that?" the girl asked.

"I don't know, but we'll have to think of something. The doctor is going to start his funny business tomorrow."

"Funny business?"

"He's not just going to take signals out of your brain—he's going to put one in. Something about trying to find out how you disappear."

"Damn!" the girl said. "I don't want that man prying around inside my head any more than he's doing already."

"That's what I thought," Delbit told her. "That's why I think we'd better get out of here."

"You'll help me?"

"Of course I will."

"You shouldn't. You'll get in trouble if we get caught."

"I have a feeling that I'm already in trouble. I think we'd better both get out of here, if we want to stay healthy."

The girl patted him on the arm. "You're nice," she said.

Delbit felt his ears go red again. "Come on," he said in a sudden burst of decision. "We'll leave now. Never be a better time, although this isn't very good. Have you anything to take?"

"Your hand," she said. "I believe I shall take your hand." She put her hand in his.

Delbit pounded on the cell door. "Going to take the girl downstairs," he told Fenton. "Let the doctor talk to her."

"I don't know," Fenton said, pausing to scratch his nose.

Delbit laughed a hearty laugh. It rang hollow in his ears. "You think I can't handle her?" he asked.

"Well, I guess it's okay," Fenton agreed, stepping aside to let them out. He followed them down the corridor and unlocked the ward door for them. "I mean, it's not like she's one of the nuts," he said.

"I should say not!" Delbit agreed.

Delbit took her around through side corridors and down the servants' stairs to the back door. It was locked.

"We'll have to chance the front door," Delbit said. "It's usually fairly busy this time of day; with luck, nobody will notice us."

"Luck is not my strong point these days," the girl said, "but let us go."

"It's a good thing you got your clothes back," Delbit

commented, leading her through the ground-floor warren toward the front door. "We'd never have gotten you out of here in a bathrobe."

They had made it to the front hall when Delbit heard the familiar high voice of Dr. Faineworth approaching down the main stairs. He paused, holding the girl back.

Edbeck was trotting down the stairs at the doctor's side. They both had their coats on.

"Quick!" Delbit whispered. "In here!"

He opened the door by his hand, and he and the girl slipped into a small, dark room.

For about ten minutes Delbit stood there with his ear to the door. "That's funny," he murmured to the girl. "Someone has just entered the building, and they're just staying there in the hall talking. Dr. Faineworth sounds angry."

They cautiously cracked the door open and peered out. The doctor and Edbeck were standing just inside the front door, talking to three tall, thin men who were wearing identical red-and-black cloaks with hoods. Dr. Faineworth was gesticulating violently. He looked angry.

"I wonder what that's about," Delbit asked.

"I don't like this," the girl said. "I think—oh, Xerxes!"

One of the thin men had turned around, and was staring right at them. He began walking forward.

The girl clutched Delbit. "The Bee!" she said.

"What?"

The man was almost at the door.

She closed her eyes and twisted her face into a strange, strained expression.

The man touched the doorknob.

There was a soft plopping sound, and the little room was empty, save for a pile of clothes on the floor.

* * * * * * *

They were surrounded by trees.

"You came with me," she said.

"You have no clothes on," he said, trying not to look. He almost succeeded.

"But you do," she said. "How unaccountable."

He looked down at himself. "That's right," he said. "Perhaps it's because you were clutching at me through my clothes that you brought them along with me. Did you do that on purpose? Shift, I mean, or whatever you want to call it."

"Not exactly. That man frightened me. I'm not sure why. But I knew him, I think, from another place. So I—reacted."

"Here," Delbit said. "Let me give you my shirt. That way we'll both be, ah, clad."

"Very kind," she said. "Now what do we do?"

"I was hoping you'd tell me," Delbit said.

* * * * * *

"We call ourselves Friends of the Bee," the tall man said, looking malevolently down at Dr. Faineworth. "The reasons will not concern you."

"What do you want?" Faineworth demanded.

The man spread his hands. "The girl," he said. "What else?"

They were now upstairs in Dr. Faineworth's office, he and Edbeck and the three tall men. A crumpled pile of women's clothing rested on the desk. Faineworth and Edbeck sat together on the red couch and tried not to look frightened as the three men with their faces hooded towered over them with strange-looking weapons in their hands. The weapons, as Faineworth had discovered when he made a dash for the door, made only a slight barking sound, but gave out a beam of intense brightness that charred what it touched. The one tall man seemed to be the spokesman for the three; at least the other two did no questioning, although they seemed just as interested in the answers.

"You saw," Faineworth said. "She is gone. She has left her clothing behind. It seems you know more about it, and her, than I do."

"Where did she go?"

"I don't know," Faineworth said.

"She just disappeared," Edbeck said, waving his hands in the air. "Poof! She has done it before. The doctor thinks she goes sideways in time."

Faineworth glared at his friend.

"She has been back here at least twice," the questioner said, looking back and forth between them. "How do you bring her back?"

"She just comes back," Faineworth said. "We don't control it." Edbeck nodded his agreement.

"Now, why would she do that?" the man demanded.

"I don't know," Faineworth said.

"We think she is in some sort of loop," Edbeck said. "That her mental condition makes her cycle between here and wherever else she goes."

Faineworth turned to glare at his friend, but said nothing. Edbeck appeared not to notice.

"Mental condition?" the man asked.

"She has amnesia," Faineworth said unwillingly.

"Ah, yes. Of course." The man turned to his companions. "I am leaving now. Stay for two weeks to see if the girl comes back. Bring her unharmed to the hive. Then kill these two. Destroy the city."

"New York?" one of them asked.

"Whatever."

Wait a minute!" Edbeck screeched. "You can't do that!"

The man paused for a second and turned to him. "You are mistaken," he said. Then he left.

CHAPTER FOUR

Castimere Parr. Preceptor of the Overline, rose from the streaming water and slowly stepped out of the octagonal sunken tub. He wrapped himself in yards of blue cotton towel and crossed the tessellated floor of his hot room to inspect himself in the huge mirror set into the blue-tiled wall. "Tell Miss Viola I am ready to be poked and prodded," he told Drom, his squat body servant, who stood by the door.

As Drom silently padded from the room, Preceptor Parr used one edge of the towel to wipe off the mirror and stared at his reflection. A wiry, muscular man of medium height, medium age, with more than the usual number of scars and the hint of an incipient potbelly, stared back. His face was not unusually ugly, but it was not one he would have chosen; it was narrow, with a high forehead below thinning brown hair and above wide-set brown eyes, and what he regarded as an overly large nose. Despite the reliability of the rejuvenation process, his middle-aged body looked subtly and unsatisfactorily different to him than when he had actually been merely middle-aged. He was not pleased with his appearance, but then he had never been, and he had more meaningful things to worry about.

Parr turned away from the mirror, glad that whatever vanity he possessed was not dependent upon his appearance. He was vain about the quickness of his mind, the responsiveness of his body; the fact that, with a bit of practice and conditioning, he could still hold his own or better in a duel of either wits or foils against any but a true master. He was vain about the depth of his knowledge, hard won over a century of service to the Overline, and his ability to make decisions on what seemed to the conscious mind to be too little information. He had long ago learned to trust his unconscious mind's winnowing of information and the conclusions it drew.

The Overline continued to exist, fat and sluggish and happy, through the constant watchfulness and prompt actions of its preceptors, backed up by the ready response of the Overline Security Service. There was a time a few centuries ago when this one strand in the vastness that was the time continuum believed itself to be the only one possessing the secret of hopping about the Paraverse, and in its conceit it had named itself the Overline. But now it knew that other machines traveled the Paraverse. Some were controlled by men whose knowledge of the secret had turned them into complacently evil exploiters of those on time strands unfortunate enough to come under their control; some by nonhuman intelligences that had no more regard for mankind than mankind had for water beetles. Some of these, if they ever stumbled across the home strand of the Overline, would destroy it reflexively and without compunction.

Everyone on the Overline knew of the threat, but most thought it such a remote possibility as hardly to be worth considering, if they thought of it at all. The others believed that if by some strange accident they were attacked, the Service would destroy the menace in short order. After all, what were they paying their taxes for?

But Castimere Parr and his fellow preceptors, charged with the safety of the Overline and its interests in the rest of the Paraverse, knew how thin the protecting wall was, and how close the barbarians were to the gates. Any strand on which the Overline Import Complex was firmly entrenched had to be defended, lest a captured transporter reveal the location of the Overline itself. Any strand that was only partially exploited would be abandoned rather than chance losing a transporter or conveyer—an action about which the merchant lord doing the exploiting was never pleased.

Parr closed his eyes and stretched out prone on the marble massage table. He tried to focus his thoughts on one of the larger problems that awaited him in the worlds beyond his bath. Brisk exercise followed by a steaming tub had usually served to clear his mind and bring his thoughts into focus. But it hadn't been working of late, and today he found himself unable to concentrate on any one question for more than a few seconds before it was brushed aside by another. What he needed, he decided, was a vacation.

The curtain parted and Viola entered. A brief white dress was wrapped around her slender form with an artless simplicity that only the highest art can achieve. She looked desirable. For Castimere Parr she always strove to look desirable. But then, for Castimere Parr she always looked desirable, whether she tried or not. She carried a stack of fresh towels and a bottle of body oil. "Your slave, Preceptor Parr," she said, bowing slightly. "What do you require?"

Parr rose on one elbow to look at her. "It is impossible," he told her, "for such perfection of beauty, grace, and wit to be enfolded within the slight body of a single twenty-six-year-old female. Surely there must be five of you."

She laughed. "If I weren't your slave already," she told him, putting the towels down at his feet, "such words would go a long way toward capturing my heart. But since you already have my body, and my personal services covenant for the next sixteen years, what would you do with my heart?"

Parr smiled. "You don't love me?" he accused.

"Not a bit."

"You'd leave me?"

"In a flash. Just unlock the ankle chains."

"You aren't wearing ankle chains."

Viola looked down. "That's so." She pushed Parr's head down onto the table and surrounded it with her arms. "Then, perhaps I love you," she said.

After an appropriate pause, she took the bottle of oil and began massaging his neck and shoulders. "Your muscles are still tense," she told him. "What's the point of boiling yourself for an hour in that sunken pot if it isn't even going to relax your neck and shoulder muscles?"

"The problems won't go away just because I immerse myself in steam," Parr said.

"You let more of the world sit on your shoulders than any man should carry," Viola told him. "It's going to age you before your time, and you know how I hate old men."

"Yes," he agreed. "Indeed. I can see that in your every gesture." He rolled over, nearly upsetting the massage oil. "The problem, my love, is that you should be the problem. What to do about you—us—should be of paramount concern, and my mind should occupy itself with nothing else until it is solved. But somehow I can't seem to drop these other, lesser concerns, and they crowd into my mind unbidden and leap about, demanding attention."

"There's no rush about us—about our problem," Viola said. "It will keep for years unchanged, as I am indeed your slave as well as your lover; and we can neither of us do anything about the one, nor do we wish to do anything about the other. Concentrate on the problems of the rest of the Paraverse; ours will wait, Preceptor Parr."

Parr shook his head. "It is unstable," he said. "And as it can change in but one direction, that is the direction it will choose."

"Our relationship, you mean?" Viola asked.

"That is so."

"You fear that as I can't leave you, I will grow to resent your lovemaking?"

"Something like that."

Viola pushed his legs over and jumped up to sit on the table. "But I can leave you whenever I wish," she told him. "At least I can leave your bed. You didn't drag me into it, you'll remember. It took me quite a bit of work to get you to seduce me. You were much too honorable to bed a slave."

"I was not prepared to believe that you really cared for me," Parr said. "You saw me from the inside, so to speak, with all my defenses down. People are not heroes to their own servants."

"Sweet Mother of Ishtar!" Viola said. "You thought I was just trying to get out of work by hoisting my skirts for the boss?"

"The culture you were brought up in seems to have had a penchant for colorful language," Parr commented, swinging his legs over the side of the table and rotating his arms at the shoulders to loosen them up.

"Here, let me finish the massage," Viola said, moving behind him and attacking his shoulders with her thumbs. "The culture I came from sold me into slavery," she said. "I grew up in Menashas, a dirty little town in a dirty little kingdom called Babistron, where my father spent fourteen hours a day making cowhide sandals and selling them for not quite enough money to feed his family. He couldn't support a daughter, and he had no hope of getting me married. He tried giving me to the temple when I was twelve, but the priests of Ishtar wouldn't take me. I was too skinny for them. The priests of Basht would take me, for the offering of only a few silver coins. But my father heard what the priests of Basht did with little girls, and he couldn't go ahead with it. Bless him. So when I was fourteen he sold me to a slaver."

"I thought that you didn't like talking about this," Parr said.

Viola shrugged. "You have it on file from my hypno sessions," she said.

"I've never looked at the disks," Parr told her.

When new slaves were purchased on any time strand they were routinely given complete suprahypnotic regressions, and their past history was put on disk in their own voices, along with a continuous psychoreading. The practice served the triple purpose of preventing direct infiltration by the various enemies of the Overline; spotting anomalies and anachronisms that would indicate penetration of the time strand by another Paraverse-traveling people; and building up a verbal cultural history of that strand. The intercultural anthropologists would build up a generalized history of the timeline strand by strand. They used it to define the event boundaries that separated one line from the next. Often a seemingly innocuous event would be the one that set off a cascade of change resulting in a continuing history so different from those surrounding it that it established a new line.

"The slaver took me to Constampoli, where I was sold into the harem of a young man named Priato Belesareus," Viola continued. "Priato had to maintain a harem to maintain his dignity. All the fellows had harems. But he didn't seem to be very interested in any of the girls. As far as I could tell, he wasn't any more interested in any of the boys. He liked me to give him massages, and he liked one of the other girls to kiss his feet. Occasionally he would beat us; I think he enjoyed that. Occasionally he had one of the girls beat him. He dressed in white robes and knelt before an image of his god—in the form of a young man stapled to a cross—and allowed himself to be beaten. Thus, he claimed, atoning for his sins. But I think that he liked that even more."

"I don't think I need to hear the rest," Parr said.

"But the rest is truth and beauty," Viola told him. "Priato died accidentally, while whipping one of the girls—it was either apoplexy or poison, they never knew which—and we were all sold at auction. An Overline recruiter—I think it's so lovely that they call themselves recruiters—bought a few of us. We were taken and examined, vaccinated, inoculated, irradiated, taught Lesh[1] by suprahypnotic induction, told our rights while in the service of the Overline, and brought to the Seventh Level. Then you bought me, and I came here."

"As a slave," Parr said.

Viola shrugged. "You know, my dearest love," she said, "it is a bit hypocritical of you to regret the circumstance which made me your slave, when you don't give a damn about the status of the seventeen other servants in this household."

"It isn't the institution of term-slavery that I'm bitter about," Parr said, "but merely our entanglement in it. Every servant on

---

1. The language of the Overline

Overline—and there must be twenty million of them—is better off with us than in the world he left. Usually much better off. Their rights may be minimal, but they are strictly protected. They are paid for their services. They receive free medical care. And in twenty years the contracts are up and they are released from service, usually with a good bit of money put aside, and do whatever they want with the rest of their lives."

"On the strand of their choice," Viola said.

"Yes," Parr said. "Within very proscribed limits, yes."

"Except Overline," Viola said.

"Yes," Parr said.

"Can't have overcrowding," Viola said.

"Can't have noncitizens who might be troublemakers around," Parr said.

"This is the best of all possible worlds," Viola said.

"I don't claim that being a term-slave is the Platonic ideal," Parr said. "Merely that it is a vast improvement over what they left. Life is an imperfect bargain for all of us. You and I are in an intractable bind, and I'm one of the highest of the high-muck-a-mucks on this best of all possible strands."

"Your massage is done," Viola said. "And I forgive you your trespasses. Or, better, the trespasses of your officious government and your pompous culture. But you I love. You must get dressed—there's an official visitor."

"Nice of you to tell me," Parr said, standing up and redraping the latest towel around him with an approximation of dignity. "What sort of official visitor?"

"I wanted you to get your massage first," Viola said. "I wanted to spend a minute alone with you first. I didn't want to discuss our situation, since it always distresses you. Perhaps it even distresses me a little. I'm sorry."

"I also," Parr said. "From now on we'll stick to words of love and comments on the weather."

"A very serious young man from the Overline Import Complex Directorate is waiting to see you in the library," Viola said. "I will be waiting to see you in the bedroom."

"That will be very late," Parr said. "I have much to do."

"Wake me," she said.

Parr dressed carefully, taking his time. Very serious young men from the OIC Directorate had to be kept waiting. If they got to see a preceptor within the first half hour of their arrival, they would become even more serious and self-important, and by the time they were middle-aged men from the OIC Directorate, they might expect that sort of thing.

PART TWO
HITHER AND YON

CHAPTER FIVE

Delbit turned slowly around. He saw birch trees, and walnut, and maple, and dark-colored trees he didn't recognize. They were well separated, and the space between them was covered with a mat of fallen leaves spread loosely over dead tree limbs, and live tree roots, and an occasional thorn bush. The sun was low in the sky, and long slender tree shadows groped across the ground like fingers. The wind was chill.

Delbit stared at the shadows, and then slapped himself in the face with his left hand.

"Why did you do that?" the girl asked, looking up. She was sitting on a fallen tree, using her fingers and teeth to construct a pair of sandals for herself from the inner bark of a nearby birch.

"I was making sure I'm awake," Delbit explained. "Although this would explain itself more easily if it were a dream."

"It is disconcerting," the girl agreed. "To be suddenly thrust somewhere else. I have found it so." She stood up and stamped each foot, and then sat back down to readjust the bark wrappings.

"The time is different too," Delbit said. "When we, ah, left, it was lunchtime. Here, the sun is going down."

"If we are on another place on the earth, then the sun would be elsewhere in the sky," the girl pointed out. "You do know that the world is round, don't you?"

"Round, you say?" Delbit attempted a smile. "That would explain why the *Santa María* didn't fall off the edge."

"The what?" the girl asked, looking interested.

"The *Santa María*," Delbit answered. "Columbus's ship. You know—the *Nina*, the *Pinta*, the *Ferdinand*, and the *Santa María*."

"Columbus who?" the girl asked.

"Okay," Delbit said. "It's your spin. No more sarcasm."

"I don't understand," the girl said. "But there is much I don't understand. Perhaps we should prepare to settle down for the night."

"Night may be approaching here," Delbit said, "but it's lunch-time in my stomach. I'm going to see if I can find us something to eat. To be suddenly thrust somewhere else is shocking. To be somewhere else without food could lead to real unhappiness."

"Toward the sun is a river," she told him. "Can you eat fish?"

"If I can catch them," he said. "How do you know there's a river west of here?"

"We are, I believe, where I have been before. Three times before. Those times, there was a river."

"Oh," Delbit said. "Well, let's go to it while there's still daylight."

They started west. After a few steps Exxa paused to readjust her foot straps.

"Tomorrow I'll make you a pair of sandals," Delbit promised her. "It's one of my few useful skills."

"It would be welcome," Exxa replied, standing gingerly and testing the new configuration. It seemed satisfactory, and they continued toward the west.

The river was almost a mile through the light forest, and the sun was still above the horizon when they arrived at a small hill overlooking the river's edge. The girl stood with her arms wrapped about her chest, staring at the cliffs on the opposite side.

"Are you cold?" Delbit asked.

"Yes," the girl said. "And it will get colder during the night. But as there is nothing I can do about it, there is little point in discussing it."

Delbit considered, He was clad from the waist up in a sleeveless cotton undershirt, but at least he had a pair of heavy twill breeches on. His outer shirt, which was now the slender girl's only garment, was a thin cotton pullover which came down to mid-thigh on her, and could not provide much protection from the chill wind which tugged at them.

But, as she said, there was little to do about it. Perhaps food would warm them. A roast fish, if he could catch a fish, if he could start a fire. He looked out over the river.

"Bedamned!" he said, staring at the shore opposite.

"What?" The girl stared at him.

"Those cliffs across the river. I saw them first a few weeks ago, when I came here from Philadelphia. I'm sure they're the same."

"When you came here?"

"Yes. We are not moved through space. Those cliffs are the Schuylkill Palisades. This is Manhattan Island." He sat on a stone outcropping and stared at the river. "I venture that the clearing we appeared in is the site of Dr. Faineworth's clinic. This must be another time. I venture that we have traveled through time, not space. What a strange notion. We are in the distant past."

The girl sat next to him. "You're saying that I travel through time," she said. "I must consider that. It doesn't sound right, somehow, although certainly I must travel through something. Why do you say it's the past?"

Delbit waved his hand. "Look about you," he said. "The island is totally wild. No streets, no houses, no lights, no ships on the river. Surely in the future Manhattan will get more signs of human occupation, not less."

"Surely," the girl agreed. "And yet, how strange."

"Dr. Faineworth said something about your having traveled through time," Delbit said. "But I didn't follow what he said. I paid little attention. Perhaps I should have listened."

"Right now you should fish," the girl told him, "while there is something of sunlight left."

"True," Delbit agreed. He looked around him thoughtfully. "I don't see how I can manage a hook and line," he said, "but I've heard that the Indians spear fish with a sharpened stick."

"It sounds worth the attempt," the girl said.

Delbit found a thin sapling about six feet long, and broke it off. Then he stripped it and put the best point on it he could managed with the blade of his small pock-pocketknife. The light was fast disappearing, so he scrambled down the hill to the water. Ten minutes later he was back, clutching a large salmon to his chest.

The girl was crouching down by the side of a log, her hands occupied in front of her. She looked up without pausing in what she was doing. "You must be an adept spearsman indeed, to have accomplished so much so fast," she said.

"It wasn't me," Delbit said. "I mean, the fish were waiting for me down there. There's a sort of pen made from netting in the water, and it's full of fish. I just took one. What are you doing?"

"Firemaking," she said. "It should be another minute or two. If you like, you can prepare the fish while I'm getting the fire going."

Delbit peered at what the girl was doing. She had a small sapling-and-vine bow in her hand, and was using it to twirl a stick back and forth against a block of wood on the ground. Bits of dried moss were in readiness to feed the first hint of a flame. "Very clever," Delbit said. "Where'd you learn that?"

She thought for a moment. "I don't know," she replied. "For an instant I almost knew, but the image fled. I don't know." There was a strange, unhappy sound in her voice.

"Oh," Delbit said, for lack of anything better. He cleaned the fish, quartered it, and spitted the pieces on green branches, by which time she had a fire going. They held the slabs of fish over the fire, turning them until they were black all over, and then ate them from the branches. It was, curiously enough, as good a meal as Delbit could ever remember having.

"What sort of people do you suppose made the fish traps?" Exxa asked, carefully scooping dirt over the fire to put it out.

Delbit shrugged. "Indians, I venture," he said. "But there's nothing to worry about; all the eastern tribes are friendly."

"That's another time, friend Delbit," she said. "It may not hold true here-now."

"That's so," Delbit agreed. "We'd better keep out of their way until we see whether they're with us or against us."

The sun had been down for a while, and the last vestige of light was disappearing in the west. They found a clear space big enough to sleep in by the side of a large rock and spread a layer of dried leaves and fresh-picked grass over it. Delbit removed his boots, and Exxa unwrapped her sandals, and then they lay down, huddling together for warmth.

Exxa went to sleep with her head on Delbit's shoulder, and for a long time thereafter he stayed awake, staring at the stars overhead and feeling protective and manly and useful in a way he never had before. He felt also the stirring of sexual interest, of a desire to caress this lovely girl whose life and now whose body had become so entwined with his. But he restrained the urge. Either she'd stay asleep and not know about it or, even worse, dream it was someone else, or she'd wake up and be angry and know she couldn't trust him. Or so Delbit thought. But how could he sleep with this distraction on his shoulder, her breath against his arm?

How—

He slept.

The city stretched to eternity in every direction, and its buildings were tall and crystalline and each had its distinctive color, and each rang with a distinctive note when struck. They strode together through the amber passageways, the Prince and Princess of Loth, and all who saw them bowed low before the aura of their presence, and tinkled small bells fastened by silver bands to wrists and ankles, and all were gladdened by their happiness, and all rejoiced in the eternal city.

And the horses ran before them on the endless plain, to the shores of the mighty river. And the one horse, Nimber, the king of horses, awaited them to take them on his back. Royalty to royalty: the human prince and princess astride the king of horses. It was more than fitting.

But the Calla Gods were not happy. Invisible they went forth, and poked and prodded to express their displeasure. Subtle gods. A pressure sharp-pointed in the side of the prince, to cause pain, to distract, to pull him from the princess's side, from this land, from this dream. This dream....

Delbit woke, and the dream fled before his conscious thoughts. He discovered that a wayward branch was poking into his side, and he pulled it out of the leafy mattress and tossed it away. It was still night, and now there was a moon, or at least a quarter of one, which cast its pale light over the forest. Exxa still slept curled up next to him, her head in the crook of his arm. He puzzled over what of the dream he could remember. It was like one of her dreams. Was it merely that his sleeping mind had remembered—or could it be that they were somehow sharing their dreaming thoughts without being connected by Dr. Faineworth's grotesque machine? He thought of waking her and asking her what she was dreaming, but decided against it. For a while longer he stared up at the stars, and then sleep returned.

Exxa shook him gently. "Wake up, friend Delbit!" she said urgently. "Please, wake up!"

He stirred, groaned, and opened one eye, which refused to focus. It was light. The blur of Exxa was sitting next to him on the grass, leaning over him and shaking him. A blurred pair of legs reached the ground somewhere behind her.

Legs?

He shook his head and opened the other eye. There was a man standing behind Exxa. A slightly bowlegged, bronzed man in cross-tied sandals, a leather breastplate with shoulder pads, and a skirt of vertical leather strips layered over loose-fitting pantaloons of some sort.

Delbit sat up. "What—" He rubbed his eyes and looked around. There were four other men, similarly dressed, standing around them, staring curiously down at them. The men all wore leather helmets that came to a front-to-back knife-edge peak and covered their ears, and they carried spears. Two also had unstrung bows in their hands. They were obviously warriors of some sort, but what were they doing there? And what were their intentions? They didn't look unfriendly, but they didn't look all that friendly either. At least they weren't brandishing the spears and muttering threats.

"Satspot symat chindow mugwump," one of the men commented to another in a curiously rhythmic intonation. If this was language, it wasn't one that Delbit had ever heard. Not that he had ever heard that many languages.

"Lychew natagow," the other man replied calmly. It sounded like an instruction, or an order. He had a silver device on the left side of his breastplate, and his right shoulder pad bore three parallel strips of red fabric. He was probably an officer or chief, or leader of some sort, Delbit decided.

Delbit stared at the four strangers. "Bedamned!" he said softly.

"Don't be afraid, Delbit," Exxa said. "They mean us no harm."

"How can you tell?"

"I don't know," Exxa said. "I guess I just sense it."

"I hope you have good sense," Delbit commented. "I'm not afraid. Not overly afraid, at any rate. It's just that these men aren't Indians. At least, they don't look like any Indians I've ever seen."

"Indians," Exxa said. "That's your name for the natives that inhabit this continent. These persons are of a different ilk?"

"I'd say so," Delbit said, pushing his feet into his boots. "I've seen a lot of Indians. The Six Tribes come to Philadelphia for Peace Day, and besides, we buy hides from the Iroquois factors. And these aren't they."

The apparent leader of the five warriors leaned forward during this conversation, listening to their speech with interest. *"Nagatu primi uganchip?"* he asked.

"Sorry," Delbit told him, "we don't speak whatever that is. Do you understand English? At all?" He turned to Exxa. "Do you speak any foreign languages?"

"I think so," she said. "But at the moment I can't think of which. I'm sure I don't understand this one."

The warriors held a brief discussion. Then the three-striper turned back to them. *"Gink penyan helma ra,"* he said firmly, with an explanatory gesture.

"He wants us to get up," Exxa said.

"Well, we can't sit here all day," Delbit said, pushing himself to his feet. Exxa stood up next to him and dusted her meager garment off. Then she knelt and began re-wrapping one of her birchbark sandals around her right foot.

The three-striper examined them from all sides, seeming surprised and possibly amused by their general appearance, size, complexion, age, and hair color, and especially their clothing. He stared at Exxa's footwear for a moment, and then picked up the birchbark sandal she wasn't holding and examined it. He said something to the men with him, and they nodded. One of them pulled a knapsack off his back, reached into it, and produced a pair of leather sandals much like the ones he was wearing, held on by a thong between the toes and a strap around the leg. He tossed them to Exxa, with a laughing comment, and she gladly strapped them on.

The man, with word and gesture, made it clear that he wanted them to follow him, and then he and his companions turned and trotted off single-file through the underbrush.

"Should we follow?" Exxa asked.

"We might as well," Delbit said. "We have nowhere else to go. Besides, they'd probably just come back for us."

Delbit let Exxa go first, and they followed along after their captors or rescuers or whatever the five men would turn out to be. The men set a rapid pace, but one that was not difficult to keep up with. Particularly after they had cleared the way with their bodies and flattened the path with their feet.

In five minutes they reached a well-defined trail, and quickened their pace. They headed inland, away from the river, moving quietly and purposefully and with an easy grace, despite the heavy armor they wore. It still was not difficult to maintain the pace, but it seemed to Delbit that these men could go on like this all day, and he wasn't sure he could.

After twenty minutes the path swerved back to the west. Shortly it broke clear of the forest and descended a steep, rocky incline to the river. There was a boat dock at the bottom, and the strangest boat Delbit had ever seen was tied up alongside it. The craft was wide and shallow, about forty feet long, with a double prow. There were two bowsprits jutting out from the front, and a carved mythical beast under each bowsprit. It had one stubby mast amidships, with a furled lateen-rig sail. Behind the mast was a deckhouse, and in a cockpit atop that was the ship's wheel.

They jogged out onto the dock, and the three-striper yelled something up at one of the two men visible on the boat—Delbit assumed they were guards. The man nodded and disappeared inside the deckhouse.

Now that they had stopped, Delbit was having a hard time catching his breath. The life of an indentured apprentice doesn't allow for a lot of running, and he was out of practice. None of the other men, who looked to be at least ten years older than he was, were even slightly out of breath from their half hour's jog, and Exxa had a healthy glow about her face and an evenness of breath that indicated that half-hour jogs were merely a good warm-up for some serious exercise.

An older man in a green toga-like garment came out of the deckhouse with the guard and yelled something down at the three-striper. He sounded annoyed. The three-striper answered back, pointing to Delbit and Exxa. He sounded insistent.

The older man climbed down a rope ladder from the deck and stomped over to where Delbit and Exxa were standing. He walked twice around them and looked them over speculatively. Finally he stopped in front of her nose. *"Pronzi nigo res!"* he said, positively. *"Lea vit talu Poff!"*

"I would, you know," Exxa told him, "if I had any idea what you wanted. It seems my fate of late to be accosted by men who are loud, positive, and incomprehensible."

The man turned to Delbit and fingered the stitched hem on his undershirt curiously. *"Satspot,"* he said.

The three-striper replied, talking urgently. It sounded to Delbit as though he was working to convince the older man of something. Finally the older man nodded and yelled up to the guard on the ship.

The three-striper beckoned to Delbit and Exxa, pointed to the boarding rope, and made climbing motions.

"I think he wants us to get on board," Delbit said.

"I hope it's not a sea voyage," Exxa said. "I don't think that would be wise."

As they climbed the rope ladder, a gong sounded from somewhere above them: three beats, and then a pause, and then three more beats, and then a longer pause, and then it was repeated; and the sound reverberated back to them from the cliffs across the river.

The others climbed up behind them, and the gentleman in the toga led them to a small cabin in the deckhouse, motioned them inside, and closed the door.

"Do you suppose we're prisoners?" Exxa asked.

"Hard to say," Delbit said. "I didn't hear the door lock, but they may have posted a guard outside." He went over to the door and peered out. "Nobody's visible. Let's give them the benefit of the doubt and assume we're honored guests. I've always wanted to be an honored guest. Why do you hope that we're not taking a sea voyage?"

"Because if you're right, then I travel through time, not space, when I blip. And if that's right, then if I'm in the middle of an ocean when it happens, I'll probably drown."

"I didn't think of that," Delbit said.

Groups of men appeared out of the forest and ran out to the dock, to the accompaniment of the beating gong, and clambered up onto the boat. After a while the gong stopped.

The three-striper entered the cabin with an armful of clothing and dumped it on the stretched-canvas bunk. Behind him was a man carrying a large basin of water in his two hands, with several towels draped over his arms. He set the basin and towels on a small table jutting out from the far wall. The three-striper pointed to the basin, and then the clothing, and then to Delbit and Exxa, and said something in a friendly manner. Then he and the other man left.

"Clean clothes," Exxa said, "and a sufficiency of them, by the looks of it." She sorted through the pile and pulled various articles out for closer examination. "The dress, I assume, is for me. And these various undergarments, such as they are, seem to be of the feminine bent. The explanation I favor is that there are other women on the boat. Whereas this is clearly masculine in intent.

"I shall wash and dress while I have the chance," she continued, stripping off Delbit's shirt and standing in front of the basin. "These people, whoever they are, are very thoughtful, and very cleanly. There's a sea sponge here, and a block of soap. And the water's hot, by Xerxes!"

Delbit flushed and turned away, fighting the desire to stare at her long-limbed body. "I won't look until you're dressed," he said.

"Why not?" she asked, wringing out the sponge and starting to wash the dirt off her arms and legs. "Do you find me ugly?"

"On the contrary," he told her. "It's just that, er, we don't look at each other without clothes on. Especially not people of the other gender."

"You have a social constraint against nakedness," she said. "I thought so."

"You don't where you come from?" Delbit asked.

"It would seem that way," she said. "I don't like being stared at by people I'm not fond of, like Dr. Faineworth or his fat friend. But nudity among friends seems natural to me."

"You must come from an interesting place," Delbit said, continuing to stare at the opposite wall.

"I certainly hope so," she said. "I noted that Dr. Faineworth seemed to think that taking my clothes away gave him some sort of power over me; but even then he felt impelled to give me a bathrobe. That made me think that your civilization probably has a strong and pervasive inhibition against nakedness."

"It's true," Delbit said. "Until this moment I had not ever considered an alternative."

"There's no preference," Exxa said. "Every civilization has its built-in rules, that's all. They are usually invisible to the people living them, unless they are pointed out."

"Like what?" Delbit asked. "Besides taking your clothes off."

"Like food," Exxa said. "You think that those things that you find edible are the natural things to eat. Some people eat dogs, or locusts, or termites. Some people don't eat meat at all, and would get sick if they watched you eat a steak."

"Dogs?" Delbit asked.

"Even so."

"That's horrible! How do you know all this stuff? I thought you'd lost your memory."

"You can turn around now," Exxa said. "I'll tell you what: I'll stare at the wall while you wash and change clothes."

Delbit turned around. Exxa was wearing a flowing white dress, belted at the waist, and looked pure and lovely and untouched. Delbit told her so.

"Untouched, is it?" Exxa said, smiling. She lifted the skirt of her dress and stuck out one newly clean but very scratched leg. "Look at what's happened to my legs in running along that path. I've been touched by every thorn bush in the forest. I was about to say that I've never been so cut up, but of course that may not be so, as my memory is less than two months old."

"You didn't answer my question."

"How do I know so much? I don't know that. I remember all sorts of facts, but nothing about myself."

Delbit changed places with Exxa and took his clothes off, after self-consciously making sure she was facing the other way. He busied himself with sponging the dirt off his body. "By the facts you know," he told her, "we could probably figure out a lot about where you come from and what your past is—or was."

"That may be so," Exxa agreed. "It's certainly worth trying."

"There is one thing," Delbit said. "I was wrong about us going back in time."

"You were? How do you know?"

Delbit thought about his answer while he finished his sponge bath. He felt a slight jarring motion, and realized that the boat was leaving its mooring. "As far as I know, these people are not in the past of my country. And yet I could swear that this is, indeed, Manhattan Island." He stuck his feet in the pair of baggy trousers that he found on the bed, pulled them up, and tied them around his waist. "They are not Indians. Neither are they Norsemen, Celts, Egyptians, or any of the other races claimed to predate Columbus's arrival in Nova Isabella."

"I wonder what they are, then," Exxa said. "And where we are. And where they're taking us."

CHAPTER SIX

The boat moved steadily upstream, propelled by the strong arms of forty rowers, twenty on each side. A drummer on the quarterdeck beat the time as the eighteen-foot oars rhythmically lifted and dipped. Delbit and Exxa stood on deck watching the Hudson, or whatever it was called here, flow by. The warriors who had been recalled to the boat were doing the rowing, their spears and bows hung in racks along the railing and their heavy leather armor folded neatly at their sides in case of need. Six armored warriors served as lookouts, standing along the rail and casting suspicious eyes on the passing scenery.

Delbit watched as the six lookouts changed places with six rowers, one at a time so the boat would never be eyeless. The procedure took place about every half hour, and was the only break that the rowers got.

"Those lookouts are serious about peering into the forest," Delbit commented to Exxa. "And notice how the rowers keep their arms and armor by them. I venture these people have active enemies. I hope we don't find ourselves in the middle of a battle."

"I hope they keep thinking we're on their side," Exxa replied. "They seem to be awfully anxious to figure out who we are."

"You think so?" Delbit asked her.

"This is all for us," she reminded him. "These forty men toiling through the day, rowing under this hot sun, when they had planned to be hunting, or whatever, in the cool forest. They're taking us somewhere to be identified. Haven't you noticed that there's an armed guard discreetly hovering in that doorway, watching us?"

"Well," Delbit said, "after all, they're all armed. You can't expect one of them to put his sword away just because he's watching us."

"That's so, I suppose. But I still think they're very concerned about us. They would like very much to find out where we're from, and when we get wherever we're going, they're going to try real hard. That's what I think," Exxa told him.

"How can they hope to know where we're from when we don't?" Delbit asked.

"An interesting question," Exxa said. "Maybe they think they already know."

"I'm afraid that there is no way that their assumptions can coincide with our realities," Delbit said.

The scenery passed as they went upriver, mostly heavy forest with an occasional meadow thrown in for relief. They saw a wide variety of water birds, and an occasional deer crashed noisily off into the woods as they passed. Once they saw a pair of moose, a heavily antlered bull and a winsome-looking cow, that paused in their drinking, standing up to their knees in the river, and looked curiously up at the passing craft. Later they passed a pier, jutting out into the river, with several men on it who seemed quite surprised to see them go by. Shortly after that they smelled wood burning, which caused a lot of excited murmuring among their escorts, and sent a lookout up to the top of the stubby mast. But he couldn't see smoke anywhere, and shortly afterward the smell passed.

The rowers rowed steadily, hour after hour, until early evening. Then, as the sun was poised to drop below the horizon, the trees on the left bank parted and a village surrounded by a high wooden palisade came into view. The boat pulled up to a dock under the watchful eyes of a squad of crossbowmen atop the palisade wall.

The three-striper who had found them gathered an escort of three guards and hurried Delbit and Exxa through the gate and into the village. The men they passed were all warriors, Delbit noted as they made their way down the central street. There were some women visible, dressed in long, dark-colored robes, belted at the waist, but no children—at least none in view. No one they went by showed the slightest curiosity about the passing strangers.

The buildings were well-constructed rectangular structures of roughly hewn wood, with the framing poles jutting out an extra two or three feet at each of the upper corners. They had an impermanent look to them, as though they hadn't been there long and didn't plan to stay. The streets were unpaved, and although they were wide enough for vehicles, there were none in evidence. At each intersection one of the corners had a life-size statue of a man with a bird's head—Delbit thought it was a hawk—hewn from a log and painted lifelike colors. Each bird-headed man statue was dressed and arrayed differently; this one a warrior, this one a worker, this a patrician.

"I've never seen anything like this," Delbit murmured to Exxa.

She nodded. "This is a Kalgash war village," she told him. "We are among the Kalgash."

Delbit stared at her. "Who are the Kalgash—and how do you know?"

Exxa considered. "The Kalgash," she said in a positive voice, as though she were reciting a lesson, "are a warlike people who settled the Northwestern Continent—what you call North America—in their section of the Paraverse some three thousand years ago. They came originally from somewhere around the Black Sea and crossed Europe before making it to the Northwestern Continent. They probably crossed in boats much like the one we were just on, starting from some northern point where the distance is not excessive. The various Kalgash tribes war against each other and against the Asian people who settled the continent from the west. Those are probably the people you call Indians."

"Bedamned!" Delbit said. "How do you know all that?"

Exxa stopped. "I don't know," she said. 'It's just.... I don't know. I recognize the building style, and the street-corner statues. I know I'm right, but I don't know how I know or how I learned. I certainly don't understand their language. Not even a hint."

"What's a Paraverse?"

"A what?"

"You said something about 'their section of the Paraverse,'" Delbit told her. "What's a Paraverse?"

She stared at him. "I have no idea," she said.

"*Meshak,*" their escort said firmly, beckoning to them. "*Meshak!*"

At the three-striper's urging, they meshaked their way down the street to a two-story central building, larger but no more elaborate than any of the other buildings. There was a statue of a woman in a niche to the left of the doorway: a full-breasted wide-hipped woman with an impossibly narrow waist and the head of a cat. She was wearing a dress that flared at the hips and fell into neat pleats at the ankles, with a pair of dainty sandaled feet peeking out below. Above the waist, the dress rose to cup the large breasts from below, pushing them up for inspection. The whole was painted in lifelike colors, and Delbit noted that the lips and nipples were rouged.

"The Earth Goddess, probably," Exxa said, noticing him staring at the statue. "A fertility symbol."

"I'll say," Delbit agreed.

"There's a good chance that this civilization is a matriarchy, if the Earth Goddess is given this prominence," Exxa said. "If so the person who decides whether we are to be accepted or not will be a woman."

"Is that good?" Delbit asked.

"I much prefer men," Exxa said. "Women are much less trusting, and much nastier when aroused."

"Aha," Delbit said.

The three-striper led them into an inner room, where there was a long, low table and half-dozen low stools with woven straw seats. He indicated that they should wait there, and went away. One small window was set in the far wall, but it was too high to look out of. As the sun was already below the horizon, it let in little light. The room was cold, and draped in shadow.

Exxa sat down. "What do you think we should do?" she asked.

"I don't see that we have any options," Delbit told her. "But you know more about these people than I. If you think they're going to kill us outright, or sacrifice us to the hawk-headed god, then I guess we might as well try to escape."

"I don't know any more about these people than what I've told you," Exxa said. "At least, I don't think I do. If any more random facts pop into my mind, I'll voice them to you."

"You think maybe you're starting to get your memory back?" Delbit asked.

"I don't think so," Exxa said. "That recital about the Kalgash wasn't recovered memory. It was always there—it just needed the sight of a Kalgash war village to bring it out. It's like, say, the word 'accordion,' or 'parallelepiped'; the words are in your memory, but unless you see or hear one, they probably don't spring unbidden into the conscious mind."

"What's a parallelepiped?" Delbit asked.

"A six-sided solid, with each side a parallelogram," Exxa explained.

"Oh."

"Well, I was looking for a word that didn't occur every day," she said.

"You found one," Delbit said. "But you see what that means: there are clues to your self—to your missing memory—hidden in the memories you've retained. That bit about the Paraverse, for example. Whatever a Paraverse turns out to be when you open the box."

"The box?"

"Like a birthday present," Delbit explained. "You open the box and look at it, and then you say, 'For me? Why, how nice! Just what I've always wanted—a Paraverse. What does it do,

Uncle Percy?'"

"I hope you're around when I open the box to my memories, Delbit," Exxa said, reaching her hand out and taking his. "I think I'm afraid of what I might find inside."

The door opened, and the three-striper returned, followed closely by a short, skinny, elderly woman dressed in black, who was carrying a lighted taper and smoking a long, skinny, twisted cigar. The three-striper waved an identifying arm at them, said a few brief syllables to the woman, and left. The woman smiled at them, a thin-lipped smile, and circled the room, lighting four oil lamps that were set into sconces in the wall. Then she blew out the taper and went behind the table to sit down. Delbit found himself fascinated by the thin, twisted column of smoke rising from the taper after she blew it out. He had once heard that seers divined the future from the shapes to be found in rising smoke. What, he wondered, did this one foretell? It looked for a second like a fist, to his intense stare, and then it resembled a monstrous bird. And then it looked merely like a thin column of smoke.

The woman produced a roll of paper from her robe, which she unrolled on the table, holding it flat with two brass turtles. Then she looked up at them and said a short, interrogative sentence. The oil lamp flickered slightly with the evening breeze, Delbit noticed, casting ever-changing shadows on the bare walls.

Delbit shook his head. "I, at least, didn't understand you," he said, smiling at her to show that there were no hard feelings.

Exxa leaned forward. "Do you speak Anglic?" she asked the woman, speaking as clearly as she could.

"English," Delbit said. "We call it English."

Exxa looked at him. "Really?" she said. "That's strange."

The woman leaned forward and looked intently at them. Then she said something in a new language, clearly different from the one she had been speaking. It neither made sense nor sounded in the least familiar to Delbit. He shook his head and shrugged.

She tried again, mouthing the guttural sounds of yet a third language and looking expectantly at them. "It sounds like a cat gargling," Delbit told her.

The woman spoke a few words in her original tongue that carried an aura of displeasure about them despite their lack of specific meaning, and beckoned them over to the table. She pointed down at the unrolled scroll. It was, Delbit realized, a chart. The writing on it looked to him like chicken scratchings, and the marked-off areas conveyed nothing. It was hard to make out detail in the flickering light. He stared at it and shook his head. "I'm sorry—" he said.

The woman said something sharply to herself, and turned the scroll around to face Delbit and Exxa. Delbit suddenly realized that he had been staring uncomprehendingly at a map of the world. It was centered somewhere toward the eastern end of the Mediterranean Sea. Delbit recognized the boot-and-ball-shaped Kingdom of the Five Sicilies, and the inked-in boundary lines divided Europe into a quilt of unfamiliar areas; but it was a map of the world for all that. North America was divided roughly into thirds by dotted lines running north and south.

"It's the world," he said.

"It's a world," Exxa agreed. "In general outline it seems to be the one I'm familiar with, but the various boundaries seem capricious."

"The country divisions do seem to be a bit, ah, arbitrary," Delbit agreed. "They are not the ones I am familiar with. Nonetheless it is our very planet."

"It verily is," Exxa agreed. "And what are we to do about it?"

"What do you mean?" Delbit asked.

The woman took an ivory stylus from her robe and pointed to roughly where they were now on the map. Then she handed the stylus to Exxa and smiled at her, waving a hand over the rest of the map.

"I see," Delbit said. "She wants us to indicate where we're from."

"We can't tell her the truth," Exxa said. "Even if we were sure just what the truth is, we have no way to communicate it to her. We're going to have to very carefully pick a place to point to. A place where they speak a language nobody here understands, and a place that these people aren't at war with."

"That should be easy," Delbit said, bending over the map. He paused. "Hmm," he said. "I see what you mean. We don't know enough."

"And no way to learn," Exxa said. "Well, I have to tell her something." Exxa pointed to an area on the east coast of the Baltic.

The woman took the pointer and pointed to the same spot, and then to Exxa and Delbit. *"Sensa Bashkavid?"* she demanded.

"I guess so," Exxa said. "Whatever."

The woman spewed out a couple of rapid-fire questions and then, realizing that they could neither understand nor respond, she shook her head, said something else, and left the room. A minute later a young warrior entered carrying a wooden platter, which he set down on the table. *"Smerjif,"* he told them, indicating the platter, and then he left the room.

On the platter lay a medley of roasted bits of chicken and various vegetables, and two earthenware mugs filled with apple juice.

"I never truly realized the importance of language before," Delbit said, taking a piece of the chicken and popping it into his mouth. It was peppery but good.

"I hope I picked a part of the world that these people are fond of," Exxa said, holding a piece of chicken neatly between two fingers and chewing on the other end.

"How can they have any opinion on a place they've certainly never been?" Delbit asked her.

"Everybody has such opinions," Exxa said. "They become part of the folklore. 'You can't trust an Etruscan,' or 'If you have a Banth for a friend, you don't need any enemies.'"

"I see what you mean," Delbit said. "Like 'You can tell a New Dorset man by the color of the egg on his shirt.'"

Exxa looked at him. "Like that," she agreed. They finished the chicken and drank the juice, and sat there wondering what was going to happen next.

The door opened, and a small clay lamp with a lighted wick

entered the room, followed closely by a young man in a brown robe. The man nodded at them and beckoned with his free hand, talking to them in a clear, high-pitched voice. They followed behind as he trotted down the dark corridor, the weak light from his lamp contrasting and thus intensifying the gloom. He kept up the one-sided conversation, turning to smile at them pleasantly every few steps.

"He's not dressed as a warrior," Delbit said. "He's the first man we've seen since the boat's captain that wasn't dressed as a warrior."

"I'd guess he's a clerk or scribe, or whatever they call them in this culture," Exxa said. "Whenever you have writing, you have records to keep, and you need a person to keep them. In some cultures they become a semi-priestly class, in others they are slaves. It all depends on the people's outlook on such things."

Their guide finished what must have been an amusing anecdote, chuckled briefly, and then preceded them up a knotted-rope ladder to the second floor, maneuvering neatly with one hand until he could rest the lamp on the floor above. Exxa had little trouble following him, but rope-climbing had not been included in Delbit's apprenticeship. His school had offered rope-climbing during the hour of compulsory torture it called gymnasium class, and most of the boys had enjoyed it. It was certainly more fun than such alternate gymnastic enterprises as throwing the large leather ball full of sand about in a circle, or hopping on one foot and then the other while lunging at your classmate with a cotton-waste-filled baton. But Delbit had always totally disliked the enjoyments of "most boys," including all contact sports and any form of exercise. In any possible future that he had envisioned for himself, the ability to run mile after mile without tiring or to climb a rope had not seemed a high priority.

He had been mistaken.

Delbit pulled himself laboriously up and sat on the floor to catch his breath. The man made what might have been a pointed comment on Delbit's rope-climbing prowess—or possibly merely a remark on the fine weather they were having so late in the year—and took them to a pair of small adjoining rooms at the rear of the building, lighting a tiny oil lamp in each room. The rooms each had a cot and a low table with a pitcher of water. Then he showed them the back door, with its rope ladder coiled beside it, and pointed to the courtyard below, indicating a small shed-like building in the center.

"The privy," Delbit guessed.

"Of course," Exxa agreed. "And it has a roof. How civilized of them."

The scribe told them another funny story, laughed at it, and then went away, dropping dexterously back down the indoor rope ladder.

"It is strange not knowing whether he was just saying 'There were these two Frisians walking down the street' or 'They're going to take you out and shoot you tomorrow morning,'" Delbit said. "I do wish I knew which it was."

"Since we know nothing of his sense of humor, either is possible," Exxa agreed. "But I prefer to think that if they were preparing us for execution, they would indulge in a more somber ritual. And they'd probably lock the door."

They abluted and prepared for bed. Delbit went into his room and lay supine on the hard cot with the one thin blanket pulled up to his chin, staring at the flickering shadows on the ceiling and thinking. His life, humdrum for so long, had become hectic; and the hecticity was increasing at an exponential rate. Two months ago he had been placidly, if not contentedly, spending his days sweeping the floor of a Philadelphia shoe factory. Two weeks ago he had become apprenticed by right of sale to a doctor in Manhattan, and was traveling about in someone else's dreams. Two days ago he had suddenly blipped into another place— that was somehow the same place—with Exxa, and here he was lying on a hard cot in an upstairs room in the central building of a Kalgash war village, whatever that was. Life, he thought, could hold no more surprises.

He was mistaken.

Exxa came into the room with her blanket wrapped around

her thin body. "Are you awake?" she asked softly.

Delbit sat up. "Yes," he whispered.

"I don't want to be alone," she said, coming over to his cot. "Let me sleep with you."

"Sleep with me?" Delbit felt his heart beating suddenly, and something was caught in his throat. "You mean—?"

Exxa sat down next to him and stroked his cheek. "Perhaps," she said. "Perhaps I do. Although I doubt whether either of us is up to lovemaking tonight. I find the touch of your body very pleasing, and lying in your arms very comforting. I think I like you. How much of this is due to circumstance and propinquity is impossible to tell. We could at least start there, and if anything more happens, then it was meant to be."

"If you come into my bed—cot—after saying that, and nothing else happens, I shall be very surprised," Delbit said.

"So be it," Exxa said, kissing him on the forehead. Leaving her blanket at the foot of the cot, she gently pushed him down and lay next to him, fitting her body to his. She was naked under the blanket. "Hold me," she said.

And so he did.

Delbit's experience with women was limited to reading and imagination, but some things require no practice. Holding a lovely girl snuggled in your arms is one of these. His mind raced and thought of many things, obscure irrational things that had little to do with a boy and a girl lying together on a small cot with no clothes on. But her physical presence, and the smell and feel of her next to him, overwhelmed his senses.

She moved slightly and wrapped an arm around him, and murmured something to him in a language he didn't understand. He was startled briefly, but did not say anything. Not now. Later he would ask her what she had said, and what language she had spoken, but now he didn't want to do anything to alter the feeling that had enveloped them both.

She took his free hand, the one her head wasn't lying on, and kissed it. "Well?" she whispered. "It's your move, my dear friend."

"I'm afraid to start," he said, realizing as he said it that it was true.

"Afraid of me?" she asked.

"No. Well, maybe a little. But mostly afraid to start making love to you."

"Why."

Delbit searched for words. "This is going to sound strange," he said. "But if I—we—start, then after a while it will end. And I want this moment to continue forever, and never end."

"All things must end," Exxa said softly. "And if we do not begin, then it will simply end without ever having happened, which would be sad indeed." Her hands moved on his body, and her lips met his.

After a while they slept a dreamless sleep.

CHAPTER SEVEN

A cry or alarm pierced the still night, close followed by another.

Delbit stirred. Exxa shivered in her sleep.

Silence—

—broken by a shriek.

Delbit opened his eyes. The lamp had gone out, and it was as dark on one side of his eyelids as the other.

In the distance, someone yelled in an unknown tongue. Then several other voices took up the cry. Commands? Threats? It was impossible to tell.

Exxa rolled over. "Are you awake?" she whispered, holding his arm.

The sound of many running feet came through the window, along with more distant thudding and cracking noises. Someone screamed.

"I am now," Delbit said.

"What do you suppose is happening?"

"I have several guesses, all of them unpleasant," Delbit whispered. "Can you find your room in the dark?"

"You want me to leave?"

"I want you to go get dressed. If the lamp is still burning in your room, blow it out first. Then come back here."

She swung her feet around and sat up. Wrapping her blanket around her, she bent to kiss him on the nose, which she found with unerring accuracy in the dark, and then she was up and through the door.

Delbit rose and groped his way across the small room to the low table and felt around until he located the pitcher of water. He poured the ice-cold water over his hands and splashed it on his shoulders and face, wiping them with a small square of fabric that might have been a towel. Then he dressed as rapidly as he could manage in the dark.

The noises were louder now, and more directed, coming mostly from somewhere off to the left of the window. Thuds and clanks, and hollered commands, and yells, and a strange high-pitched keening sound, and an occasional scream. A few bright flashes of green and blue light winked briefly in the sky.

This was not a situation Delbit was prepared for. As he dressed he tried to figure out what to do. Exxa had taken his direction immediately, with no discussion. This extremely competent woman seemed to think him capable of making reasonable decisions, and he didn't want to disappoint her. But it would be a lot easier to make a reasoned decision if he had some idea of just what the hell was going on out there. Loud clanging and yelling in the night was certainly the manifestation of some dark evil, but just what it might be he could only guess.

These people were probably under attack. But by whom? And with what purpose? And just what should or could he and Exxa do about it? He didn't even know which side they should be on—if either.

Exxa came back to the room. "It's getting louder," she said. "What now?"

"A good question," Delbit said. "My experience with other people's battles tells me that the best thing to do is to keep out of the way. I will admit that the only battles I'm personally familiar with involved boys with snowballs, but I think the principle is sound."

"Just what I was thinking," Exxa said. "Now all we have to do is find out just where 'the way' is, so we can continue to keep out of it."

"Sounds right to me," Delbit agreed.

An arc of light crossed the sky out their window, shortly

followed by a second, and then a third.

"Fire arrows!" Delbit said, going over to the window to see if he could tell where they were landing. For an instant a blue light flickered against the sky. It didn't look like any sort of flame Delbit had ever seen. "Those people are serious, whoever they are," he said.

"The wood in these structures is remarkably green," Exxa commented. "They're not going to burn easily."

"That's true," Delbit said. "Still, fire arrows are a pretty uncivilized way to fight a war."

"Judging by those pretty-colored flashes, someone is using beamers out there," Exxa said, "and that's very civilized, but very nasty. Especially against people who obviously don't even have guns."

"Beamers?"

"Light-beam weapons," Exxa said. "They come in different sizes, from hand-held to as big as a house. They cast powerful beams of light or other energy."

"How can a beam of light hurt anyone?" Delbit asked.

"Truth be known, I don't know how they work," Exxa said, "but work they do. If the beam hits you, it'll burn a hole right through you and set fire to whatever is on the other side."

Delbit stared at her. "I'll trust you on that," he said.

"I exaggerate," Exxa admitted, staring out the window into the darkness below, "but not much."

The battle grew noisier and closer. The enemy had broken through the palisade walls, and warriors could now be heard running through the streets beyond the enclosure.

"Whatever we're going to do," Delbit said, "we'd better do it now. There's no point in running, and besides, we have nowhere to run to. But it would be prudent to keep out of the way of whatever's happening." He thought for a moment and then said, "Let's see if we can get up on the roof."

"Take your blanket," Exxa suggested. "I'll go get mine."

Delbit stripped the blanket off his cot and joined Exxa in the hallway. They felt their way along the wall in the pitch dark, checking each room as they came to it for the access rope to the roof, which would, Delbit thought, probably be tied off against one of the walls.

"This isn't going to work," Delbit whispered when they reached the window at the far end of the hall. "The rope may be tied off too far to reach in the dark." He peered out the window, while Exxa went into the last room in the line. It was still pitch dark, and he couldn't make out anything of what was happening below. An occasional flash of blue light lit up the sky, but for too brief a time for any detail to be carried to the eye.

"I found it!" Exxa announced from inside the room. "Here, against the far wall."

Delbit went over to her and felt around where she indicated. There, right up against the wall, was a knotted climbing rope descending from the ceiling, looping around a hook on the wall. Exxa unhooked it so that the free end dropped to the floor, and then scrambled up it like an athletic young girl climbing a rope. "There's a trap up here," she whispered down to him. "Wait a second—I'll open it."

Delbit heard a scraping sound and suddenly felt a cold breeze.

"It is the roof. I can see stars," she said. After a couple of bumping noises, she called down, "There! I'm sitting on the roof now. Come on up!"

"Be careful where you step," Delbit called. "It's probably only strong enough to support rainwater, not people. Here I come!"

Delbit slung his blanket over his shoulder and used all his strength to pull himself up the rope. Exxa helped him over the edge of the trap, and they pulled the rope up and closed the trapdoor. There they huddled on the main roof beam, sitting on one blanket with the other wrapped around them. From their position at the front of the building they listened to the fighting going on below.

In a little while they heard the sounds of people thrashing their way about in the building below them. The sounds continued, getting louder and closer.

"Whoever is down there, they're not exactly trying to be

quiet," Exxa whispered. "It sounds like they're breaking every lamp, every pot, and every stick of furniture they come across."

"And a few bones, I venture," Delbit said. "Let's try not to be noticed."

There were people in the building now. They heard the sounds of fighting from somewhere below. In a short while they heard voices and footsteps coming from directly under the trap. Then they saw white light coming up from around the edge of the trap cover.

Delbit grabbed hold of Exxa's arm. "Disappear," he told her. "Take a deep breath and let's go somewhere else."

"I'll try," Exxa said. She closed her eyes and concentrated.

The trapdoor suddenly flew upward, letting a bright white light flare up through the trap like a beacon into the night sky. A horned helmet thrust up to roof level, and a pair of eyes like angry almonds peered about the rooftop. Delbit and Exxa froze where they were and found themselves staring at the man who was now staring at them. That part of him that was visible below the head was covered with an armor made of thick leather slabs, overlapped all around and studded with brass rivets.

The armored man grasped both sides of the trap and pushed himself onto the roof. Without a word, he grabbed Exxa with one hand and pulled her toward him, then swung her around and dropped her bodily through the trap. The action showed a precision and economy of motion that, in other circumstances, Delbit might have admired.

"Hey!" Delbit yelled. "You can't just—"

"Mushk!" the man said firmly. He reached his hand out with the speed and accuracy of a striking snake and grabbed Delbit by the collar of his shirt. Dropping suddenly to his knees, he swung Delbit in an arc over his head and released him over the trap, headfirst. Time moved slowly as Delbit waited for the approaching floor to crush his head. But at the last possible second he was grabbed at the waist and shoulders by the two men in the room below. They dropped him roughly to the floor, knocking the breath from him. He lay there quite unable to

move, waiting for whatever would happen next.

The man on the roof dropped lightly back through the trap and barked a brief series of guttural orders to the two catchers. They produced leather thongs from about their heavily armored persons and tied Exxa and Delbit securely by the wrists and ankles. Then one of them picked up Delbit and the other Exxa, and they tossed them over their shoulders like two sacks of grain and started out the building. At the trap to the ground floor they went down the rope ladder as if the extra weight meant nothing to them.

Delbit felt himself in the grip of a blinding rage, and a desire to do something—anything—to get himself and Exxa out of this horrible, painful, and humiliating situation. He had been treated badly in many ways during the course of his brief life, but never before had he ever been being treated like a sack. It was galling, it was humiliating, it was very frightening.

Gradually, as he bounced along on the shoulder of his captor on his way out of the camp, the feeling of rage was replaced with one of supernatural calm. Anger would not get him out of this. He would have to stay alert and watchful, and wait for the right moment. And hope that he could recognize it when it came.

CHAPTER EIGHT

Ensirs Donnesby and Pollock, two members of the Overline Import Complex Directorate, sat facing Preceptor Castimere Parr across the ancient walnut table that he used for official business. Their hands were folded across their chests, and their expressions were bland. Parr gazed speculatively at them across the table, wondering what they wanted, and why.

Even more than the other lords of the Overline, the merchant princes of the OIC considered themselves the born rulers of the Paraverse and resented any interference from the preceptors, or even the Great Council. As they were here, they wanted something. The questions were whether it was something he could give, and what they planned to offer in return. After all, no matter how princely they behaved, they were at heart merchants, and merchants believe in bartering as others believe in their household gods.

They were in Parr's office in the Preceptory, a complex of buildings gathered around the Preceptors' Court, which was a large formal garden in which the preceptors were by tradition supposed to wander while solving the more subtle problems facing the Overline. Like many of the structures in Lyander City, the Preceptory was in the pseudo-Greek style, popularized two centuries before, known as Assumptive.

Lyander City, the seat of government of the Overline, had been growing for the past two hundred years according to the carefully structured plans of the Planning Board, subject to the approval of the City Council. Were it not that these carefully structured plans were radically altered at the whims of each new City Council, which appointed each new Planning Board, the city would be a masterpiece in marble, a fitting backdrop for the self-styled rulers of the Paraverse. But despite a recurring preference for use of the Assumptive style, Lyander City was a fascinatingly diverse hodgepodge of official, semiofficial, and unofficial buildings, differing wildly in style, scale, ornamentation, and placement. In the two hundred years since the Overliners had moved to that strand and established Lyander City, it had grown so large that even longtime residents usually consulted a map when going to a less familiar part of town.

The oak-paneled walls of the Preceptor Parr's office were hung with oil paintings by Van Rijn, Van Dyck, Vermeer, and other seventeenth-century Flemish and Dutch masters of Fifth-Level, Alpha-area C-Line, which was properly identified as the Claudius-Charlemagne-Elizabeth line, and generally known as Fifth-Alpha-Charlie. Parr had a fondness for the painting of this particular area in this particular period of this particular line, and rescued it from any strand where its continued existence was in doubt.

Ensir Pollock had requested the meeting in subdued, almost respectful tones, with only muted sarcasm in his fleeting mention of the Preceptory. This was uncharacteristic of any of the lords of the Overline, particularly unusual from any of the mercantile princes, and decidedly unexpected from this pair. They surely wanted something, Parr thought, probably something they weren't supposed to have.

In an attempt to keep the moral high ground, Parr had on his official silks—a flowing jacket and trousers in gold-trimmed imperial red—and he wore the engraved ruby Orb of Office of the Preceptory on a golden chain around his neck. A preceptor needed and used every psychological edge possible in dealing with his (or her) fellow lords.

The lords of the Overline felt that any sensible sentient entity would recognize them as the Gods' Elect; after all, could they not control the destinies of quintillions of people on billions of

Earths? Were they not the invisible rulers of tens of thousands of nations on thousands of strands on hundreds of lines in dozens of areas of the Paraverse?

Some of the more thoughtful, or more perverse, among the lords considered their position as more analogous to that of parasites than that of the gods' emissaries; but such opinions were suppressed or ignored by the other lords, an overwhelming majority.

Most members of the OIC, those arrogant princes of Paraversal commerce, strongly resented the exercise of any authority over themselves, even such authority as had been designated by their own Great Council. When they had to appeal to such authority for help, they resented it even more. The nine preceptors found it necessary to maintain a psychological and moral superiority over the Overline nobility in order to serve them. Thus the trappings of office. Thus the armed fancy-dress Preceptorian Guard at the door, and the somber secretaries in the waiting room. Governing did not demand such trappings, but keeping the consent of the governed did.

Ensir Donnesby, a thin, intense, tight-lipped man well into his second century, had an apparent age of about forty-five; but he was a man with a low threshold of irritation, and a century of irritation showed in his face. There were scowl lines at the sides of his mouth and a hint of cosmeticized frown lines straddling his eyes. His nose had an angry peak, and his chin jutted stubbornly forward. He was leaning back in his chair, pursing his lips in concentration, and staring intently and unblinkingly at Parr. A black leather document case fitted with gold hardware was by the side of the chair, and he kept his left hand resting casually on it.

His companion, Ensir Pollock, was even older and looked even younger, if less well kept. A round-faced man with no hair at all on his head, he clad his portly body in a loose-fitting red toga and wore wristlets of diamonds on each arm and chunky diamond rings on almost every finger. He looked, Parr thought, like a flustered matron at a garden party. This was his most recent look, and was largely affectation. Pollock was reputed to have one of the finest mercantile minds in the Overline, which he artfully concealed under a facade of constantly varying affectation.

"You should marry, Ensir Parr," Pollock said, reaching to a small ornate silver plate on the table and taking a tiny sweet-meat daintily between his thumb and ring finger. He examined it, sniffed it, and then popped it into his mouth. "Really you should. How is the Overline to breed the highly intelligent capable youth it needs to replace those it loses by attrition if its finest minds produce no offspring?"

The favorite conversational gambit in Overline these days was the oblique attack.

"Ah!" Parr said, leaning back and lacing his hands together behind his head. "And what of yourself? Are the permissible pair of Pollock progeny even now springing off to one of our institutes of higher education?"

"You know, Preceptor, that I lack the inclination, the enthusiasm, for the rather strenuous activity that engenders progeny. I am given to understand, through the most casual and innocuous of rumors, that you have been known to indulge in the sport. But you play it with one of the females of your household staff, and thus any brats you may get are half-bloods, and therefore, according to the collective wisdom of our Great Council, not to be considered of the Overline. This is of no aid to our decreasing population."

Suppressing an urge to hit Pollock in his fat face, Parr merely raised an eyebrow. "I had not realized that my amatory affairs were matters for common gossip," he murmured. "Do you have pictures? Should I put shades on the windows?"

"Nonsense," Pollock said, dismissing the thought with a shake of his massive head. "Don't be annoyed at my pleasantry, Ensir Parr. The Paraverse is so large and there are so few of us that we of the Overline are of necessity all one great family. And all families gossip interminably; it's one of the habits that deters internecine homicide. It is a good thing that you practice the, ah, skills of procreation with a female partner, Overliner or not. We seem to be becoming an effete culture, requiring stranger, more intense, and more perverse entertainments every year to keep our interest in playing the mating game. The gods know I certainly do. Ensir Donnesby here finds the game greatly stimulating, but only as a spectator sport, I fear."

So, Parr thought, we're all one big happy family, are we? This must be something serious indeed!

Donnesby's perpetual look of annoyance increased. "That's ridiculous, Pollock," he snapped. "When I go to one of your orgiastic affairs I find myself merely watching because the boys you supply are too young." He bore down heavily on the word "boys."

"Ah, yes," Pollock said, his voice syrupy with sympathy. "And the girls, I suppose, are too old. Speak to my majordomo in advance next time, we'll try to supply your specialized needs. If we don't have what you want in stock, we'll send out. For you, my dear friend, no request, no matter how bizarre, will be denied."

The two men kept looking at Parr even as they exchanged insults. It was as though they were afraid he would disappear if given the chance.

As indeed I would, Parr thought wryly.

"I consider entertaining my fellow lords one of the privileges of my office," he told the other two. "And I enjoy nothing more than listening to you bandy badinage about. But surely you had some more immediate reason for requesting this meeting than discussing our various amatory proclivities? Some important matter to discuss, perhaps?"

"Important?" Donnesby sniffed. "I wouldn't call it important, precisely. We have some information for you, my dear friend, that you might find useful in the pursuit of your duties."

"We merchants of the Paraverse believe it essential to maintain close, friendly relations with the Preceptory," Ensir Pollock added. "Whenever we find some small act, some morsel of information, that would interest you, we scurry right over here with it, heedless, momentarily, of our own interests or desires. For what helps the Preceptory helps the Overline, and thus helps us."

"Well said," Parr told them dryly. "I would that some of you merchant princes were such public-spirited citizens. It would make our jobs here much easier." What, he wondered, were they leading up to?

"Princes?" Pollock waved a depreciatory diamond-studded hand. "I wouldn't call us princes. Just poor toilers in the vineyard of the Paraverse. We have been luckier than some, not as lucky as others; more astute than some, more obtuse than others."

"And it was in this metaphorical vineyard that you ran across these useful morsels of information?"

"Surely not a bad metaphor for the Paraverse," Pollock observed. "Think of each separate grape as one alternative earth, one time strand, isolated in time and space. Think of each bunch of grapes as a cluster of alternate Earths, each coming from the same stem—say the French Revolution, or the Prague Autocracy, or the Peh Wen Interlude."

Parr smiled and leaned forward. "Ripe for the plucking, eh, Ensir Pollock?"

"There the metaphor fails," Pollock said, blandly studying the ring-studded back of his right hand. "We poor merchants engage in barter, nothing more. We trade, and all noncoercive trade is, by definition, equitable. We Overliners possess the Maberippe Device, and can travel through the Paraverse. But this gives us no more unfair an advantage than that of the wayfaring merchants of the past who traveled to distant shores in their precarious lateen-rigged barques. We give goods of a certain value to us, and receive goods of greater value. Those with whom we trade do the same, and all are winners. My surplus is another's need, and his useless, outdated artifact is another's *objet d'art*. And so the Paraverse spins. If it does spin. Does it spin, Preceptor?"

Parr nodded. "In twelve dimensions," he said.

"There, you see?" Pollock spread his arms wide.

"Is there a point to this?" Parr asked. "If not, I must get back to one of my other more pointed, if less enjoyable, activities."

"We have stumbled across an apparent anachronism," Pollock said, "In a time strand of peripheral interest to us. We believe it to be a xenosode,[2] although there is, as yet, no proof."

"'Us?'" Parr asked.

"Poldon Rarities and Specialties," Donnesby explained. "A registered outline enterprise, doing business in seventeen strands at the moment," Pollock expanded. "The Khazachamar group mostly—Level Four. We've been researching and establishing a market in possible pharmaceuticals—local variants of useful herbs—and in rare metals."

"One of the strands we have a site on has produced an anomaly worthy of study by the Preceptory," Donnesby said. "We happened, ah, to notice it, so we're bringing it to your attention."

"What sort of anomaly?" Parr asked, smiling. He thought he saw a glimpse of the light at the end of the conversational tunnel. A bright, shining light of deceit and evasion. He would maintain his attitude of friendly confusion until he found out just how many Overline laws and precepts these two had broken before coming to him.

"We have pictures," Pollock said. "Perhaps rather than prejudicing you with our opinions of what is happening, we should let you look at the pictures."

"Yes," Donnesby agreed, lifting the document case into his lap. "The pictures will speak for us." He unlocked the flap and unfolded the case. "Have you a viewer?"

"Disk or crystal?" Parr rested his hand on a particular spot on the table and a compact control center blinked into fuzzy existence above the table in front of him.

"Disk," Donnesby said, producing a five-centimeter circle

---

2. An object or event in one strand caused by people or objects from another. An inadvertent sign left by a Paraverse traveler.

of a highly reflective plastic-coated metal from the case and handing it to Parr. "That's a new-model visualizer, isn't it? Second-Level A-Line Alexandrian?"

"A little farther over," Parr told him. "They're specially made for us on Two-level, C-Line Corinth. Very good work. The holograph is just an aid to concentrating my thoughts in the right pattern. After I get used to it I can, supposedly, dispense with the display. Of course, they don't know they're making it for us. They think it's a children's game."

"I should have recognized the workmanship," Donnesby said.

"Indeed you should have," his tubby partner agreed. "We may not handle upline technology, but we should certainly be aware of it, and have some idea of what equipage is currently in favor in Overline. In some intricate trading accommodation, it may be the difference between profit and disaster."

"That's why we're partners," Donnesby said in a clipped voice. "Because of your encyclopedic knowledge of everything under the sun, and your constant willingness, even eagerness, to share it with the rest of us."

"Even so," Pollock agreed, complacently folding his chubby hands over his stomach. Parr dropped the disk into the slot that had appeared on his desk and stared at the control-board hologram, concentrating on manipulating the controls with a series of triggering thoughts. A screen dropped neatly into place next to the far wall, and the room lights faded out. Parr turned to look as a picture blinked onto the screen.

He was looking at a temperate-zone forest, which slowly panned by as the camera turned to give him a full-circle view. Pollock's voice, deep and firm, sounded from the screen: "These scenes were taken by OIC standard perusal devices on the strand registered with OIC as Poldon Six, which in standard Overline nomenclature is Level Four, Area Epsilon-Alpha, commonly known as the Khazachamar group, line B-B, strand three two five point seven one, no noticed variables.

"The strand vectors ninety-seven degrees, fourteen minutes,

fifty-three seconds from the meridian, to within an arc-second, at a distance of nine hundred thirty-seven years, ninety-seven days, four hours and a quarter, plus or minus fifteen minutes."

The scene shifted, the spy device lifting above the trees and moving forward over the forest at an impressive speed, until the trees below were just a blur.

"The beginning few scenes are from our original coverage, shot two years ago when we first established a Poldon factory. We are looking at a forest on the Northwestern Continent," Pollock's voiceover announced. "On this time strand it has been settled by the Kalgash and Prishnath from the east about five hundred years ago, and the Nishon-ga from the west about a hundred years later. The two eastern groups are at about the same stage of civilization: nomadic hunter-herdsmen. The Kalgash practice slash-and-burn agriculture and have a limited matriarchy, with power vested in a high priestess who speaks for Astrita, the Earth Goddess. The Prishnath worship Baalal, have a priest-king, and grow corn.

"The Nishon-ga have a very complex religion, and an even more complex social structure. They have seven positions between serf and king, and two below serf...."

A well-laid-out village came into view below the spy-eye, with rows of identical huts lining the regular, rectangular streets.

"Their lives are completely structured," Pollock's voice continued, "and there is no upward mobility. Therefore the society is stable but completely stagnant. Their industrial level is late feudal: they have no machinery beyond simple clock-works, used mostly as toys or religious devices. They have the compass, and a bit of forged iron, and paper, and simple printing from wooden blocks. Below you see a Nishon-ga agricultural village."

Parr leaned forward, his elbows on the table, and watched as the spy device, probably disguised as a soaring bird, circled the town. He had seen a thousand like it in his decades in the Overline Security Service, working his way up to the preceptorship. He had lived in probably a dozen of them for periods of up to a year while on one assignment or another. This village was a microcosm of the human condition for much of the span of human existence. He knew the dirt, the squalor, the disease, the hunger, the fear, the monotony; and also the subtle satisfactions and joys that made up the life of a villager over most of the Paraverse throughout most of history. Although joy was difficult for anyone living in such a village who knew there were better things.

In short order he was shown overhead shots of the other two groups which were colonizing the Northwestern Continent. They looked about as he would have expected them to look. Then a Poldon Company terminus was reviewed by the overhead camera. It was, Parr noted, fairly well set up, as such things go. There were no blatant anachronisms in evidence, nothing that would make a native decide that these people weren't from anywhere around there. More to the point, there was nothing that would cause a Paraverse traveler from an alien time line to immediately conclude that here were more people who hopped sideways through time.

The scene faded to black. "The pictures you will see now," the amplified voice of Pollock told him, "were taken within the past few weeks, in accordance with the scheduled yearly rescreening of the strand, according to OIC routine."

The scene that came up showed a railroad under construction. A group of Nishon-ga coolie laborers were doing the constructing, with a few sturdy-looking warriors wearing what appeared to be Mongol armor standing around doing the overseeing. The background was desert, and the tracks stretched off to the horizon, which was a good distance away.

The overseers came in two distinct types. Most of them had leather armor, and carried short swords and long lashes with which to beat the coolies. But a few, probably officers or tribal chiefs, wore silvery metal armor, and carried short, baton-like weapons. As Parr watched, one used his baton on a coolie who was insufficiently enthusiastic about his work. He jabbed it at the coolie's chest, and the coolie went rigid, and then dropped as though suddenly deanimated. The victim remained unconscious, although apparently still alive, while the officer ordered two other coolies to carry him to the side of the work area and dump him on the sand.

The scene changed to a raid on a Prishnath village by a slaving party of the Mongol warriors. Through decades of viewing similar perusals, Parr was inured to scenes of carnage, but he found this one impressive—not for the earnest viciousness of the ongoing rapine and pillage, but for the orderliness and precision of it. The device hovered over the village for about twenty minutes, during which time the warriors destroyed the village and bound the surviving villagers with thin, strong ropes, dividing them into two groups, one of men, and the other of the women and older children. The younger children were methodically killed where they were found. Although most of the attackers made do with swords and crossbows, several sudden pencil flashes of intense light showed that someone was using an energy weapon.

When the scene changed to yet another village under attack, Parr sent a strong thought to the visualizer. The picture switched off, and the room lit up. "You've made your point," he told the pair of merchants, "although perhaps it isn't the one you thought you were making, or intended to make. I am certainly convinced that we have an intervention problem on the Khazachamar group, strand three two five point seven one. Or, if you prefer, Poldon Six."

Pollock smiled a concerned smile. "I'm glad we brought it to your attention. We didn't wish to just abandon the strand when this, um, situation appeared. I believe in working closely with the Overline authorities on any little problems that crop up."

"I thank you for bringing your little problem to my attention," Parr told him, pushing back his chair and rising to his feet. "With any luck, and if you both work closely with the Preceptory and the Overline Security Service on this, I may be able to keep you out of prison."

Pollock's mouth dropped open. "Prison!"

"I don't see how you will avoid the mandatory confiscation of fifty percent of your assets," Parr continued blandly, "but I think you may stay out of prison."

Donnesby looked as though he had just swallowed something that had a horrible aftertaste. "Such a jest is in bad form, Ensir Parr," he said. "Perhaps we do need your help more than we liked to admit. After all, it goes against the grain to run to the Preceptory every time we run into trouble—"

"You didn't run into trouble on Poldon Six," Parr told him, "you married it. Let's start with the fact that you never did an initial survey, as required by both OSS and OIC regulations."

"But—you saw—the first few scenes—"

"Were shot at the same time as the later ones. You just used someplace where the vandals had not yet penetrated. You discovered them by accident, probably when they attacked a village you trade with. I hope it was merely a village you trade with. If they attacked one of your termini—if they captured a transporter or conveyer—then you're both in real trouble."

"No, no," Donnesby said, sounding ill, "nothing like that, I assure you."

Pollock leaned back. "How did you know?"

"A lot of things," Parr told him. "But the clearest, the example I'd use in court, is the railroad. If you had done your perusing when you moved onto the time strand a year before, as you were required to, you would have spotted it then."

"You can build a railroad in a year," Pollock objected.

"We can, but they couldn't. It would take them at least a decade to build up the technical support base for such a project. A couple of perusers in low orbit couldn't help spotting the rail foundry, or the plant where they're making locomotives and rolling stock."

"Perhaps they brought all that from their home strand," Pollock said.

"Would you?" Parr asked. "Even assuming you had a conveyer large enough, the energy cost of transporting a loco-motive any distance through the Paraverse would cut your profits to the vanishing point—not to mention a few thousand miles of iron track."

"We did a hasty job," Pollock admitted. "But who could imagine, out of the infinite number of strands in the Paraverse, we'd hit one that was already being exploited? We'll cooperate fully in whatever investigation you have to make."

"You certainly will," Parr told him. "The very fact that this has happened before should have told you that it could happen again. We are aware of—what is it?—fourteen other peoples that have the secret of Paraversal travel. And this one looks like a second-degree situation, which makes it all the more dangerous."

"What do you mean, 'second degree'?" Donnesby asked.

"It's the OSS term for a culture that has taken over someone else's Paraverse transporters. We know of three such."

"You mean they stole the secret of the Maberippe Device?"

"In one case, apparently, that is what happened. In the other two the cultures were too low in technology to even vaguely comprehend the secret. They merely stole the device itself. Which is what I believe has happened here. A group of people on a time strand that was being exploited by an advanced Paraverse-traveling culture took over one or more transporters. They were probably slaves or servants of the owners of the device. Presumably then they fled to a strand where they could be the masters instead of the slaves."

"Ah!" Pollock said. "Then they should be fairly easily handled."

"They seem to be a warlike, nasty group of people," Parr said. "They have no reason to like any other people possessing transporters. And they know enough to be on the lookout for them. They seem to have brought some natives in to work with them, to play soldier to their officer. And the natives don't seem any nicer than their bosses. You can get killed just as dead by a crossbow bolt as by a beamer. Plus we have the additional job of trying to capture their transporter intact to determine whom they stole it from. We may well find a brand-new Paraverse-traveling race. Which is going to please the Great Council no end."

"You're right, of course," Pollock said. "It's going to be a nasty business. What do we do?"

Parr aimed a thought at the device on his desk, and all the lights in the room turned red. "Damn," he said. "That's not what I intended." He turned the lights back to white and then tried again. The fuzzy face of Salvar Donevan, his chief assistant, appeared on his desk.

"Yes, Preceptor? What do you need?" Donevan asked.

"Call OSS and alert the intervention staff to put a crew together. I'll send them an annotated disk to show them what they'll be up against. Triple-star priority. Then come into my office."

"Yes, chief." Donevan's face disappeared.

"I've got to practice using this visualizer," Parr said. "When it takes me two tries to make a phone call, that's a good sign that the technology is progressing faster than I'm keeping up."

"What do you want us to do?" Ensir Pollock asked.

"I'm going to send you into another room to be debriefed under suprahypnosis by an OSS psych officer," Parr told him. "We need to know everything you know, starting with the local languages. Then you're going to sign transition papers, turning over all your property and claims on strand three two five point seven one of the Khazachamar group to the Overline Security Service. Given the circumstances, you will not be reimbursed. Then, if you cooperate fully, I will try to keep charges from being filed against you."

"All our property?" Donnesby asked plaintively.

"Shut up, Donnesby," Pollock said. "We agree, Ensir Parr. Here's my hand on it."

"We will also do a routine investigation of all the other strands you have filed on," Parr told him, taking his hand. "So I suggest you do it first."

"We've already begun," Pollock assured him.

CHAPTER NINE

Delbit had never walked so fast for so long in his life. He was connected to a group of other male prisoners by a long rope that snaked between them, fastening to a leather thong around each of their necks; the arrangement left just enough slack so that they wouldn't quite choke each other as they moved. Their wrists were tied behind them, and they were prodded along by their fierce and surly-looking guards at a pace somewhere between a fast walk and a trot.

His rage had left him. What he felt now, as he stumbled through the woods doing his best not to trip and strangle himself, was a slowly building hatred that started somewhere down in the pit of his stomach. He would revenge himself on these people, whoever they were, however long it took, and whatever he had to do to stay alive until he had the chance. And if they so much as touched Exxa, he would spend years devising new and horrible tortures.

He still had no idea who his captors were, what they intended with him, or what their relationship was with the Kalgash group that had taken him and Exxa in, and were now trotting along with him in these ridiculous leather necklaces. He also had no idea what had happened to Exxa, and, even as he ran gasping for breath and half choking every time he stumbled, that worried him more than his own predicament. Which says a lot for young love. Or old love, for that matter.

The sun came up and rose steadily in the sky, and still they moved along, creating their own trail through forest and meadow, but mostly through forest, prodded by the pointed swords of their tireless guards. When the sun was about a third of the way toward the zenith—say thirty degrees above the horizon—they came to a stream, and were allowed to pause for a brief drink of water. When it was at roughly sixty degrees they reached a large cleared field that was occupied by the manifold paraphernalia of their captors. Ahead of them to their right, a haphazard group of tents of various sizes and degrees of ornateness spread over the field. To the left were stacks and piles of logs and boards and crates, and mounds of things covered with canvas tarpaulins.

They were poked and prodded over to a corner of the field, where they were allowed to collapse together. One man was left to guard them, but their hands were not untied and the rope was not removed from the thongs around their necks.

Delbit occupied himself for the first little while with lying still and breathing hard, but eventually he regained his interest in the world around him. He sat up and looked around. There were a lot more of the short men garbed in rough leather armor with brass studs. They seemed to be overseeing gangs of workers of various other peoples in the far corner of the clearing, but just what sort of work they were doing Delbit couldn't tell. They were going to and from stacks of supplies, which were uniden-tifiable to Delbit, who was several hundred yards away from the action.

After a while Delbit and his ropemates were stood up and lined up, and a short, barrel-chested, self-important man in a breastplate of gleaming brass, obviously an officer of some sort, slowly walked down the line, carefully examining each of his new acquisitions. Two of the leather-plated guards walked behind him, swords drawn. He held neither sword nor spear, but carried an air of complete assurance, and a black rod about a foot and half long and two inches thick, which had a handgrip at one end and several buttons placed where they could be oper-ated by the thumb and forefinger.

The officer pulled each man one step forward from the line, which was as far as the neck yoke would allow, and poked and prodded at him, peering into ears and mouth with an air of expectation, as though prepared to be startled by what he found there. He also examined the men's clothing with care, but Delbit couldn't tell what he was looking for.

He came along the row of men slowly, pulling each forward and pushing him back when he was done. At the fifth man from Delbit he paused, stared intently at the man's face, and then poked him in the chest, yelling something at him in a sharp, guttural, unfamiliar language. The man stood stolidly where he was. The officer barked a command, and his two followers grabbed the man, unfastened his neck thong from the rope, and forced him to a kneeling position on the ground. The nearer guard swung his sword up in an arc over his head with a two-handed grip and brought it down on the prisoner's neck.

Bright arterial blood geysered into the air. The prisoner's head dropped and, not completely severed, dangled grotesquely from the stub of a neck. Slowly, as though moving through a thicker atmosphere, the almost headless body sprawled over onto the bare earth.

Delbit suddenly found himself throwing up. In a few seconds the meager contents of his stomach were on the ground beside him, and his mouth was filled with bile and his throat burned. He swallowed, forcing the bitter bile back down, and wiped his mouth with his sleeve. It seemed unreal. It must have been unreal; a trick, a joke. People didn't really do that to each other. But the corpse just lay there. It did not rise and reattach its head, and say it was all a joke.

The prisoner next in line to the corpse, a tall, muscular Kalgash warrior, clenched and unclenched his hands as he stared down at his friend's body. His face turned beet-red and the veins in his temple bulged. Suddenly, with a roar of rage, he leaped forward and clutched the barrel-chested officer's throat between his large hands.

The officer calmly raised the black rod he carried and jabbed the man in the chest. The man dropped like a stone at the touch. Before his shoulders had reached the ground the two guards had slashed him with their swords. He lay there supine and unconscious, and blood welled from gashes in his chest and side.

Delbit swallowed again. This was a place and a time when it was better not to be noticed. He would work at being unnoticeable until he had a better command of just what was happening and how it all worked. Why had that man been killed? How had the next man been suddenly felled like a rotten log? The warrior had clearly been unconscious before the guards reached him with their swords. He seemed to be breathing still, but he was taking no interest in his surroundings.

The barrel-chested man continued down the line, examining the remaining prisoners, as though nothing unusual had happened. And, Delbit realized, in this time and place, nothing unusual had happened.

When the man reached Delbit he stared at him for a moment, and then stepped back, a look of surprise on his face, as though he had just run across a strange and possibly poisonous lizard. He barked a couple of guttural commands to his swordsmen, and they unfastened Delbit's neckpiece and thrust him forward.

This is it, Delbit thought, trying to devise an instant plan of defense. When he raises the sword, I'll dive between his legs and head out toward the woods. Running away didn't have much chance of success, but staying still had even less.

The two swordsmen stepped back, keeping their swords pointed in Delbit's general direction. The officer peered closely at Delbit's face, first his nose, then one ear, then the other. He said a couple of brief words to Delbit.

Delbit shook his head and shrugged.

The officer repeated the words slowly, as to a backward child. Then, when Delbit showed no more understanding than before, he backed up two steps and yelled an instruction to the shorter of the two guards, who turned around and dog-trotted off toward somewhere else in the clearing.

It seemed to Delbit that he was going to live, for at least a little while longer, and suddenly that fact blotted out all else. He felt a great sense of release, and went very weak in the knees. It was with a tremendous effort that he remained standing.

A thin old man with a scarred face returned with the short guard and took his turn examining Delbit. Judging by the ornate markings on his breastplate, he was some sort of high-ranking officer in this group of murderers.

He peered even closer and poked and prodded and did not seem entranced by what he found. After a few moments' conversation with his barrel-chested subordinate, he turned back to Delbit and tapped him on the chest. *"Ulgash!"* he said.

"I have no idea," Delbit assured him.

Scarface nodded, satisfied. He turned and issued a short burst of instructions, then wheeled about and headed back in the direction he had come from.

The barrel-chested officer bellowed the same instructions to his guards—at least they sounded to Delbit like the same instructions—and the taller guard tied a short length of rope around Delbit's neck and trotted off across the clearing. Since he was still holding the other end of the rope, Delbit trotted after him.

As they approached the far end of the clearing, Delbit could see that behind the tents was a railroad track, running along the middle of a wide swatch of cleared land and disappearing into the forest on either side. Sitting on the track was a three-car train, minus the locomotive. The first car was rounded and ornate, with three puffy little cupolas on top and small windows placed high up on its sides; it was painted a deep red and trimmed in gold. The second car was more utilitarian, especially if there were enemies lurking in the woods: it had heavy timbered sides with long slit windows, and a pointed roof. Rows of iron spikes surrounded the car at different levels, and the roof had hundreds of nails protruding point-outward to a length of six to nine inches.

The third car was a flatcar with drop-away sides. Several large iron rings were fixed to the floor of the car, and Exxa was tied to one of those rings.

The guard grabbed Delbit by the waist and neck and hoisted

him onto the flatcar like a sack of noodles. Jumping up after him, the guard checked his wrists to make sure he was still well tied, and then fastened him to a ring at the front of the car, about four feet from Exxa.

Having secured Delbit, the guard stepped over to Exxa and leered down at her. He patted her hair twice, and was ready to commence a more personal exploration when one of the brass-breastplated officers walking by the train turned and yelled at him. He straightened up immediately, looking frightened, and jumped off the flatcar.

"If it isn't one thing," Exxa said calmly, "it's two or three others equally nasty. Hello, Delbit, my friend. How are you?"

"Exhausted, frightened, and angry," Delbit told her. "I don't think I like this world we've blipped into. Let's blip into another one."

"I would that I could," Exxa said. "If I feel it coming on, I'll tell you. But we'd better be touching when I go, if you're to come along. Can you reach me?"

Delbit experimented, twisting his body this way and that to test the bounds of his bonds. "With my feet," he said. "And if you can lie down pointing this way, we can probably touch heads."

"That might be wise," she told him.

"But as it is we're both still here," Delbit said, "and it looks like we're going to have to work at staying alive until we can blip to somewhere else."

"Back to that man who wants to stick pins in my brain," Exxa said.

"We'll be miles away from Manhattan Island," Delbit told her.

"That's so. Oh, Delbit, I hope I don't pop through to somewhere else without bringing you with me."

"I hope so too," Delbit said. "I really do. On the other hand, I venture you'd better do whatever it is you do pretty soon, with or without me. It would be nice if one of us survived this experience."

"Don't talk like that," Exxa said. "Years from now we'll both look back on this and smile with amusement."

"I venture we will look back on this," Delbit said, struggling to find a comfortable sitting position that wouldn't strain his arms, "but it will be a long while before I laugh at anything again."

A faint and distant whistling and chugging slowly grew louder, and a few minutes later a sudden thud shook the flatcar and threw Delbit to the floor. "I think the locomotive has arrived," he said, rolling over and sitting back up as best he could.

With many more thunks and clanks the locomotive was hooked up to the front car, and then there were ten minutes of much yelling and cursing and running about by those in the tent camp. Then six female prisoners and a guard were hauled up onto the flatcar with Delbit and Exxa, and the train started heaving and puffing down the track. The six women were fastened to rings on the other end of the flatcar, and the guard stationed himself halfway in between. As soon as the train was out of sight of the camp, he piled up some canvas sacking, stretched himself out on it, and went to sleep.

Delbit felt the track bumping rhythmically under the car, but he was not soothed. It had not been a soothing day. "I wonder where they're taking us," he said to Exxa, "and in what way it's different from where we've been."

"I wonder why they're taking us," Exxa said, staring thought-fully off at the passing trees, "and in what way we differ from those they are not taking."

"I don't think I want to think about that," Delbit told her.

The train chugged through the forest for hour after hour. Aside from figuring out that they were heading basically west, Delbit learned nothing from the continuing journey. The guard kept sleeping. The other women sat silently, staring at whatever their eyes happened to be looking toward. Their posture spoke a stoic apathy as loud as words.

"Listen, Delbit," Exxa said after a long time. "Whatever

happens, I want you to know that the time we had together was good. Possibly the only good thing that has happened to me within my brief memory is knowing you."

"Thank you," Delbit said. "And remember, this is just the beginning. Whatever happens, we will find a way to get out of it and be together. If we are separated, we will find each other again." He spoke earnestly and sincerely, but the words rang false in his ears.

"Of course," Exxa agreed. "I would like to say I will always remember you, but I can't be sure of even that, can I?" For a moment she looked as though she was going to cry, but she bit her lip and held her breath, and it passed.

After several hours they stopped while the locomotive took on water for its boilers. The guard freed the women from their rings, untied their hands, and took them, including Exxa, off the car to a clearing on the side of the water tower, where a slit-trench lavatory had been dug. When he brought them back, he sent Delbit to the trench in the care of another guard. Then he handed out hunks of black bread the size of a man's fist, which had been dipped in some sort of rancid-smelling grease. That, washed down with foul-smelling water from a dirty leather bucket, was the evening meal. It was also, Delbit suddenly realized, the first food he had eaten all day.

The guard retied his prisoners' hands behind their backs and refastened them to the iron rings in the floor of the flatcar. In a short time the train started up again, heading into the setting sun.

Delbit was suddenly overcome by a wave of fatigue. Lying down as best he could with his hands tied behind him, he twisted and turned to find a comfortable position, and then fell asleep almost immediately.

He awoke to a thumping, bumping, and jostling of the flatcar under him, accompanied by yelling and banging from somewhere to his right. Dawn was a hint in the distance behind, and the predawn light showed that they had passed beyond the forest. The land they were crossing was reasonably flat, covered with a dense underbrush, and scattered with clumps of trees in the near distance. Farther away than a couple of hundred yards all was still shrouded in the black of night. Delbit shivered in the predawn chill and looked around to try to figure out what was happening.

The train had slowed to a crawl, and there was much yelling and cursing coming from the front, and from off somewhere to the side. Suddenly four men jumped up from behind a passing bush, ran over to the side of the flatcar, and leaped on board. The guard pulled his sword out as he jumped to his feet and stood, legs apart, swinging the sword in great arcs, defending his flatcar.

There was the noise of fighting coming from the front of the train. Delbit heard the noise and saw an occasional flash of blue or green light streak across the sky, but from where he was tied he couldn't tell who was attacking whom, or with what effect.

"What do you suppose?" Exxa whispered, leaning toward him. "Are we about to be rescued, murdered, or taken by a band of even nastier people than those we're with?"

"I don't see how any other group could be worse," Delbit said, thinking of the beheading he had watched. "Maybe, if we're lucky, these new people will cut us loose and we can run off into the woods."

"I don't see any woods nearby," Exxa said. "But if we get loose, we'll find them."

The attackers quickly overpowered the guard and threw him over the side. Then they ran to the six women tied at the far end of the flatcar and sawed at their bonds with the edges of their swords.

"Hey!" Delbit called. "Over here, men! We could use a hand."

One of the attackers suddenly clutched at his side and fell over; the shaft of an arrow was visible between his hands. His companions swung around. There were two slit windows in the fighting car in front of them that faced back toward the flatcar, and someone inside was shooting arrows out of the slit on the left.

Delbit and Exxa dropped to the floor of the car. There was nothing to hide behind, and they were on the side of the flatcar closest to the fighting car, which put them between the two combatants—always an uncomfortable place to be. Whoever was shooting from the fighting car was well above them, but when the raiders began shooting back, who knew what would happen?

The archer inside the car was not able to aim well through the thin slit of a window, and his arrows were going well wide of the mark, except for the one that was sticking out of the downed attacker. Several shafts were already stuck into various parts of the flatcar, now that Delbit looked for them. The archer in the fighting car had apparently been at work for some time without effect, and the arrows that came after the lucky hit were no closer than the ones before.

The attackers hastily finished cutting the women free, and then, carrying their wounded companion, they all scrambled off the flatcar and ran away. The bowman in the car let fly a few more arrows just for luck, and then gave up.

The locomotive had made its way through whatever was slowing it down. Delbit guessed that the attackers had rolled a few logs across the track, which had now been pushed aside. The train was again gradually building up speed.

"We're alone," Delbit said, leaning toward Exxa as much as he could. "If we could manage to get loose, we could jump off and get away."

"I don't think I can manage to get loose," Exxa said, "but I'll try."

Delbit twisted and turned, trying to work the rope loose, or reach one of the knots that tied his wrists behind his back. "It's no use," he said after a while. "I suppose a people that spends much of its time capturing other people learns how to tie knots."

At the next water stop, a guard came out and took Exxa and Delbit into the middle car, where they were thrown into a corner and ignored by the dozen warriors in the car. After several more hours of travel the train stopped, and they were pulled out of the car.

A tent city stretched in front of them; they could see disorderly rows of large, ornate tents, with no two alike or even vaguely similar in anything but basic shape. The streets were full of people, most of them men in armor, bustling back and forth in a complex weave of endless motion.

After some conversation among their captors, they were pushed into a small blue-orange-and-white tent a few hundred feet from where the train stopped, tied to a ring on the tent pole, and left. The last person out closed the tent flap, leaving them only a thin sliver of light coming in from the outside world.

"We could probably pull down the tent," Delbit observed wryly, examining their tiny surroundings. "But it wouldn't do us any good. We'd still be tied to the pole, and we'd be dragging the whole tent around with us."

"It might be noted by some passerby," Exxa agreed. "And they might take offense."

They waited patiently in the tent, for lack of choice, for several hours until the tent flap was opened and someone peered in at them. Then the flap was closed again, and another half hour passed.

The next time the flap was opened a fat man entered and released them from the tent pole. *"Mughughragh!"* he commanded, indicating with an unmistakable gesture that they were to get up and go outside.

Delbit stumbled to his feet as best he could with his hands tied behind his back, and did several deep knee bends to get the circulation back into his legs. But the fat man was impatient and pushed Delbit roughly out of the tent with his chubby, muscular hands before Delbit was done. A few seconds later Exxa followed, stumbling into him.

The man led them from the rear, pushing them along and indicating with grunts and nods which way and when he wanted them to turn. The tents had not been laid out in any rational manner, and the path between them was haphazard and twisting, and of irregular width. As they went on the tents grew larger and more ornate, and the spacing between them got wider, if no more regular.

"You can tell a lot about this society from these tents," Exxa said, as they rounded the corner between a large octagonal tent, flamboyant red with a row of tassels around the top, and an even larger circular, bulbous structure done in wide blue and gold diagonal stripes.

"You can tell that these people have disorderly minds," Delbit replied, ducking between two tent ropes and stopping to allow a pack of hungry-looking dogs to run by.

"That, too," Exxa agreed.

"*Grughagh!*" their chubby escort insisted, shoving them along.

They came to a large, cleared area amid the tents, with one great round orange tent in the middle like the yolk in a giant sunny-side-up egg. There was a semicircular door in the yolk, with two guards standing just inside. Past the doorway there was a secondary barrier of brightly multicolored curtains that shielded any view of the tent's interior. Delbit and Exxa were pushed inside the door and left in charge of the guards while their escort parted one of the curtains and disappeared into the mysterious interior.

Two minutes later the curtain parted again, and the escort reached out with both hands and pulled them inside. He wheeled them around and shoved them through another curtain, where-upon two more guards grabbed them and pushed them to a kneeling position on the floor. Then Delbit's head was pushed forward until his eyes were staring at the carpet from a distance of less than an inch. A quick glance out of the corner of his eye showed that Exxa was being subjected to a like indignity.

Remembering the sudden murder he had seen that morning, Delbit's first impulse was to panic and grab Exxa and run blindly through whichever of the curtains they could reach. Then he noticed that the man who had brought them was kneeling on the floor next to him. It must, Delbit decided, be a custom of the country, and it didn't necessarily mean instant death. But still his heart beat faster. After what seemed like an eternity of staring at four square inches of carpet, he gathered his courage and looked up.

The room was empty, except for a pile of cushions in the right-hand corner, and it was lit by a cold white light, brighter than sunlight, that emanated from a long, thick stick hung high on the center pole that held up the tent roof. Delbit had never seen anything like it. He wanted to take a close look, but somehow doubted, given the present circumstances, that he'd get much of a chance. At that moment one of the guards saw that his nose was raised from the carpet and pushed his face back down.

After another eternity Delbit heard someone pad-pad-padding over to them in soft-soled shoes. He peered cautiously over and saw that their escort was still clinging firmly to the ground, his face down. Delbit decided to continue in a similar position until someone indicated that he could rise. After all, he had been put in many more humiliating positions in his days as a 'prentice, and by people who didn't hack your head off if they disliked your face.

The person who had pad-pad-padded over now shuffled around them twice, looking closely at them and stopping often to think about what he was seeing. This kept up for a while, and then he whispered a command, and the escort scrambled to his feet. The two guards grabbed Delbit and Exxa by the arms and pulled them up.

The man they faced was short and incredibly wrinkled, with folds of skin on his face as though he had once been very fat and his skin had not shrunk with the rest of him when he lost the weight. He was dressed in red robes with yards of gold trim that hung loosely on his form and trailed on the carpet. On his head was a red skullcap supporting what looked like a minia-ture many-branched gold candelabrum. His face was fixed in a scowl, and whatever he saw in the two prisoners before him was doing nothing to make him wish to rearrange his features.

It was clear that there was something about Delbit and Exxa that displeased him greatly. He stared at them, muttering intensely guttural complaints in a raspy undertone, and the escort and the two guards shifted from foot to foot and looked nervous. He gestured and whispered an order, and the guards pulled out their knives and cut away Delbit's and Exxa's clothing, letting it fall in a pile at their feet.

Delbit was too startled to complain, which was probably a good thing. Exxa stood there stoically as though this sort of thing happened every day, and didn't much matter. It seemed to Delbit to be the only wise course in the circumstances, so he tried to emulate her attitude. He felt foolish, and he knew he looked foolish, which made the attempt difficult.

The old man circled the two of them, peering, poking, and prodding as he moved. What he was looking for was impossible to tell. The sight of Exxa naked did not seem to interest him except as it afforded him a better chance to decide whatever he was trying to decide. The sight of Delbit naked had, if anything, even less interest for him.

The guards were trying their best not to look interested in Exxa's naked body. Indeed, after a sharp whisper from the old man, they were doing their best not to look at all.

The curtain in back of the room was pushed aside, and a huge man in full armor strode in. He spoke sharply to the old man, who whispered a reply, pointing to Delbit and Exxa.

"Hah!" the huge warrior said, striding across the room and standing, legs wide, arms akimbo, to stare at the two naked people in front of him.

The old man murmured a few words of explanation, and the warrior nodded his agreement. He took his right forefinger and gently prodded Exxa. He prodded her again. Then he laughed and announced something.

The old man disagreed in a harsh whisper.

The huge warrior slapped his thigh, pinched Exxa's face, roared with laughter, and then, as though a switch had been flipped, suddenly turned to the old man and screamed at him, his face puffy and red with anger. Then he turned and stormed out of the room, almost ripping the curtain that was the far wall as he passed through it.

The old man stared thoughtfully into the space that his huge friend had lately occupied, then turned and whispered to the guards. One of them went out, and returned in a moment with two white robes. The old man took them and draped them over the shoulders of Delbit and Exxa, closing them with a row of loops and hooks down the front.

The two guards left the room at a gesture from the old man, who then went over to Exxa, sighed sadly, patted her gently on the cheek, and whispered to her in a hoarse, earnest voice. Delbit had the feeling that the old man was trying to explain something that was important to him and that he was not happy about.

"I don't think I like what he's trying to tell me," Exxa said softly when the old man turned away.

"I don't think I like any of this," Delbit said. He thought of heroic things to do, but couldn't think of how to accomplish any of them, so he just stood there. A real hero, he decided bitterly, would not be daunted by the fact that he was in the midst of an enemy encampment, without weapons, with his hands tied behind his back.

The old man walked through the far curtain, leaving them standing alone. A few minutes later they heard him arguing softly with someone in the other room. Then the other person roared a reply, and they knew it was the huge warrior.

The argument continued for some time, and then suddenly it stopped. The curtain parted, and the warrior strode in. The old man was in the other room, and he stared through at them for a moment, then, with a shrug, allowed the curtain to fall closed.

The giant warrior strode over to Exxa and grabbed her by her hair. He cupped her face in his other hand and pulled her forward until her nose was touching his. Then he announced something to her, loudly, clearly, and positively. Then he laughed.

"Your breath is beyond bad," Exxa said.

Delbit stood where he was and silently raged. There was nothing he could do that was worth doing. He could spring forward and kick the warrior—and be beheaded a second later for his trouble. He could rush blindly out of the room through some random curtains—and be caught within seconds, and probably beheaded for his trouble. Or he could stand there and hate. He stood there. He hated.

The warrior dragged Exxa over to the right-hand side of the room and tossed her roughly down on the pile of pillows. Laughing, he unbuckled his sword belt and tossed it to the side. Giggling, he undid his brass breastplate and tossed it to the side.

Suddenly he screamed.

Delbit stared, and suddenly began laughing. On the pillow where Exxa had been thrown, there was now only an empty white robe.

Once again Exxa had disappeared.

CHAPTER TEN

The giant wheeled and glared at Debit. Then, with a cry of rage, he turned back to the now empty pile of pillows and glared at them. He examined the discarded robe. He poked at the pillows, first with his hands and then, as he grew increasingly puzzled and angry, with the point of his sword. Feathers puffed into the air as his sword ripped into the pillows. Then he picked up each pillow and shook it and threw it back, causing clouds of feathers to billow about the tent. As the feathers settled he turned to Delbit and stared suspiciously at him, muttering imprecations in some primal language.

Delbit quickly stopped laughing and tried to look somber and worried. This was not difficult, as he was worried. When yon hot-tempered giant warrior stopped prodding at the cushions with his sword, what was he going to poke at? Who was he going to blame for the sudden mysterious disappearance of the object of his lust?

The giant sat on a mound of pillows, ignoring the feathers that gradually settled all over his body. He stared at Delbit and held his breath, trying to think. After a few long moments of intense consideration he stood up, pulled a short, curved knife from a sheath on his leg, and slowly approached Delbit. He had found a focus for his anger and frustration. There was a murderous gleam in his eye.

Delbit backed away. "It's not my fault!" he yelled. "I wish it were, but it's not."

The giant was not impressed. He steadily approached, leaving a trail of feathers behind him. He was in no hurry to exact his revenge from Delbit for the way the young female had disappointed him. That what had happened was manifestly impossible according to everything he had ever learned was a fact that the giant's brain was not prepared to deal with, so he ignored it.

Delbit had to do something fast. And the possibilities were limited, as his hands were still tied behind his back. He took a deep breath, then rolled his eyes and fell to the floor, kicking his feet and forcing spit to drool out of the corner of his mouth. "Catamount!" he screamed. "Nemesis!" he shouted, shaking his head from side to side. "Octahedron!" he choked, rolling around on the rug. "If rabbits were lions would anyone know," he yelled, "unless a grammarian said it was so? If lions were rabbits would anyone care, unless you attempt to grab one by the hare?!"

The giant stepped back.

"I'm crazy!" Delbit yelled, trying to stand on his head and falling back to the floor. "I'm intensely bewildered! Rubba dubba hubba hubba boo bah!" He got up and danced around, sticking his tongue out and twisting and waving his head insanely. He moved his arms from side to side as best he could with his hands bound. "Better leave me alone. It's bad luck to kill a loonybug."

The giant put his knife carefully back in its sheath and stared with a blank expression at Delbit capering in front of him. Then he leaned forward and slapped Delbit a solid blow across the face with a right hand that was covered with large, sharp finger rings. It was like being slugged by a jagged brick. Delbit screamed and fell back on the floor. "I think you just broke my jaw," he yelled, sitting and licking blood from the corner of his lip. "Don't you people have any respect for the insane?"

The giant backed up to the cushions, not taking his eyes off Delbit, and groped around behind him among the feathers for his sword.

"Shit!" Delbit yelled, with feeling.

The giant paused and looked up.

A bugle sounded a series of triple blasts from somewhere

outside, and then came the clamor of a large kettle being beaten on by two large and heavy ladles.

The giant stared about him wildly, as though trying to remember where he was, and then grabbed his sword and raced off through one of the curtained walls of the room, taking the curtain down as he passed. Delbit noted that the old man who had examined them was hiding behind one of the displaced curtains, and wondered about that. But he wondered more about the interruption, and what was causing it, and how long it would last, and if he could sneak off while it continued. Cautiously he climbed to his feet.

The old man seemed to have lost interest in events in that room when the giant ran off, and had himself disappeared into the world beyond the curtains.

From outside now came the sound of gunshots. And galloping horses. And screaming men.

Delbit slowly got to his feet, breathing hard. The crazy act had taken a lot out of him. And except for the timely interruption of whatever was happening outside, it wouldn't have worked anyway. What was happening outside? Well, he'd find out soon enough. He looked around for something to cut the ropes off his wrists.

* * * * * * *

Troops B and C of His Majesty's Eleventh Cavalry Regiment, Royal Army of the United States of America (OSS Reconstituted), regrouped on the far side of the tent city, the men pausing to reload their lever-action Sharps carbines. Captain Rotsler stood up in his stirrups and looked around. The initial objective, to take out the guards and create confusion, seemed to have been accomplished. There hadn't really been any formal guards, just some casuals standing about on the perimeter of the tent city. And the confusion was just about complete. The enemy, clearly not expecting any sort of attack, had been taken completely by surprise and was still not reacting in force. A number of individual warriors in various stages of undress had run out of the tents brandishing one weapon or another, but there was no attempt at leadership, and they had been cut down as fast as they appeared.

"Take them through again," Rotsler told his lapel microphone. "Sabers out. Hack at the tent ropes. If those tents come down, the fight is over. Remember—as many prisoners as possible. Take them individually as they work loose from under the canvas."

The troop lieutenants relayed the order, and the horse soldiers slid their carbines back into their saddle boots and drew their sabers. Most of them hefted their heavy long-barreled O Sullivan .48 caliber service revolvers in their other hands.

The captain lifted his saber, waved it once about his head, and dropped it, and the men and horses galloped haphazardly back through the gaudy tent camp, hacking at tent ropes and shooting at running warriors as they went. The surprise was almost complete, and the enemy remained totally disoriented. Most of the Mongol horde were caught under mounds of collapsing canvas, and those that made it outside were outgunned and too startled to fight effectively.

One of the enemy officers raced out of his tent, black baton in hand. But before he could raise it, a passing trooper neatly removed it from his arm, hand and all, with a swipe of his saber. The officer looked surprised and then fell over. The trooper jumped from his horse, rolled the man over, and put a tourniquet on the stump. They were supposed to be careful with officers and anyone using anachronistic weapons. Major Sepple needed such people to interrogate.

The battle lasted about twenty minutes, and that long only because some of the warriors buried in the collapsed tents came out fighting when they were disinterred. Then the prisoners were divided into four groups: the standard run-of-the-tribe Mongol-type warriors; those who might have been in charge; prisoners or slaves of the Mongols; and others. The last group was very small, consisting of one frightened-looking young man with his hands tied behind his back who clearly belonged somewhere else. He had been found lying among the folds of a collapsed tent, trying to look like part of the upholstery.

CHAPTER ELEVEN

It was a full day before his rescuers showed any interest in Delbit. In the meantime they had untied him and given him soap and water and some clothes—a clean light red fatigue uniform that had been so well starched that he had to break the two sides of each leg apart to get into the pants—and a few decent meals. But nobody had tried to talk to him, except for making soothing and comforting noises in yet another language he couldn't understand. Then, in late afternoon of the next day, a slender trooper of indeterminate age in a sharply pressed uniform, a very wide-brimmed hat, and highly polished boots opened the flap of his tent. *"Framish dopar,"* he said, beckoning.

"What's that?" Delbit said, without thinking.

"I said 'come along,'" the trooper said in a clipped, nasal voice. "Hey—you speak English!"

"Well, I'll be," Delbit said. "So do you!"

"I never heard such an accent before, but it is, by the lords, English," the trooper said, slapping his hands together in either surprise or approval. "What in the king's name are you doing here?" he asked. "Aren't supposed to be anyone speaking English on this strand. Not that we've been told about, leastwise."

"What king?" Delbit asked.

"What king indeed," the trooper agreed. "Last I heard it was Benjamin the Third, but it might well be George the Seventh by this time. We haven't been back to our own strand for it must be six years now, and it mayhap we never shall. But that's why only those of us with no familial baggage—wives and children, or such—signed up for the Eleventh. After the War of Reunification it was, or the War of the Spanish Alliance, whichever you like to call it, when so many of us were at loose beginnings with naught else to look forward to. Although the time has been when I did miss my mother more than I would have thought."

"What's a strand?" Delbit asked, deciding to retire the royalty question until later.

"Why, what we're on. This unique hunk of the Paraverse that binds you and me and these Mongols and everybody together. It's where you live if you can't travel between the lines. I wouldn't talk so free to you, only seeing as you speak English, albeit oddly, you don't belong on this one any more than we do. How'd you get here, if you don't know where you are?"

"I kind of blipped," Delbit said. "One second I was somewhere else, and the next I was here. I don't know how it happened."

"It does seem like that, doesn't it?" the trooper asked. "Those transporters are scary machines for the unwary. Were you not wary?"

"What machines?" Delbit asked.

"Say," the trooper said, "mayhap I talk too much. I think the major is going to want to speak to you even more than the major thought she wanted to speak to you. Which is fortunate, as I came here to bring you to the major. Come along with me."

Delbit trotted after the trooper, thinking that perhaps he, also, had talked too much. What did he know about these people except that they had captured the other people? The people around here seemed to spend their time capturing other people; it was the norm. Some of these people even killed other people, although this group didn't seem so bloodthirsty. And besides, they did speak English. From what Delbit could see, their prisoners were being well treated, and not one had had his head cut off. They were being systematically questioned, one at a time, although about what Delbit had no idea. Perhaps he was about to find out.

The major was sitting at a small portable table that had been set up outside the command tent. She was a tall, slim woman with a touch of gray in her auburn hair and an aura of kindly wisdom that surrounded her like a fuzzy coat. Her uniform was a different cut as well as a different shade of blue from that of her compatriots, and there was something else different about it, or perhaps her, that Delbit couldn't, for the moment, put a name to. She seemed interested but not at all surprised to find that he spoke English when the trooper relayed this information, and merely beckoned for him to sit down across from her and waved the trooper away.

"So," she said, leaning on her side of the small table with her elbows and lacing her fingers under her chin as she stared at Delbit, "a fellow traveler through the vastness. I'm Major Sepple. Who are you?"

"Delbit Quint's my name," Delbit told her. He noticed that the small black box by her left elbow had tiny red, blue, and amber lights glowing on its side, and he wondered what it was for.

"A pleasure to meet you. Where are you from, Mr. Quint," Major Sepple asked, "and how did you end up a captive of our nasty friends out there?"

"I'm from Philadelphia, originally," Delbit told her. "But for the past few weeks I've been living in New York. That is—ah—until New York, ah, disappeared."

"I see," the major said. "So you went one way while New York went another. Were you kidnapped?"

Delbit noticed that her accent, which had been much like the trooper's, was shifting to one a lot closer to his own. Or, as he thought of it, her accent was gradually disappearing.

"No," he said. "I venture the best way to describe it is I was kind of running away."

"I see. And you ran into a little room somewhere, and the door closed, and you couldn't figure out how to open it. You found something like a control panel in the room, and either accidentally or experimentally pushed a few dials and levers. And you suddenly felt sick to your stomach. Then you did manage to work the door, and when you got it opened New York had disappeared from outside, and you were somewhere else. Was it like that?"

"No," Delbit said.

"No?" The major sounded surprised. "In what way did my description differ from reality?"

Delbit paused. What should he say about Exxa? Should he mention her at all? How could he explain how he got here without mentioning Exxa? "I went into a room," he said, "but it was just a room. There were no knobs or levers or anything. Then I kind of blipped, and I was somewhere else. In the middle of a forest, actually."

"No knobs or levers?"

"None."

"The room just disappeared?"

"Just," Delbit agreed.

The lights on the small black machine flickered. Major Sepple looked at him thoughtfully, her face showing nothing of what she was thinking, but Delbit had the feeling that she was suppressing something. "I need greater detail on this," she said. "Tell me everything you can remember, even if it seems unimportant. Were you alone?"

Here it was. "Yes," Delbit said.

"And you just—blipped? "

"Yes," Delbit said. He could tell he was sounding defensive, but he couldn't help it. The lights on the machine did a jig. Delbit decided it was some sort of truth-perceiver, and it knew he was being less than honest.

If that was so, the major ignored what the machine told her. She reached out and patted his hand. "I'm sorry. You've had a rough few days, I'm sure. I shouldn't be trying to tell your story for you. You tell it, however you like. Take your time. If there's anything you don't wish to talk about, then by all means don't talk about it. Perhaps you want to know us better before you decide."

Delbit couldn't help breathing a sigh of relief. He nodded.

"Perhaps," he said.

"What would you like to know about us?" Major Sepple asked. "There are a few things I'm not to talk about, but they are obscure and I doubt if you will ask about them."

"Who are you?" Delbit asked. "And where are you from?"

Major Sepple leaned back in her chair. "Well!" she said. "That is rather basic, isn't it? I hardly know how—or where—to begin."

Delbit suddenly realized what had been bothering him about the major's uniform. "You're not the same as these other soldiers, are you?" he asked.

The major looked at him sharply. "What do you mean?"

"The soldier who brought me here and all the other ones I've seen are wearing the same uniforms. Not identical, I mean, because I guess they all have different ranks and such, but it's like they're all from the same group—the same family. Yours is somehow from a different family. It's not just the color or the cut that's different, it's the thinking behind it. It's like it's from a different country, with a different way of thinking about uniforms. Even the medals are of a different design. You're not in the same army as these other people."

"Curiously enough I am," Major Sepple told him. "But your observation is well taken. I am the intelligence officer with this outfit, but I was assigned right before the mission, and I had no chance to get a matching uniform. Most of our units have distinctive uniforms almost identical to the ones they wore in the strands they were recruited from. But I'm still in my OSS blues."

"OSS?"

"Overline Security Service. We are of the Overline. We sometimes find it necessary to intervene in the affairs of other strand-hoppers, as for example rescuing you from these barbarians. The Eleventh Calvary is what we call an Intervention Group."

"What's an overline?"

"It's what we, in our egotistical way, call the particular strand we come from."

Delbit shook his head. "I hate to go around in a circle, but what's a strand?"

"You really have no idea of how you got here? That is, how you left the city you call New York?"

"I sort of blipped," Delbit said.

Major Sepple sighed. "We'll have to talk about that. But as far as your explanation goes, I think I'd better begin at the beginning, as they say. I'm not good at describing this, but I'll do my best. Let's start with where you are now. Do you have any idea of where 'here' is?"

"No," Delbit admitted. "For a while I thought that I must have traveled backward in time, but for several reasons that doesn't seem to be the answer."

"That's very perceptive," the major commented. "You could look at what happened to you as a form of time travel. But we'd have to consider it as moving...let's call it sideways, not backward. I know that sounds strange—"

"The doctor said something like that," Delbit interrupted, suddenly remembering.

"Doctor?"

"Dr. Faineworth, from back where I came from," Delbit said. "Sorry to interrupt. Please go on. I need to know this, I really do."

The major got up and went into the tent, returning with two tin cups, one of which she handed to Delbit. "Coffee," she said.

"Thank you," Delbit said. He sipped at the liquid in the cup, which was hot and bitter, and wondered whether it would be polite to ask for sugar. He decided not to.

"I shall start at the very beginning," the major said after taking a gulp of coffee, "as I am not sure how much understanding you have of basic cosmology. If I knew which of the myriad of New Yorks you have come to us from, I would have a better idea of your belief structure. I can pin it down to the line, by your accent, but there are countless strands on that line, and I haven't the time right now to close in on it better than that. It's amazing how much variation there is from one side of a line to the other, and even sometimes from strand to strand. And much as you'd like to help, I'm sure you have not even an understanding of the question."

"What do you mean, 'which New York'?" Delbit asked. "How many New Yorks are there?"

Major Sepple smiled. "That's what I was afraid of," she said. "As I said, I shall start at the beginning. Bear with me patiently."

"Yes, ma'am." Delbit would have borne with almost anything for an explanation of what had been happening to him for the past few days. With particular reference to a girl named Exxa, and how she blipped from one place to another. And possibly who she really was, and where she was from. And where she was now, and how he could get to her. Surely not much to ask.

"The universe, or what we think of as the universe, began several billion years ago, in one way of measuring time, as a tiny speck," Major Sepple said, holding up her right thumb and forefinger as though grasping between them a tiny speck. "But it rapidly expanded. In but a few milliseconds it was a meter across. Within a second it was the size of Earth, and within an hour, the size of the Solar System."

Delbit shifted uncomfortably in his camp chair.

"Are you squirming for a reason," Major Sepple asked, "or is it merely an attribute of youth?"

"Beg pardon, ma'am," Delbit said, "but I was raised a Congregational. It's not that I don't hold with other religions, you see, but, well—"

"You aren't here to be converted, is that it?" the major asked, looking amused.

"Not exactly," Delbit said. He thought for a minute. "It's more that—well—I don't want to insult you or anything you believe, ma'am, honest I don't. But when you said you were going to explain what had been happening to me, I didn't expect theology."

"That's fair," the major said. "And I wasn't about to stuff any down your throat. What I am telling you is independent of religion. That is, I'm going to explain to you how the physical universe works, according to the best guesses of the most brilliant scientists in the Paraverse. Or at least the most brilliant ones we've run across. But as to why it works that way—whether it's the hand of God; or the many hands, claws, tentacles, pseudo-pods, or other appendages of a pantheon of gods; or a dream of the Cosmic Mind; or an eructation of the Cosmic Gut; or any other manifestation of a Higher Power—I leave up to you to determine as you feel best. Agreed?"

Delbit nodded. "Yes, ma'am," he said, feeling foolish. "I'm not actually much into religion anyway."

Major Sepple smiled again. She had a nice smile, but Delbit had the feeling he was amusing her, and it made him uncomfortable. "I see," she said. "You just want to be sure that I'm not trying to feed you my theology to replace your own, since you aren't all that excited about your own anyway. Is that it?"

"Yes, ma'am, I suppose it is." This lady was not Delbit's vision of an army major. The only army officers Delbit had ever seen where he came from either shouted at you or ignored you. They certainly wouldn't pay attention to anything you had to say, even if it was only to gently point out the flaws in your thinking.

"Okay, no attempt at theology, no matter how well disguised," Major Sepple said. "I'm merely trying to explain to you where you came from, and how you got here." She suddenly laughed. "Although, come to think of it, that's what religion claims to do, isn't it?"

"I guess so, ma'am."

"Please stop calling me ma'am. It makes me nervous. Call me Major. I worked hard for it. They don't give rank easily in this person's army." She finished her coffee and set down the cup. "Now let's get back to the speck that will become our universe. Starting as a bunch of proto-basic particles, which someone else can explain to you, it rapidly coalesced into bigger particles called quarks; and they then made up electrons, protons, neutrons, and a bunch of strange little things that flew about.

The space expanded rapidly in as many different directions as it could find. We will call each of these directions a 'dimension.' There are, to name a few, up and down, and forward and backward, and left and right, and into the future."

"What about into the past?" Delbit asked.

"A logical question. There is reason to believe that although the universe passes through the past to get to the future, the arrow of time is not reversible."

"Why not?"

"Because the universe is moving in the direction of increasing entropy. Things break by accident, but they don't ever fix by accident. So the direction of the time arrow is from the fixed to the broken."

"Then how do things get made in the first place?"

"Well, most complex things either are forms of life or are made by living things. Living things make things, including each other. Intelligent living things make even more things. You might think of life and intelligence as very localized anti-entropy devices."

"Oh," Delbit said.

"But if we continue along this line, we'll be a long time getting back to that part of the explanation you're most interested in. So I will end this digression and return to the subject of dimensions. The expanding universe creates within it a series of vectors or tensors that we call dimensions. One of them is the dimension we call time."

She extended her right arm and pointed off to the right. "Let's call that way 'the future.'"

"Okay," Delbit agreed.

"So here we are in a universe consisting of matter, in fairly large amounts, and energy in various forms, in even larger amounts, which are essentially interchangeable—"

"What do you mean?" Delbit asked.

"Aha," Major Sepple said. "That narrows it down. Have you ever heard of a chap called Einstein? Albert Einstein?"

"No," Delbit said. "Should I have?"

"Not at all," Major Sepple reassured him. "It just eliminates the Einstein intersection, and thereby a good chunk of the Fifth-Alpha-Charlie Line. Don't worry about it. And for now, either take my word that matter and energy are interchangeable, or ignore it entirely. There's nothing you can do about it anyway.

"So. We have matter, and we have energy, and we have directions; these three things define the physical universe. And of these directions, one of them which we call time has an arrow that says you can only go one way along it. Is that reasonably clear?"

"I guess so."

"But you have no idea where I'm going with this, or how it's going to answer your question. That being so, you're amazingly patient."

"I like learning things," Delbit said.

"Good!" the major told him. "We like people who like learning things. So I'll teach you something more. Picture this universe I've been describing to you. It exists in many dimensions beyond those we are immediately aware of—some say as many as forty-eight. In most of them it just is. But in one of them—time—it progresses along at a steady rate. Or at least the now of it does."

"The now," Delbit said speculatively, savoring the expression.

"Yes. The now, which rides the border between the past and the future, and carries everything that is of us, and everything that is external to us, and everything we are aware of along with it."

Delbit's eyes opened wide. "That's something," he said. "The now. That is something."

"So picture the universe as it would look from somewhere outside it, through the eyes of some creature that could see in forty-eight dimensions. Perhaps as sort of a long sausage, with one end emerging from that primordial dot at the beginning of time and the other constantly riding the crest of now into the future."

"Sausage," Delbit said. He had the look of a boy just being introduced to Santa Claus. Cosmological discourse does that to some people.

"Now the Paraverse," Major Sepple said, "is the universe of universes. A set of twelve superdimensions within which a limitless number of these forty-eight dimensional universes can extend. Picture if you can a vast room full of universe sausages, all stacked up together and pointing in the same direction."

"A universe of universes?" Delbit's eyes opened even wider. He was being introduced to the concept of infinity in a way that made it of immediate and practical interest, and therefore much more than an intellectual exercise. Many lives have been changed by taking infinity seriously. "There is such a thing?"

"You have traveled about it," Major Sepple told him. "You, yourself, in leaving your New York and coming here have jumped from sausage to sausage—or, as we would put it, from strand to strand."

Delbit thought this over for a minute, while the major went into the tent to refill the coffee cups. "I hope you don't mind a few questions," he said to her when she returned, "but if I have gone from one universe to another, as you say, then why are they so similar? Why are there the same trees, the same geological features, the same animals? Why, for that matter, are there two almost identical planet Earths, in exactly the same place in their orbits around an identical—as far as I can tell—sun?"

"Because these multiple universes all evolved from the same cosmic speck," she told him. "Each strand which is a universe split off from a similar strand at some point in the past until, if you look far enough back, they all merge into that primeval mote.

"The splits take place at what we call event nodes, and most of them are so minor that the two universes remerge within a few seconds, or at most hours, of the split. But sometimes the divisive event causes a cascade that so alters history from that point that a new strand is formed. Every atom is constantly having event nodes, where it either does or doesn't emit a beta particle, or a photon, or something. Usually, since these events are unrecorded, and effect nothing beyond the atom, the two universes formed exist only for the length of time it takes light to travel from one side of the nucleus of the atom to the other. And since nothing travels faster than the speed of light, the alternate universe has no time to propagate."

"You mean that one atom can evoke the existence of a whole new universe?" Delbit asked.

"It's a very complex notion," Major Sepple told him. "If you ever formally study the subject, your understanding will be far greater than the explanation I am struggling with, and I'm sure you will find this wrong in most respects. Nonetheless, it conveys the flavor of the situation. It goes like this:

"Atoms and various basic particles exist on a level of probability rather than actuality. When the probability that they are in any one place becomes unity, or close to it, then they could be said to be in that place. But there is always a chance, a probability, no matter how small, that they are actually somewhere else."

She paused and stared at Delbit. "Does that make sense?"

"No," Delbit told her.

"You're right," she agreed. "However: what seems to happen when one of these nodes is passed, and a new strand is created, is that a probability wave is propagated from the zero point, giving all particles equal probability of being in either universe. Eventually the probability of their being simultaneously in both causes each of them to replicate as a duplicate set of probabilities, although they never are actually in both, or probably in either."

"I'm sorry, ma'am, but you've lost me entirely," Del-bit said.

"I lost myself somewhere in there too," she admitted. "The basic idea is that each of these universes is related, having sprung off from the one next to it at some point where a major event happened one way instead of another. In one, General Washington crossed the Delaware; in another, he didn't. In one, Hitler issued his troops invading Russia with winter clothing;

in another, he didn't. In one, Goldstein discovered the seventh force, and in another he didn't. And then around each of these basically different universes spring a cluster of look-alike strands where the differences are so subtle that they're hard to find. And these strands all bunch together in the Paraverse, the universe of universes."

"I see," Delbit said.

"Do you?" Major Sepple asked. "Congratulations. Now, one last concept for you to grapple with. If you were to slice through these bundles of strands at right angles, and examine the cut end, you would find that on one side—let's call it the right-hand side—the strands travel just a paltry bit slower through time than the left-hand side. And the strands at the top have just a wee bit more energy than the ones at the bottom."

"What sort of energy?" Delbit asked.

"A repulsive energy that separates the strands that are universes in the Paraverse. It's known as the seventh or Paraversal force," the major told him. "Its existence is suspected, or even confirmed, in several lines. But its function is known only to Paraverse-traveling groups. The potential difference between universes is what separates them, and at the same time what makes Paraverse travel possible."

"I think I have the picture," Delbit said.

"Fine," Major Sepple told him. "You're a fast study. Ponder it while I go take care of some necessary business. Why don't you go eat dinner in the mess tent—which is that one over there—and after dinner I'll get to ask you some questions. It is, after all, my turn."

"Um," Delbit said.

"Gilden!" Major Sepple yelled.

The trooper who had brought Delbit to the major's tent ran over, and Delbit realized that he had been keeping discreetly in the background the whole time. To be available for the major's orders, or to keep an eye on the prisoner? Delbit wondered. Not that it mattered.

"Yes, Major," Trooper Gilden said, coming to attention in

front of the table and saluting smartly.

"This young man is to have the run of the camp," Major Sepple said. "Make an effort to keep him out of trouble, answer any reasonable questions, and take him to the mess tent. Let him go where he will, but stay with him and protect him. He is more important to us than he knows, or than you can imagine. I shall continue my interview with him at nineteen hundred hours."

"Yes, Major," the trooper said, saluting again. "Come along— ah—"

"Delbit," Delbit said.

"Delbit," the trooper repeated. "Come along, Delbit."

CHAPTER TWELVE

The dinner was pieces of what Delbit sincerely hoped was chicken, which had been baked into submission and covered with a sauce compounded of squashed tomatoes, peanut oil, peanut butter, hot peppers, tiny cubes of unidentifiable vegetables, and various spices. The whole was ladled over a bed of rice on a tin plate. And to Delbit's surprise, once he got used to the pepper, it was very good.

They sat at a long table in the mess tent with several other troopers, who showed surprisingly little curiosity about who Delbit was or where he had come from. They were polite enough, and even friendly; but after they found out that he couldn't ride a horse, couldn't load a carbine much less shoot it, and probably wasn't going to join the Eleventh, they lost interest.

Every once in a while one of the troopers at the table would remember Delbit was there and try to include him in the conversation. But it was trying for everyone, being pretty much limited to "Well, and aren't you glad we rescued you from those beastly Nishon-ga?" and "What do you think of the grub?" and "So you speak English, do you? Where you from?"

By the time Delbit had explained that he didn't know just where he was from, and that it wasn't any place they knew anyhow, for the fourth time, everyone was willing to grant that the conversational amenities had been preserved, and enough was enough, and Delbit was thenceforth ignored.

The conversation going on around Delbit was fascinating to him. He sat quietly so the troopers would forget he was there, and just listened to their talk. Some of it was the perpetual griping of the soldier, much the same from the army of Xerxes the King of Kings to the present, on all strands at all times. Some of it was personal, the sort of in-group commentary that makes little sense to one outside the group. But some of it offered tantalizing hints of a life, a civilization, a science, and a philosophy as much outside of Delbit's experience as his own was beyond that of a Seleucidic serf. The serf, if intelligent, might have understood an explanation of the principle of expanding steam, or rising gas, but he could hardly have thence imagined a locomotive or the string of silver balloons that was an airtrain.

So Delbit listened, and made what sense he could, and imagined wonders of the rest.

"Have you seen the new beamers they're using on Beta-Beta? They have almost no beam ionization, but they'll bally well vaporize anything they hit up to two kay."

"I'll stay on these primitive levels. The big stuff frightens me. Carbines and sabers and a good retirement after twenty is good enough for me."

"Yeah, Smitty? What's it to be—a farm on Under-Four?"

"Nah! I'm going to open a racetrack on Under-Two. Mayhap a pleasure dome on the sideshow. Let the Overliners keep me in cabbage."

"A racetrack, is it? Haven't you had enough of horses?"

"Look who's talking! You put in for a commission in the propolly, didn't you? Haven't you had enough fighting?

"They don't fight! They use reason and suasion. Then they break heads. It's policy."

By the time the mess sergeant came around with a giant bowl of bread pudding and scooped some into everyone's tin plate, telling them they could call it desert or anything else they liked, Delbit was stuffed with food and partly digested overhears. He relaxed and drank a mug of coffee, which seemed to be the universal beverage of the Eleventh.

His dinner companion turned to him. "We've been leaving you out of the talk," he said. "Sorry 'bout that. Anything you need?"

"You could tell me a few things, if you would, Trooper Gilden."

"Call me Melvin. I will if I can. What do you want to know?"

"Just general curiosity, I guess." Delbit said. "Like, where did you fellows come from?"

"Me and my 'sociates of the Eleventh, you mean? We're all from the same line, and mostly from the same strand. The Eleventh was empted about eight years ago, right after the Spanish Alliance Fracas. We had beat the tin-plates right back down to Mechico, and were getting ready to invest Ciudadela Mechico herself, when His Majesty called the whole thing off. He had made a deal of some sort with King Juan. At one hit we were all redundant, and His Majesty wasted no time turning us off. One week I was a trooper in His Majesty's Ninth, and a week later I and twenty thousand of my 'sociates had our one-for-one in one hand, a ticket back to our place of 'listment in the other, and a stunned look on our collective phizzes."

Delbit felt like someone with an imperfect knowledge of a foreign language. Their English was not—quite—his English. "What is, ah, 'empted,'?" he asked. "And what's a one-for-one?"

"'Empted' is Overline-speak for *en*listed." Gilden emphasized the part of the word he usually left out. "It's not clear where it came from. Maybe from 'preempted,' or maybe from 'empressed,' like with a press gang."

"Where I come from, 'empt' means leisure," Delbit told the trooper. "Like, if you're empt, you're not doing anything in particular."

"Is that the snuff? Well then, mayhap it comes from us being at leisure at the time we're empted. Although sure not for some time after. And what was the other word? Oh, yes— 'one-for-one.' That's what we called being paid out or disenlisted from His Majesty's Forces. Benjamin the Third was ever a tight man with the privy purse. We were paid a bonus of one week's pay for every year we'd been in service. An amount of money, I admit, hardly adequate to excite the avarice of your average mendicant."

"Thank you," Delbit said. "Go on."

"With what? Oh, the story. Well, there I was in Arnold, Hamilton—"

"Who's he?" Delbit asked.

"Who's who?"

"Arnold Hamilton."

"Oh." Trooper Gilden gave a "don't you know anything" shake of his head and raised his left thumb. "Arnold," he said, pointing to the thumb with his right forefinger, "is the town, probably named after Benedict"—he raised his left forefinger and pointed to it—"which is the capital of the State of Hamilton, which is certainly named after the Alexander of that ilk."

"I see," Delbit said. "Thank you."

"So there I was in Arnold, along with thousands of my 'sociates, spending our one-for-one in riotous living, 'cause there isn't enough of it to bother hanging on to, until we run out, and then hocking our travel tickets. So this 'vertisement appears in the Arnold paper: 'Men wanted for dangerous, well-paid work in foreign lands. Must be unattached. Interviews daily, one to six, at Burr Hotel. Only the brave need apply.'

"So we talked it over that night at the boozerie, and decided that it was a shuck, that it was some sort of strange come-along that could do none of us any good. 'Only the brave need apply'! At best it was a joke, and at worst a trap. It was best ignored, we decided.

"So the next morning at around eleven the line began forming in the lobby of the hotel. I was nowhere near the front, I must admit, as I didn't arrive until almost noon."

"I don't understand," Delbit said. "You decided that the ad was a trick, and yet you all still went for interviews? That doesn't make sense to me."

Trooper Gilden stared off into as much space as there was between him and the far wall of the tent. "Tell you a story," he said, leaning back on the bench and lacing the fingers of his two hands behind his head. "It was in the little town of Tashkent,

Kentucky, fifteen, mayhap twenty years ago. I was but a small boy...."

Delbit noticed that at Gilden's "tell you a story," the other troopers at the table had nudged each other and paused to listen to Gilden talk. He decided that Trooper Gilden must have quite a reputation as a storyteller.

"There was a personage in the town by the name of Yapley at this time, Bart Yapley," Gilden continued, "who loved beyond all else games of chance. He would wager on the lay of the pasteboards, he would bet on the rattle of the bones, he would lay odds on the relative merits of one horse against another over the distance of three or four furlongs. He would wager on which lump of sugar a fly would land on. And he'd give you six to five and take either lump.

"Every Thursday and Saturday night without fail Yapley would retire to the back room of the Golden Egg saloon for an all-night euchre game with Gross Ned, who was the owner of the saloon, and the mayor, the town marshal, and such other celebrities as would happen to be about. Are you with me so far?"

The question was addressed to Delbit, but the audience had increased now to a hushed crowd which surrounded the table.

"So far," Delbit assured Trooper Gilden.

"Good. This story has an uplifting moral, as all stories should, but on my word there won't be a quiz after. Now one day it happened that a stranger rode into town and during the day Yapley happened to do him a favor in the course of business. It wasn't much of a favor, something involving livestock, I believe, but nonetheless it was a favor.

"Now that night the stranger, whose name, I believe, was Preston, happened to sit in on the euchre game for a few hours. During which he lost a small sum of money. And Yapley also lost, perhaps a bit more. At about three in the morning the game adjourned for a half hour for the room to air out, and the gamesmen to partake of refreshment.

"Now during this break, Preston, the stranger, took Yapley

aside and said to him, 'Friend, you have treated me as a fellow Christian during the course of this day, and for that I thank you. And I feel that I should tell you something. I am an expert at plain and fancy card manipulation, something I do not ordinarily reveal while I am engaged in a friendly game. But friend Yapley, I am going to quit this game now—and I'll tell you why: this game is crooked! You and I were both being cheated. The marshal feels that the second card from the top is the only card worth dealing, while the mayor favors the card on the bottom of the pack. Both decks are marked in at least two different ways, and the deck that Gross Ned switches in with the pair of expanding tongs which is concealed under his coat is so educated that it can probably do everything but spit grapefruit juice on command.'

"'I realize that, friend, for I have been in this game now for some years,' Yapley told the stranger, 'but I thank you for the kindness of spirit you have shown in informing me.'

"'Years?' the stranger inquired. 'And yet you yourself do not cheat?'

"'That is correct, sir, I do not.'

"'Then why on earth, friend, do you stay in the game?'"

Here Trooper Gilden leaned forward toward Delbit, and spoke slowly and distinctly, as though sharing with him a great secret. "'Because, friend, it is the only game in town!'"

The other troopers leaned back and nodded their heads in satisfaction. Evidently the story was as they remembered it. Gradually they dispersed and went back to what they had been doing, mostly drinking coffee.

"Oh," Delbit said.

"It was about three o'clock before I was interviewed," Gilden said. "There were a man and a woman in the room. They were dressed like city folk, and they talked like they were from back east somewhere, but somehow I sensed even then that there was something different about them, as if they were from somewhere far, far away. Or mayhap that's only my memory of it now, in the afterlight. At any rate, they asked me my name, my outfit, and what experience I'd had. They asked me if I had any family living, or anyone I was particularly close to. I told them I had a mother in Garrett City. They asked me whether I was willing to go to distant parts where there was a good chance I'd never see my mother again. I told them that I was, but I'd like a chance to say goodbye."

"Did they tell you about the Paraverse and the time strands and all that stuff?" Delbit asked.

"Not then. They merely said that I would be well paid, if accepted, and that I would have to sign up for six years for my first hitch, and that if I stayed twenty, I would get an admirable superannuation. I asked them where we'd be going, and they said that they would promise that I'd never be asked to fight against anyone who I presently regarded as a friend, but beyond that they stood mute. I said I was interested. They gave me five sovereigns in gold, and two weeks to think it over, during which time I went to see my mother."

"And when you came back, you enlisted?"

"I had a whole list of further questions, as when I thought it over, their offer made little sense to me. Where could they be needing troops bad enough to 'cruit them from Hamilton, in the United States Empire? The pay they had quoted was not precisely a fortune, but they could have 'cruited far cheaper elsewhere. Why were they being so mysterious about where we were going? I wanted to know all that before I bottomed my name to any 'cruiting paper they might wave at me."

"As would I," Delbit agreed.

"They assured me that all would be explained, and that I would have one chance to back out after the explanation, and they pointed to a door, saying I should go in there if I was still interested, and that I could leave with their blessings—and keep their five sovereigns—if I had any misgivings. So I entered the room.

"There were about ten of my 'sociates sitting around the room, several of whom I knew well. After a while one or two more ex-troopers entered. Then the woman came in and warned us that we might feel a mite queasy in a moment, but it weren't nothing to worry about. Then she opened a sliding panel in a table by the wall, and dialed a few dials and pushed a few buttons, and I threw up."

"A fine introduction to the Paraverse," Delbit said.

"I thought so at the time," Trooper Gilden agreed.

CHAPTER THIRTEEN

His hands held behind his back, Castimere Parr walked slowly and pensively past the fallen marble pillars of a long-ruined temple at the edge of a long-deserted city and stared out at the sea below. The beach was brilliantly white, and the water painfully blue. Sea birds strutted along the beach eyeing the jetsam.

His companion strode alongside and watched him as they walked, trying to read in his face some emotion, some reaction to her words.

"Are you sure?" he asked her finally.

"Sure? Of course not, Preceptor. How could I be sure?" She kept her voice carefully neutral, as befits one whose chief value is in her studied objectivity. But then, it was not she who would have to make the decisions that would affect the fortunes—and possibly the safety—of the Overline for centuries to come.

"I have given you the information I have," she told him, "and my evaluation of it. If you can reach another conclusion, I would not be insulted. Indeed, I would be delighted."

"We of the Preceptory have worried about so many things," Parr said. "We have prepared for so many eventualities, we have developed so many contingency plans. And yet nobody planned for this! Not in two hundred years. But then, how could we? How does one plan for the entirely unexpected? I'm still not sure I believe it. Not that I doubt you, my dear Major—"

"You could—it wouldn't bother me," she said. "I doubt myself. But after allowing for my doubting, the facts remain unchanged."

"You are asking me to believe in magic," Preceptor Parr said.

"Magic is merely anything that you can't explain," the major told him.

"No, it's more than that," Parr said. "Magic is something that appears to violate the laws of the Paraverse, as you understand them."

"It does that," she agreed. "Obviously our understanding is incomplete."

"Obviously," Parr agreed.

They walked in silence for a while.

"You have not interviewed the lad very deeply," Parr commented.

"I saw no point in pushing," the major replied. "He is predisposed by events to be on our side. We must draw the story from him gently and gradually."

"Of course, of course," Parr said. "Certainly gently, if not gradually. I'm just wondering what he can tell us—how much he knows."

"He knows something remarkable has happened to him," Major Sepple said.

"But he has no idea how remarkable. I had best go and speak with him. Luckily English is one of my languages, as I don't want to wait six hours for a suprahypnotic induction, and I've never liked using interpreters. Incidentally, I'm placing this under preceptor's seal; you will keep all information concerning this lad and his story, whatever it turns out to be, as ultimately privileged knowledge. You haven't told anyone yet, I trust."

"Only you, Ensir Parr," she said.

"Good. Merely the unconfirmed rumor of this could cause havoc in the OIC. The merchant princes would not know what to make of this, and they would inevitably construe the worst. And hide their collective heads under the sand, leaving only their rear ends sticking up, as is their courageous wont. And when the Complex shivers, all Lyander City takes to bed. Not but that the problems inherent in this are not very real, but I would rather be free to deal with the real danger in front of me without worrying about the imagined dangers behind my back."

Parr stared out at the sea a bit longer, then the two of them retraced their steps back to the transporter, cleverly hidden in an uncollapsed section of temple. "How quickly can we get there?" Parr asked.

Major Sepple dropped the concealed control panel of the transporter and studied the active chart of the Paraverse on the shift board. She punched a few numbers into the destination computer and considered the result. Each transporter was unique, and traced its unique path through the Paraverse. There were several known reasons for this. The transporter's physical location was one; it could not come through to a strand where it would appear buried in the side of a mountain, for example. Which was a good thing for all concerned. The tuning of the particular Maberippe Device which was the drive for that transporter was another: some could take only gross hops, skipping many strands on each hop; some managed dainty steps, almost moving from strand to strand. Some hopped grossly in one area of the Paraverse and stepped finely in another. Each machine had to be individually tested and calibrated, a job closer to art than science, and no one could explain or alter the machine's aberrations once the Maberippe field had been activated. The holding field was a strange conflux of Paraversal forces in the shape of a perfect sphere no more than a few centimeters wide which existed deep inside the machine. If it was turned off, then the machine could no longer retrace its steps through the Paraverse when the machine was reactivated, but would cut an entirely new swath.

"My transporter is at the Poldon terminus on Level Four-Omega," the major said. "We can make it in three hops, I believe. It looks like we can go directly from Alpha-Alpha, which is two hops, but I can't be positive until we're there and the chart has shifted."

"Let's get to it," Parr said, pulling the door closed and turning on the internal power.

Twenty minutes, three hops, and one change of machines

later he pulled aside the flap to the tent that concealed the OSS transporter and walked out into the tent town of the Eleventh Cavalry on the strand known as Poldon Six. It was already evening here; the sun was just disappearing below the trees, and the troopers were posting perimeter guards as they quietly and efficiently prepared to settle in for the night.

"My tent is over this way," Major Sepple said, taking the lead. "Is there anything you want before you interrogate the boy?"

"Not a thing," the preceptor said, rubbing the back of his neck with his hands. "I am anxious to meet the lad. Delbit, is it?"

"Delbit Quint," she affirmed. "Here's my tent. I'll have him sent for."

Par sat down on a camp chair outside the tent. A sitting figure was less threatening than a standing one, and Parr did not want to seem threatening to Delbit Quint. He closed his eyes and used several well-learned mental exercises to relax himself in body and mind.

He opened his eyes when the major's voice informed him that Delbit had arrived. The lad who stood before him, shifting nervously from foot to foot, was slender, with brown eyes and hair, protruding ears, a prominent nose, and artistic hands. To Preceptor Parr he looked startlingly young.

"Greetings, Delbit Quint," Parr said, switching smoothly to English. "Please be seated. My name is Castimere Parr. I am a preceptor of the Overline. This fact is not relevant to you, nor should it be; I state it only for the record. I believe we have a common problem."

Delbit sat down. "We do?"

"I'd say so," Parr said. He stared off into space, some-where beyond Delbit's left shoulder. "You arrived here with a young lady who disappeared under what the natives regard as rather remarkable circumstances. You appear to have carefully avoided any mention of this young lady in your conversations with Major Sepple here." He waved his hand in the vague direc-tion of the major, who was standing behind him. "This would lead one to believe that you either have no interest at all in the lady and her welfare, or that you have such extreme interest that you wish to protect her from even potential dangers. Which are we to believe?"

Delbit stared at Parr, his mouth open.

Preceptor Parr smiled. "Had you unconcernedly said 'What young lady?' we would have had to conclude either that you were truly uninterested in her or that you were an agent of some sort, trained in dissimulation. I am delighted to discover that neither is the case. As I said, we share a common problem."

Delbit nodded slowly. "I venture we do," he said.

"Let's talk about it," Parr said. "I promise to give you at least as much information as you give me, and perhaps more. Surely that's fair."

Delbit thought it over slowly, his eyes on Parr's less than expressive face. "Perhaps it is," he said at last. "I have to do something."

"We have made the assumption that you haven't overly lied to us," Parr said. "That is, except for your omission of the existence of the young lady, the account of your travails is fairly accurate. Is that so?"

"It is," Delbit agreed. "As far as I can remember what I said to the major, I don't think I told any deliberate lies. After all, you people did rescue me from a very troublesome situation. I don't think I would be alive now had you not come along when you did. For which, if I haven't mentioned it before, I thank you."

"It was our unexpected pleasure," Major Sepple said.

"Now we would like you to put the young lady back into your story," Parr said. "To start with, what is her name?"

Delbit considered the question. "I don't know her real name," he said. "I've been calling her Exxa."

"Why won't she tell you her name?" the major asked.

"She doesn't know it," Delbit said.

The two Overliners looked at him.

"I suppose I'd better explain," he said. "But first, what do you intend to do with her?"

"Do?" Parr leaned back and managed to look surprised.

"So far everyone wants something from her," Delbit said. "From the obvious to the not so obvious. What do you want? And, if you don't mind, why do you want it?"

Castimere Parr stood up and raised his right hand. "I would like to ask her some questions," he said. "But, on my oath as a preceptor, unless she has committed some high misdemeanor of which I am not aware, I will neither harm her nor allow her to come to harm while she is in my care. That is, assuming she ever comes under my care. She doesn't seem to be around at the moment. You may ask anyone here the value of a preceptor's oath."

Delbit looked questioningly at the major.

"Preceptors do not lie under oath," she told him. "Their oath is their bond, and the bond of the Overline. Effectively, what Preceptor Parr has just done is bind the forces of the Overline to protect this girl." Major Sepple told him this with the sort of flat assurance that one would use in saying "The sun will rise in the morning."

Delbit thought this over. "I assume that as an intelligence officer, you have been trained to lie convincingly," he told her. "But I venture I have to trust somebody, so I'll start with you two. What do you want to know?"

"Start at the beginning and keep on going until you reach the end," Parr told him, "and then stop. But take your time, and don't leave out anything of even peripheral interest. We have nothing of more pressing importance."

"Very good," Delbit said. He sighed, and looked thoughtful. "I was apprenticed to a master shoemaker in Philadelphia...."

* * * * * * *

Two hours and fifteen minutes, several score questions, and two cups of coffee later, he stopped talking.

Around him, although he didn't realize it, was an aura of

awed silence, which was finally broken by Preceptor Parr.

"I don't want to believe it," Parr said, "but I suppose I must. How could such a thing have been concealed from us for all these years?"

"Perhaps we've just never run across it before," Major Sepple said. "After all, we have investigated only a few thousand of the near infinity of strands."

"Perhaps," Parr said. "Although the concept of near infinity shows sloppy thinking. But somehow I doubt it. After all, the girl speaks English."

"She calls it Anglic," Delbit volunteered. "And, if you don't mind, sir, what don't you want to believe?" Delbit found himself calling this new questioner sir, without having made a conscious decision to do so. There was something about Preceptor Parr that invited respect.

A sudden commotion at the far end of the camp by the railroad track attracted their attention, and the conversation paused. A few seconds later a horseman emerged from behind one of the cars and trotted toward them, weaving between the tents. When he reached them he leaped off his horse and stood at attention in front of Preceptor Parr, in one swift, coordinated move.

"Captain Rotsler, Preceptor," he said, saluting. "Acting CO of the Eleventh."

"Yes, Captain?" Parr said, returning the salute. "Congratulations on your promotion, by the way."

"Thank you, Preceptor. Our scouts report activity on the railroad line, about ten kilometers to the west. It seems to be a reinforced train, along with outriders. It should be here in about half an hour."

"I see," Parr said. "What do you want to do?"

"That depends, Ensir. Are we staying about for a while, or fading away?"

"I think we'd better assume that we'll be here awhile," Parr told him. "Put a note through to OSS Central over my signature asking for reinforcements. I leave it to you to handle the approaching horde."

"Very good, Ensir," Captain Rotsler said, saluting. He vaulted back onto his mount and trotted off.

Parr looked thoughtful for a moment, then shifted in his chair, transferring his attention back to Delbit. "Can you keep a secret?" he asked.

"I suppose so," Delbit said. "I don't think I've ever had the opportunity before. I didn't keep Exxa very much of a secret."

"It wasn't your fault," Parr said. "Circumstances beyond your control brought her existence to our attention. And her disappearance really seemed to bother that large warrior who was preparing to force his attentions—among other things—on her."

"What's the secret?" Delbit asked.

"Actually you already know it. The secret is that Exxa can blip from one strand to another. I like 'blip'—it's an expressive word."

Delbit looked puzzled. "But so can you," he said. "Can't you?"

"Not without help," Parr said. "You needed Exxa. We need transporters. It's like birds fly, people need airships. Exxa is a bird."

"Oh," Delbit said. He frowned, and his sense of assurance disappeared. "What are you going to do when you find her? Cut her open to see how she does it?"

Parr raised an eyebrow. "You don't trust anybody, do you, son?" he asked. "I suppose I see your point. No, I'll merely give her back her memory so we can determine who did what to her and why. Then I shall ask her help in figuring out how she got this blipping ability, if restoring her memory doesn't answer the question. If she is unwilling to help, I will try to persuade her that it is to our mutual benefit. If she will not be persuaded, I will be satisfied if she keeps the secret. I believe that is something she will gladly do. She has surely been keeping it all her life. We will, of course, pursue our search for this knowledge by other means."

"You can return her memory?" Delbit asked.

"Almost certainly."

"I'm sure she will be grateful, sir. I know I will," Delbit said. "But about her blipping ability: why is this so important to you?"

Preceptor Parr stared at him. "A fair question," he said finally. "And one that I'm not sure of the answer to yet. The idea is very new to me. Let me try to explain.

"We of the Overline possess the Maberippe Device," Parr said, "discovered by Hennery Maberippe almost two centuries ago. Apparently it was a unique discovery; if there was a Hennery Maberippe on any existing neighboring strands, he did not pursue a similar investigation. There are signs that several strands that were our immediate neighbors were somehow terminated at about the time that Maberippe was experimenting, but we have no explanation of this phenomena. We have no idea of what could make a strand terminate; it is outside our experience. It, however, has made us very cautious about making alterations to Maberippe's basic design."

"I'll say!" Delbit commented.

"The Maberippe device makes it possible for us to travel— let is call it—sideways in time. Our civilization is based on this fact. We produce nothing, or almost nothing. We trade through the Paraverse, and grow rich and content on the product, the handicraft, of others. We have convinced ourselves that we perform a useful service, and indeed perhaps we do. Therefore the device is our greatest secret, and we strive hard to keep it unknown to all those we deal with.

"Through the years we have encountered a variety of other Paraverse-traveling entities, some human and some not. The ones that captured you are an example of such."

"They seemed human," Delbit said.

"Oh, yes," Parr agreed. "Only humans tend to be that deliberately vicious to other humans. The nonhuman races treat us as we would treat insects."

"But it's still the planet Earth, right?" Delbit asked. "I mean, whichever, ah, strand you go to, the place in that universe you reach is still this planet?"

"Oh, yes. Traveling sideways in time does not seem to affect the gravity well we are at the bottom of. There are presumably millions of alternate universes where the planet Earth was never formed from the cosmic dust; and if we were to transport to one of those, we'd find ourselves in a vacuum ninety-three million miles from the sun. Or so I believe," Parr said.

"And there are Earths where people—humans—are not present? Where there are nonhuman intelligent beings?"

"There are. Many. The human possibility occupies only a small percent of the known alternate Earths. On some the dinosaurs still roam. Intelligent dinosaurs, probably descended from Compsognathus. On other lines, still further removed from our own, evolution took strange and unexpected turns even before the dinosaurs. One of our Paraverse explorers has briefly visited one replete with creatures that resemble lobsters with long necks. They communicate with flashing lights on their bulbous heads."

"Lights?"

"It is so. And they build cities, and they fight wars. We believe they have three sexes."

Parr took a deep breath. "At any rate," he continued, "there are a few other races—peoples—who have discovered the secret of traveling sideways in time. They build machines much like our own, as far as we can tell. Sometimes one or more of these machines are captured by people on one of the exploited strands, and they go managing on their own. The possibilities and permutations are, as you can imagine, endless.

"Our firm policy, when we run into another Paraverse-traveling people, is to avoid them when we can and fight them when we must. We do our utmost to preserve the Maberippe secret from any who do not possess it. We will do absolutely anything to protect the secret of the exact location of that strand that we call the Overline."

"I can understand that," Delbit said.

"We will not allow our transporters or our conveyers to fall into unauthorized hands."

"What's the difference?" Delbit asked.

"A transporter goes anywhere—or perhaps any when. A conveyer is a stripped-down transporter that just enables a link between two strands."

"Ah."

"What your friend Exxa represents to us is the fear of the unknown. She can blip between two worlds as easily as you can hop over that log over there. And we know nothing about her or her ability. How did she get this ability? How extensive is it? How easy is it to learn? How many others like her are there? Where are they? What are they doing? How would they feel about the Overline if they learned of it? Or, more to the point, perhaps they have already learned of the Overline. In which case, what do they think of it, and what do they intend to do about it? Perhaps they are already doing it, and we don't know. It would make Overliners very upset if they learned about Exxa and her ability. And with cause. Do you see?"

"I don't know," Delbit said. "I don't like to disagree with you, sir, but Exxa would never harm anyone."

"Of course not," Parr agreed. "And we don't intend to treat her as a threat. You have my oath. But from what you've told me, I agree with that doctor back in New York on your own strand: Exxa's amnesia is induced. We must assume that whoever did that is another who possesses the secret of time-blipping. Otherwise his actions make no sense. There also has to be a reason why he merely removed Exxa's memory rather than killing her, but presumably we shall find that out in time. Our first job is to find your lady friend."

"How are you going to do that?" Delbit asked.

"You are going to tell us more about the strand you come from than you thought you knew," Parr told him. "It seems that Exxa is flipping between this strand and that one. If we can establish which one you come from, we will look for her there."

"Why not wait until she reappears in this, ah, strand?" Delbit asked.

"Because yours seems more civilized," Preceptor Parr told him. "If she reappears in the middle of this forest, we have small chance of finding her. And if anyone else from this strand does stumble across her, it's liable to be a war party of our friends out there."

"Hah!" Delbit said.

"So, let's get to talking," Parr said.

"What do you want to know?"

Parr got up. "I'll let Major Sepple conduct the questioning," he said. "She is very practiced in just this sort of information gathering. As for me, I'd better see about the fighting down the track. I wouldn't want the troopers to think that their preceptors are afraid to show up at a fight, or worse, that we don't care about them. That would lead to dissatisfaction in the ranks."

PART THREE
HUNT AND PECK

CHAPTER FOURTEEN

It was almost midnight and the tents of the Eleventh Cavalry were all buttoned up to prevent artificial light from intruding on the night. There was only a thin sliver of moon, and the darkness in the clearing was almost tangible.

Delbit lay on his back on a blanket that had been spread on the ground and gazed in perfect silence at the stars. Somewhere off in the distance, down the railroad track, a bunch of maddened Mongols led by a few angry and puzzled outstranders were trying to decide whether or not to attack the encampment for the third time. If there was such an attack, Delbit's trooper guide had assured him, it would almost certainly not be launched until daylight. The enemy had already discovered to their great surprise that the troopers of the Eleventh could fight in the dark much better than they could.

The nightview monocles built into the brims of the trooper's cavalry hats gave the Eleventh a decided advantage, but even if the Mongol horde could have captured a few hats they couldn't have found the monocles, much less worked them. Fourth-level Vendakh-Prega was a line that had eschewed national warfare, but had raised the practice of individual and corporate warfare to an art. This, combined with its overpowering lust for technology and gadgets, made a culture that produced wondrous individual weapons. The Overline Security Service imported much of its personal weaponry from there.

Delbit had learned a lot during the last twenty-four hours, most of which he didn't understand yet except in the vaguest terms. But the knowledge that the information was there, that the universe—the Paraverse—was so vast, and so different from what he had ever imagined, that there was so much to yet learn, was frightening and exhilarating at the same time.

The stars looked the same as they ever had to him—distant, mysterious, and wonderful. And now he knew that the very earth he was lying on was more mysterious and more wonderful than he could have known. There were countless Earths, each slightly different from the next, and the cumulative differences made for vast changes—different civilizations, different peoples, different species, different forms of life. All interconnected in the past, and each now separate and alone and headed for its own destiny.

And it was possible to move between them! And he was one of the favored few who knew this was so. What a change for an article-apprenticed shoemaker! Think of moving between worlds as easily, or at least as rapidly, as moving between different rooms in a house.

And Exxa has done that, he then thought, and the thought sobered him. She has moved between the worlds. Even now she is somewhere—somewhen—else, where she might be in danger; and I lie here staring at the stars. And Major Sepple says I probably do not know enough for them to identify my home strand from among the many. My New York is like too many other New Yorks; my Philadelphia like too many other Philadelphias. And thus we cannot find her.

And I cannot help her.

A dark form appeared between his eyes and the stars. Someone was standing over him. "Delbit?" the person asked. "Are you awake?"

He sat up. The voice was Preceptor Parr's. "Yes, sir," he replied.

"Come into my tent."

Delbit followed the preceptor over to a large tent. Parr held the flap open for him and then entered, closing the flap behind him. Delbit noticed that the single dim interior light went off and then on by itself as the flap was opened and closed. It was such small details that he found most impressive.

"Sit down," Parr said, looking very serious as he waved Delbit to a camp chair. "I think we've located your strand."

"You have? That's wonderful, sir. But how? I thought you said there were too many possibilities—"

"There are," the preceptor agreed, "if all had remained as you described. But, apparently, all has not."

Delbit sat down and watched as Preceptor Parr sorted among various papers and photographs on the table. Major Sepple stood in a corner of the tent to Delbit's right. She nodded when he looked at her. She did not look happy.

"We sent an orbiting peruser into your line to try to establish parameters," the preceptor told him. "It took pictures of Manhattan Island from low orbit in many different strands. We were trying to narrow down the possibilities to those strands where the Faineworth Clinic building stood as you described it. If we were lucky, there would be but one."

"And that's what happened?" Delbit asked. "And the orbiting whatdyacallit found it?"

"Not exactly." Parr handed him a bunch of photographs and switched on a light that shone directly down on the table. "This is what we found. The more distant photograph is from the orbiting peruser. The other four are close-ups taken by a flying drone we sent in. We are trained to disbelieve coincidence, so we believe, with a high order of probability, that this is your strand."

Delbit had seen hundreds of photographs. His strand was going through a photography fad. There were portraits of dressed-up ladies and gentlemen in artificially stiff poses, photographs of domestic animals, pictures of rustic and urban laborers in artful arrangements, and occasional landscapes. He looked at the photographs Parr had given him. To his surprise, at first he couldn't figure out what he was seeing. And then he realized it was an overhead view, taken from very high up, of an area of ground that had been almost totally destroyed. The arc of destruction was centered somewhere in the uptown area of Manhattan Island. The lower part of the city, by the old fort and the docks, was still standing. But everything from Great Central Park north was just no longer there. Instead there was a vast circle of blasted and burned homes, sheds, shops, stables, barns, vehicles, and whatever else had been in the path of destruction.

Smoke was still rising from some of the buildings, and one of the pictures showed a fire crew pumping water onto the still-burning remains of what had been some sort of ware-house. Several ambulances were visible on the wider streets, but whether the supine figures in back were alive or dead, Delbit couldn't tell.

"My God!" Delbit said, staring at the pictures. "What on earth could have caused this? It's horrible! I can see this is—was—New York by the shape of the island, but why do you think that it's my New York?"

"The strands on both sides of this one have a Faineworth Clinic," Parr told him, fishing another picture from the pile on the table. "And the center of whatever this was is where the clinic should have been."

Delbit examined the new photograph. It was an aerial view of the Faineworth Clinic. He could even make out the large sign on the front lawn. "That's it," he said, pointing at the building. "That's the clinic!"

"Yes, but almost certainly not your Faineworth Clinic," Preceptor Parr told him. "It is, you might say, the strand next door."

Delbit stared at the picture and thought that over. "Does that meant that if I were to go down there, I'd find another Dr. Faineworth—and another me?" he asked.

"Another Dr. Faineworth, probably, but you would find him subtly—or perhaps even vastly—different from the one you were acquainted with. Another you, certainly not. As the girl you call Exxa did not appear in this strand, the good doctor would not have sent to Philadelphia for this strand's Delbit Quint. Besides, the identities of individuals in populations change rapidly from strand to strand. When two strands have been separated for as little as one century, it is hard to find *doppelgängers* under sixty or so years old. There will be many people with the same names as someone in another strand, perhaps even born of the same *doppelgänger* parents, but they won't be the same people. "

"Doppelgänger?" Delbit asked.

"A person on one strand identical with someone on an adjoining strand. A second Delbit Quint, with your genes instead of merely your name."

"Oh," Delbit said. He picked up the photograph showing the destruction at a distance. "You believe this is my strand, sir, is that right? What do you think happened there? What caused this?"

"I can't be sure, but I can make an educated guess," Preceptor Parr said. "We have checked for atomic radiation—"

"Atomic—?"

Parr raised his hand. "Never mind, I'll explain some other time. It would be a sign that a particular type of very large bomb was used. But it wasn't. And to get enough regular explosives to destroy so great an area, they would have had to have been trucking the explosives in for weeks. Surely someone would have noticed. And besides, there probably weren't enough nitrate-based explosives on the continent to have done that."

"What does that leave?" Delbit asked.

"Only one thing I can think of," Parr said. "A Goldstein bomb."

"Excuse me, sir?"

"A man-made implosion of the seventh force."

"The repulsive force that separates the strands in the Paraverse," Major Sepple contributed, seeing Delbit's blank look. "I think I mentioned it to you in my rather abbreviated basic physics lecture."

"You may well have, ma'am—I mean Major," Delbit agreed. "I'm sure I didn't retain more than half of what you said."

"Retaining half would have been very impressive," she told him. "These are not easy concepts; neither are they self-evident."

"So we are working on two assumptions," Preceptor Parr said. "Both of a fairly high order of probability. That is, we're guessing, but it's a good guess. The first assumption is that this was done by a Goldstein bomb. But I can't think of anything else that makes sense, and neither can the OSS Assessment Consort. That means that some people who understand how to travel about the Paraverse and how to manipulate its forces were loose on your strand. And they seem to have had a grudge against the Island of Manhattan."

"Why would anyone have done something this horrible?" Delbit asked.

"Would you like to hear my theory?" Parr asked.

"Very much, sir."

"I think someone is looking for your friend Exxa. Possibly those people you told us about that she called 'the bees,' or whatever. I think that they found out that she alternates between your strand and another. So they decided to clear off the area on your strand she would return to, to make her easier to find. A naked girl walking down a street in a burned-out city would surely be easy to spot."

"But that would be—" Delbit ran out of words.

"It's just a theory," Preceptor Parr told him dryly. "Luckily she has been removed from the area of Manhattan Island, so they won't find her, even if I'm right. The question is, do you want to find her?"

"Yes, sir," Delbit said. "I surely do."

"Then we'd better get about it right now, while she is still on your strand—at least we shall assume she is still on your strand for the purposes of this exercise."

"We?"

"You," Preceptor Parr told him, "and I. We."

"Oh," Delbit said.

"I can't do it without you," Parr told him, "because I've never seen the girl, and I doubt whether she will be overly forthcoming about her identity to a stranger. You can't do it without me, because you can't. I won't let you."

"Oh," Delbit repeated.

"The easiest arguments are the best," Parr said. He turned to Major Sepple. "Have you established the connectivity?"

She nodded. "You'll go through Overlook Two," she said. "I've notified them to expect you. That's where the perusers went out, so they have the parameters for Del-bit's strand. You can use the facilities there for proper costuming. By the time you're ready, they should have a transporter processed and waiting for you."

"Very good, Major," Parr said. "I'd better leave you with a formal record of my instructions. You never know." And with that cryptic comment he picked up a small, rectangular box, about the size of a pack of playing cards, and squeezed it. "Recording," he said clearly into the top of the box. "I am Preceptor Castimere Parr. Instructions follow for Major Maxinne Sepple of the Intelligence Consort and Captain—what's his name?—Willhelm Rotsler of the Eleventh Cavalry IG, who are now engaged in an OSS intervention on Level Four, Area Epsilon-Alpha, Line B-B, strand three two five point seven one.

"It has been determined by prisoner interrogation and supra-hypnotic regression that the Paraversal invaders of this strand are surrogates of the Grazond Tetrarchy. As it is current Grand Council policy to avoid the Tetrarchy, it is my unavoidable decision that we isolate this strand.

"Therefore, the group currently attempting to attack this encampment are to be captured. Then, after interrogation, all prisoners are to be transported to a suitable strand to be designated by the Preceptory. This strand is to be evacuated, and all traces of Overline presence are to be removed.

"Done on this day ninety-two of the two hundred and forty-third year of the Overline, by my seal."

Parr released his grasp on the instrument, and a small disk, like a silver coin, popped into his hand. "Have I covered everything?" he asked, dropping the disk into Major Sepple's hand.

"It will do fine, Preceptor," the major told him.

"Good. Then I'll just leave you here to finish cleaning up this mess," Parr told her. "We superior officers have all the fun."

Major Sepple came over to Delbit and took his hand. "Good luck, son," she said. "I hope you find your girl. May whatever gods you trust in remain at your side."

"Thank you, Major," he said.

She kissed him lightly on the cheek, then turned to Parr. "Good luck, Preceptor," she said, raising her right hand slightly with the fist loosely clenched, then dropping it. Parr nodded slightly in response.

Perhaps because of the contrast between her farewell to the preceptor and her farewell to him, Delbit kept a mental image of the slight hand gesture, and Parr's even slighter response. Some time later he learned that the Overline Security Service used a secret visual language of minimal gestures for security in the various unfriendly strands in which its officers worked. The dialogue Delbit observed was, roughly:

MAJOR SEPPLE: Remember that what you are about to do is dangerous. Take care of yourself and your companion. I will do your bidding here until you return or the job is done. Until we meet again, friend.

PRECEPTOR PARR: I understand. I will follow your suggestions. I trust you (to do the job here). Until we meet again, friend.

"Well, Mr. Quint, we had better get moving," Parr said. "Have you anything to retrieve before we leave?"

"No," Delbit said.

"Then follow me." Parr led him out of the tent and across the way to what appeared to be a hastily constructed storage shed. A guard who had been resting unobtrusively across from the shed's entrance saluted them as Parr unlocked the door. Parr returned the salute and shooed Delbit into the small room.

"Here we go," Parr said, pulling the door closed behind him.

"Step one of our trip into the unknown. This should prove exciting."

"You must have done this many times, Preceptor," Delbit said. "Do you really still find it exciting?"

"The thing about the unknown," Parr told him, "is that it is—unknown. You're going back to your own strand, albeit a part of the country that is unfamiliar to you. I am about to enter a world that I have never been on before. No matter how many other worlds I have entered, this one is unique. When I start feeling *blasé* about entering new worlds, then I will lose the edge, and the Great Council will have to elect another preceptor."

"Why are you doing this yourself?" Delbit asked, watching Parr making mystical passes over the control panel he was standing in front of. "In my, ah, strand, important people let others do the dangerous things for them."

"Ah, but this is not merely a dangerous thing, it is also an important thing," Parr explained. "If it is done wrong, I don't want to be able to blame anyone but myself. Hold on."

Delbit started to ask "What to?" But before he could, he felt a wrenching sensation in the pit of his stomach and suddenly his ears felt stopped up.

"Step one," Parr said. "Come with me." He unlatched the door and yelled through the doorway, "Fimblesommer! Let's not have any accidents. This is your preceptor!"

Delbit realized that the doorway had changed, beyond the door itself, and he was now looking at a tent flap. Parr raised the flap, and Delbit peered outside and saw that it was the middle of the day now, and there were six men with side arms of various sizes pointed at the door. The men slowly lowered the muzzles to point at the ground.

"It's regulations," Parr told him. "Just in case anyone nasty has captured a transporter. The guards are always ready to blast anyone who comes through the door without yelling the day's password first."

"Oh, good," Delbit said, stepping out of the door after the preceptor. They were in a clearing hastily hacked out of a forest, filled with tree stumps and packing crates, and punctuated by an occasional tent.

"This is the staging area for the operation which we just left," Preceptor Parr told him. "This continent is devoid of human life on this strand. Come along!"

Parr maneuvered them between stumps and crates to a large tent with a pointed top on the far side of the field. "Here we are," he said, pulling open the tent flap. "The second stage of our journey. This transporter will take us to Overlook Two, where we will be costumed for your home strand. Then, as quickly as possible, it's onward to find Exxa."

CHAPTER FIFTEEN

The pike to Seneca Falls, West Massachusetts, was crowded with afternoon traffic. Electric landaus and sedans and steam waggons and carriages jostled for space with the horse-drawn coaches and hacks, which tended to ignore a rather loose injunction that they stay in the right-hand lane. In the middle lane a speed of twenty-five miles an hour was permitted, and in the left lane speeds up to forty could be sustained, if achieved. At this time of day, even twenty-five miles an hour was but a fond ideal in the minds of some of the younger and more hopeful drivers. The vehicles were almost all driven by professional chauffeurs, as in this strand driving was considered menial work, and those who could afford to purchase vehicles could also afford to hire or buy drivers.

Delbit and Parr sat in the back of the small electric vehicle, which called itself a Gadabout, that Parr had purchased in Stalky, the small town closest to where they had emerged from the woods. Parr had obtained an adequate supply of local currency by selling some gold jewelry, the Overline equivalent of bartering beads with the natives. In the seat in front of them, separated from them by a closed glass partition, wearing a yellow driving coat, a black, floppy driving hat, and a pair of driving goggles with saucer-sized lenses, was Irvant Tarsipal, the short, bald, twisted, taciturn, elderly chauffeur that Parr had hired by the week from the garage that had sold him the Gadabout.

It had taken only two hours in Stalky to establish where

Exxa had turned up in this strand, and where she probably was now. When a naked girl appears at the side of the road just as the mayor and his wife and adolescent children (one of each) are driving by, and this apparition causes the horse to bolt and nearly kills everyone involved, the incident is the subject of nonstop conversation for many days thereafter. The Stalky *Express-Tagenblatt* had carried the story as front-page news, complete with an unrecognizable photograph of the girl in a borrowed house robe. It was right up there along with the stories of the survivors of the New York Disaster who were still streaming into Stalky, and Attucksville, and Seneca Falls, and points west.

The girl, who had refused to give her name or explain her presence or her lack of attire, had been taken in custody by the local sheriff. She had then, it was reported in the *Express-Tagenblatt*, been transported to Seneca Falls, the commonwealth capital, for a hearing before a General Sessions magistrate to determine what should be done with her. The good citizens of the Commonwealth of West Massachusetts did not approve of people who thwarted law and order by appearing out of nowhere with a noticeable lack of clothing and frightening respectable mayors and their families.

"What's our plan?" Delbit asked Parr, after making sure that the glass partition between the front and back seats of the Gadabout was securely closed.

"Plan?"

"Yes. How are we going to rescue Exxa? You must have some sort of plan."

Parr looked at him mildly. "You mean, 'At exactly fifteen twenty-three you will stand on the southwest corner of Kickapoo Street wearing a green clown suit'? That sort of thing?"

"I guess so," Delbit said.

"I didn't realize they had that sort of literature on this strand," Parr said, shaking his head. "But I guess it is endemic to the human condition."

"Well, we can't just walk into the magistrate's office, or the courtroom, or the jail, or whatever, and walk out with her," Delbit said.

"Perhaps we can," Parr told him. "At any rate, you have just elucidated the best reason why we can have no plan at the moment. We don't know where she is; we don't know how well she is guarded—if she is guarded at all. Maybe they let her go. We don't know what story, if any, she told them. There are so many things we don't know that it would be futile to try to establish any sort of plan at this point."

"Oh," Delbit said. "You're going to wait until we have the information before you make a plan."

"Probably not," Parr told him. "By the time we're in the thick of things, it's usually too late to plan. We'll be going by instinct, Quint. Instinct and learned response. The Overline Security Service trains both of these faculties very highly, and I spent several decades with the OSS before attaining my present exalted station. The only advice I can give you is to follow my lead, obey my instructions, and use your brain. Probably in that order."

"I shall do my best," Delbit said.

"Of course you will," Parr told him.

Twenty minutes later they were in downtown Seneca Falls, stopped across from the white marble courthouse building by a sign that said:

PARKING HERE
IS
IMPOSSIBLE

STOPPING HERE
IS
ABSOLUTELY FORBIDDEN

Parr leaned forward and tapped on the glass partition with a silver coin. Irvant Tarsipal unrolled the window with a world-weary hand, removed his driving goggles with the other, and leaned back to hear what he was about to be told. Whatever it was, he would do it, but he wouldn't like it.

"We are going to get out here, Tarsipal," Parr told him. "Take the vehicle and find a convenient place to park it. One where we may remove it at any hour of the day or night, depending on our need. Then come back here on foot and wait for us."

"I'm going to need my dinner, if that won't upset your worship's plans," Tarsipal said in a resigned voice.

"I was going to suggest that you wait for us over there, in that tavern," Parr said. "At least I assume it's a tavern." He pointed to a building on the next block where the wooden sign of the Fox & Jug swung freely from an iron bar sticking out over the street. "Eat what you will, but limit yourself to one drink. We may have farther to drive this evening." He handed the silver coin to the chauffeur. "Keep yourself available. Take a room if we don't show up before the taproom closes."

"Yes, sir," Tarsipal said, staring gloomily at the coin. "I hope they have a bit of boiled meat for dinner. Fried food makes me bilious."

Delbit and Parr got out and stood looking at the imposing four-story courthouse across the street while the Gadabout disappeared around the nearest comer. It took up most of a double-sized city block, separated from the building on its right, a two-story, unornamented block of stone, by a narrow alleyway. A flight of steps stretching the length of the building led up to a row of Ionic columns. A frieze wrapped around the building, depicting Indians and Europeans in various stages of involvement, separated every few feet by a highly stylized rendering of the letters L P C W M. Above it, surmounting the columns in front, the tympanum showed a handsome lawgiver posing heroically in a rather short toga and handing the law, in the form of a bundle of scrolls, to a mixed group of supplicant Pilgrims and Indians. Under it, in severe Latinate lettering, was chiseled the phrase The LEGISLATVRE and the PEOPLE of the COMMONWEALTH of WEST MASSACHVSETTS.

It was already growing dark, and the lamplighter was even

now working his way down the street using his long pole to light the municipal gas lamps. Delbit looked around. There were still a few people on the street, each of whom seemed intent on getting somewhere else as rapidly as possible. A couple passed them and, after a brief appraising glance by the man, paid them no further attention.

Delbit couldn't escape the feeling that he stood out, garbed as he was, that everyone who passed would take one look at him and giggle, but obviously he was mistaken. He was dressed in a green suit with wide, sharply creased trousers, a jacket with a flared collar and silver buttons, and a puffy cerise silk cravat, all topped by a floppy triangular hat—the acceptable attire for a wealthy young man-about-town but certainly ridiculous garb for an apprentice. But the costumers on Overlook Two had dressed him as a young gentleman, not as an apprentice, and it was thus that he would be judged by the passersby. And he made quite a tolerable young gentleman. Clothes may not make the man, but they certainly erect a strong foundation. Parr, in his powder-red suit and fluffy maroon cravat, looked so elegant that an order of American nobility cried out to be founded just so that he could be a member.

Parr stared pensively across at the courthouse, and Delbit alternated between staring at him and staring at the building. There were no lights visible in the entire structure. "What are we going to do?" Delbit asked Parr. "It looks like everyone has gone home."

"I don't know," Parr told him. "Why is it that your strand has electric cars, but only gaslight?"

"We have electric globes," Delbit said. "But you can't use them for street lighting. First of all, they're not bright enough and they don't last very long; and second of all, going around and recharging the batteries every day would be too expensive."

"Of course," Parr said. "Silly of me. Back to our problem. Let's approach the building and examine it from close up. Perhaps something will occur to us."

They crossed the street and climbed up the marble steps to

the imposing front doors of the courthouse. The three large doors were securely shut, with a solidity when thumped that suggested a solid core beneath their bronze exterior. No hint of inner light was visible either under or around the doors, or through the little porthole windows that were set high up in the facing wall.

Parr used a small pocket flashlight to examine the glass-enclosed bulletin board between the two doors. "Look," he said, pointing to one of the papers stuck to the board.

Delbit peered at the paper. Headed Court Calendar: Monday, April ye 17, which was the day now ending, it then listed six cases for each of four judges. Under Judge Henrie Van Pester, the third case was *Jane Doe*, who was being tried for *Malicious Loitering with Intent to Frighten Gentelmen, Gentelwomen, Childeren and Livestock.* In the Disposition column the following note had been penciled in: *Held for Confederal Government Inquisition.*

"You think that's her?" Delbit asked.

"I am morally certain," Parr told him.

"Me, too. What do we do now?" Delbit asked. They were getting close to Exxa, and it was up to them to rescue her. This was not the time for him to lose faith in Parr's ability. Surely the preceptor would come up with something.

"I don't know," Parr said. "Let's wander around to the side of the building—see what that looks like."

"That's it?" Delbit asked. He could feel himself getting red in the face. "You really don't have any kind of plan, do you? You don't have any idea of where Exxa is being held, or how to get her away. She could be in prison somewhere, or in some mental hospital—and we can't even find out where!" He sat down on the marble steps and rubbed his eyes with his fists.

Parr squatted next to him. "Listen, Quint," he said softly. "This is as important to me as it is to you. Maybe more. We will find the girl, I assure you. We will rescue her, if rescuing she needs. And I assume she does. We can't just go off lunging in all directions. We have to find out what's happening—where the girl is, and what they think they're doing with her. Then we'll get her out and take her away. Honest."

Delbit dropped his fists into his lap and nodded. "It's not just that I care about her, you understand," he told Parr. "It's that she counted on me, and even though she has no way of knowing that I'm here now, I don't want to let her down. Nobody's ever counted on me before."

Parr nodded, carefully not telling Delbit of the inconsistencies in his worldview. "*I'm* counting on you, Quint," he said. "Now get up and help me check this building out. If we don't gain access, or get some suggestion of someplace else to look, then we'll go join Irvant Tarsipal at the Fox & Jug and get a good night's sleep. Then tomorrow, when this place is open, we'll take it apart."

Delbit pushed himself to his feet. "Sorry," he said. "I'm all right now. But I hope we don't have to wait until tomorrow to do something."

They started down together, and then suddenly, when they had reached the wide place in the steps about halfway down, Delbit froze. He put his hand out and grabbed Parr's elbow. "Turn right!" he whispered urgently. "Walk to the far side of the building."

Without hesitation, and without a word, Parr swerved to the right and continued along on that level until he reached the wall at the edge of the building. Delbit stayed right behind him and, using all his willpower, didn't look back.

"Well, what is it?" Parr demanded when they had stopped.

"There are two men at the other corner of the building by the alleyway, right by the foot of the steps," Delbit told him. "They are all dressed in black and they are standing there, just standing, as though they're waiting for something."

"So?"

"I recognized them."

"From that distance? They must have been twenty yards away, and it's dark out and there's no streetlight at that corner."

"That's right," Delbit agreed. "And I've only seen them once before."

Parr looked at Delbit. "All right," he said. "I believe you. Who are they?"

"Exxa called them 'the bees,'" Delbit said. "They are the people that we saw briefly right before we blipped. The people that Exxa was so afraid of, even though she couldn't remember why."

Parr nodded. "I remember the story," he said. "How could you be sure it was the same people from this distance?"

"Well, I can't be sure that they are the exact same people," Delbit admitted. "But there's something about the way they are standing...." He paused, and then said, "I can't explain it, but I'm sure. If these aren't the same bees, then they're other bees. Whatever it is that bees are."

Parr nodded and thought for a second. "Follow me," he said, and he led Delbit down the steps and across the street. Going from doorway to doorway, they moved along the opposite side of the street until they were across from the two black bees, who still stood motionless by the side of the courthouse.

"They seem to be more interested in the alleyway to the side of the building than in the building itself," Parr said.

"They must have come here for Exxa," Delbit whispered.

"They must," Parr agreed. "And once more, they got here first. They probably know a great deal more than we do right now. Not that that would be so difficult. All we know is what we read in the papers."

"What should we do? We have to do something!"

Parr turned and unbuttoned Delbit's jacket. He pulled it aside, reached under it to the area that would have been covering the small of Delbit's back, and unclipped something. "Here," he said, handing Delbit what looked like a round cigar-like tube with a canted handle at one end. "This is your personal weapon. We didn't have time to brief you on it. Be careful with it."

"What is it?" Delbit whispered.

"Think of it as a gun. Point it at someone and pull the trigger and you'll burn a hole through him."

"Where's the trigger?"

"When you're holding it properly by the grip, the trigger extends from the barrel. Otherwise it isn't there. Remember to hold it in front of you when you fire. The energy beam is generated by a chemical explosion, which vents out the two sides."

"How do I aim it?"

"Just as you would your finger. Point it where you want to hit."

"That's it?"

"If you feel insecure with that...." Parr reached up to Delbit's hat and twisted something. A flat lens dropped in front of Delbit's right eye, suspended from the hat. "Look through that. No need to close your other eye. You'll get used to it in a minute."

The scene through the lens was as bright as daylight, although curiously devoid of color.

"Well!" Delbit said.

"Now hold the beamer as though you're going to use it and point it at that building over there."

"So this is a beamer," Delbit said. Holding it cautiously in front of him, he pointed it at one of the columns fronting the courthouse.

"Good," Parr told him. "Now the trigger is that stud under your forefinger. But you should feel another stud under your thumb. Do you?"

Delbit explored the surface of the beamer with his thumb. "Yes, I think so."

"It's subtle, but it's there. Push in with your thumb. Just your thumb."

Delbit did so. A bright blue-green spot of light appeared on the building across the street to the left of the column he thought he was aiming at.

"That's the aiming spot. It shows where the beamer will hit. You can only see it through the eyepiece. It doesn't show up as well in daylight, but if you look for it, it's there."

A third man in the black bee garb appeared from the alleyway and beckoned to the two waiting bees. They went with him back into the darkness.

"I think that if we follow them, they will probably take us where we want to go," Parr said. "Now be careful with that beamer. Don't go burning holes in inoffensive people just because they're in your way. Self-defense only. On the other hand, I'd rather one of them gets hurt than that you or Exxa does."

"Preceptor, I agree with you earnestly and completely," Delbit told him. "Let's go before they disappear somewhere behind the building."

"Quietly," Parr said. "Wherever they lead, we shall follow. Come along! Stay in the shadows."

Parr and Delbit crossed the street beyond the arc of the street-light and entered the alley. The three men in black scurried purposefully along ahead of them, serenely unaware of their two followers. At the far end of the two buildings they turned right, going behind the two-story adjunct structure.

When Parr reached the edge of the building he dropped forward onto his hands and peered around the building with his head a foot off the ground. Then he stood up and dusted off his hands. "Aha!" he whispered to Delbit.

"Aha, What?"

"It's the entrance to a jail, judging by external appearances. It may be the city jail, or perhaps it's only holding cells for the courthouse. Depending, I suppose, on the size of the prison population here in West Massachusetts."

"What are the bees doing?"

"They seem to have gone inside. Let us stroll over there, like a pair of honest citizens, and inquire of the guard what is going on."

Parr adjusted his cravat, tugged his jacket into position, and whispered, "Put that beamer in your pocket and retract the night monocle. I'll do whatever explaining has to be done."

They rounded the corner together and walked toward where the bees had disappeared. The jail had a bifurcated entrance; one door was heavily barred, with a sign saying

WARE!—FORCEMENT OFFICIALS ONLY,

and the other was an unadorned wooden door with the inscription over it:

SENECA FALLS TRAPMENT LOCALITY
Make Inquiries of Portal Official

They went to the unbarred door and pulled it open. The small room immediately inside the door was separated by steel netting from the larger room surrounding it. The door in the netting was open, and the three guards in the larger room were lying on the floor in various states of disarray.

Parr pushed through the netting door and knelt by the nearest guard. "Still alive," he said. "No visible wounds. Breathing evenly. I would guess he has been gassed."

The sounds of scuffling came faintly from behind a closed door leading into the interior of the jail. Parr motioned to Delbit to get against the wall opposite the door, then pulled his beamer and flattened himself against the wall on the other side. They waited as the sounds got nearer.

The door was kicked open and two black bees strode through, half-carrying and half-pulling a struggling young woman in a prison-striped dress between them.

"Exxa!" Delbit heard himself saying.

"Freeze right where you are!" Preceptor Parr yelled, in a firm, commanding voice, pointing his beamer at the nearest black-hatted head.

In an instant reaction, as though they had been practicing it all their lives, the two black bees thrust Exxa ahead of them and dropped to the floor. One rolled to the left and the other to the right, and they pulled thick black tubes from their belts. Parr beamed one neatly in the shoulder, and he dropped his tube. Delbit sent a sizzling energy beam into the floor two inches in front of the other one's nose.

The unhurt bee flipped to his feet and pointed his tube at

Delbit. A red-tinted beam coughed from the end. It missed Delbit's ear by a finger's breadth and went through the glass door of a medicine cabinet behind him, hitting a bottle of alcohol, which exploded.

Without pausing to think, Delbit fired again, pointing the silver tube of his beamer like a finger, and burning a neat hold in the bee's chest. With a strange grumbling sound, the man crumpled up and dropped to the floor. A black-sleeved arm appeared from behind the inner doorway and the gloved hand flung a small canister into the room. Parr swiveled and blasted the canister even as the first wisps of gas emanated through the tiny finned top. It crumped a low-pitched crump, and a sheet of flame erupted from it and briefly enveloped the room, singeing the hair on the back of Delbit's hands, and was gone.

"Well," Parr said. "Whatever the gas was, it was flammable. And so it has flammed."

"Good shooting," Delbit said.

"Thank you. I think we'd better—"

A loud explosion sounded from the corridor beyond the doorway, and a small cloud of dust puffed through the door. Parr cautiously stepped over to the door, climbed on a chair, and peered around the corner from a height of seven feet. "Well!" he said, jumping off the chair and running into the corridor. Delbit followed.

The window at the left end of the corridor, where it turned to enter the cell area, had been blown out, bars and all. The third bee was nowhere in sight.

"I think we've been deserted," Parr said. "And I think we'd better get out of here ourselves. Someone might remark on the noise."

"If he was carrying an explosive that can do that," Delbit said, "why do you suppose he didn't use it on us?"

"I imagine he didn't want to chance harming your lady friend," Parr said. "For whatever reason, it seems they want her alive."

They returned to the front room. Exxa was standing in the

middle of the room, staring down at the two bees, who were lying on the floor. Parr went over to examine the one who had been shot in the shoulder. "He's dead," he said after a minute.

"They take poison," Exxa said. "They won't allow themselves to be captured."

Parr looked up. "You must be Exxa," he said. "You're supposed to have lost your memory. What do you know that about these men?"

"The Friends of the Bee, they call themselves," Exxa told him. "They're very mysterious and keep to themselves, and nobody knows who they are, where they come from, where they go, or why they do what they do."

She paused and looked puzzled. "And I have no idea of how I knew that," she said. "These random bits from my past come to me sometimes. You must be a friend of Delbit's. Who are you? How did you get here?"

"My name is Parr," Preceptor Parr said. "The rest of the answers will have to wait. We'd better get you away from here now."

Exxa looked over at Delbit. "Hi, friend," she said.

Delbit went over and took her in his arms, and she hugged him tightly and pushed her head into his shoulder. "I'm glad you came," she said, "however you managed it. I tried to leave, to blip back to where you were, but I couldn't. I thought I was stuck here."

"Now we'll all leave." Delbit said. "But we have to do it in a more complex manner than you usually use. We have to go back to Stalky first."

Exxa looked at him, and then at Parr. "Whatever you say," she said, shaking her head. "Whatever works."

"Let us get away from this place," Parr said. "We have a vehicle waiting. And we'll have to find a change of clothes for you. That striped dress is a bit obvious."

"The mayor's wife gave me a dress," Exxa said. "When they made me change clothes they put it in a box, and I think they keep the boxes in there." She pointed to a door across the room.

"Let's look," Parr said. He went to the door and rattled the knob. "Quint, go through that guard's pockets," he said. "See if you can find some keys."

Delbit knelt beside the unconscious guard. "There's a key ring on his belt," he called. He snapped the ring free of the belt and tossed it to Parr.

The second key unlocked the door, and Exxa went into the small storeroom to find her clothes. Two minutes later she came out wearing a tight, low-cut red dress that flared at the waist, and that exhibited perhaps a bit more of her skin than was legal and proper in West Massachusetts. A pair of red patent-leather high-heeled shoes and a red leather belt completed the outfit.

"The mayor's wife gave you that?" Delbit asked, the surprise evident in his voice.

"Is it unattractive?" Exxa asked. "I couldn't find the one the mayoress gave me."

"On the contrary," Parr said. "It is perhaps more attractive than appropriate. I wonder for what offense the wearer of that garment is locked up."

"I'd rather look like a night worker than a convict," Exxa said, smoothing the dress against her waist. "I will continue looking for other garments if you like, but I doubt if any duchess's dresses are in that room."

"On the whole, we'd better just leave," Parr said. "Can you walk quietly in those shoes?"

"I just put them on to get the whole effect," Exxa said, bending over and pulling them off. "I'll wear the canvas slippers, which are more comfortable. I don't suppose anyone will recognize them as prison garb."

"I don't think anyone will notice your shoes," Delbit said.

"Come," Parr said. "We've been here too long."

They left the building, Parr leading, and rounded the corner to the alley. From somewhere in the distance came a series of overlapping honking sounds that Delbit recognized as the sirens of several constabulary steam waggons. He identified the noise for Parr in a loud whisper. As they made their way back up the alley the honking got louder.

"Someone heard the explosion," Parr said, peeking his head around the corner of the main street. "Quick! Up the steps of the courthouse."

They ran up the courthouse steps and hid behind a marble column until the three constabulary vehicles had turned, two going down the next block and one into the alleyway they had just deserted. When the vehicles were out of sight, they ran down the stairs and across the street and ducked into the convenient doorway of a closed hat and cravat shoppe, which had an entrance two steps below street level.

"You two wait here," Parr said. "Keep out of sight. I'll fetch our driver." And with that he was off down the street.

Exxa crouched down in the doorway and leaned against the yellow-painted wood to the side of the door. "I should have taken a coat," she said. "It's chilly tonight."

Delbit took off his jacket and wrapped it around her shoulders. "We'll be away from here in a couple of minutes," he said.

"Who is your friend?" Exxa asked. "And how did you follow me here? I left you elsewhen."

"It's a complicated story," Delbit said. "Which I'm sure will be explained to you in exasperating detail later. But we did come, which is all that matters right now. Did they treat you badly?"

"Not really," she said. "I don't think any of them had any idea of what to do with me. Did you hear what happened to that city—New York?"

It was about ten minutes before the Gadabout pulled up in front of the store and picked them up. The three hour trip back to Stalky was smooth and mostly uneventful, punctuated only twice by the honks of passing constabulary waggons, racing up and down the roads for reasons of their own. The Gadabout was not stopped, nor even seriously examined by either passing pride of constables. Their mental image of escaping convicts was obviously quite different.

It was two in the morning when they pulled up to a patch

of woods two miles out of town. Parr rolled down the window to the chauffeur's compartment and handed Irvant Tarsipal an envelope full of documents. "I have deeded this vehicle over to you," he told the wizened chauffeur. "You can either sell it or go into business for yourself. Goodby, Irvant, faithful traveling companion. I would suggest that you don't tell anyone where you left us, or they will suspect you murdered us and buried the bodies in the woods. It would prove inconvenient for you."

"You're getting out here?" Tarsipal asked.

"Even so," Parr admitted.

They did so. Tarsipal shrugged and drove off.

They walked into the woods about a quarter mile and found the clearing the men had arrived at. Delbit and Exxa lay down and slept on the grass by the side of the clearing, wrapped in a light blanket from the survival kit that had been left behind. Preceptor Parr sat against a tree and stared silently into the dark.

Shortly after dawn the air shimmered, and a metal cage appeared in the clearing.

CHAPTER SIXTEEN

The overline was beauty and truth and love and honesty and safety in an unfriendly Paraverse. The Overline was smugness and force and chicanery and indifference and foolish regulation in an uncaring Paraverse. It was the best of worlds, it was the worst of worlds. It rescued people in trouble on alien and savage strands. It practiced chattel slavery. It taught and professed to believe in the highest ideals of public utility and the common good. It allowed any sort of behavior of its traders when on foreign strands. It was easy to understand. It was impossible to understand. Delbit was confused.

Delbit and Exxa stayed with Preceptor Parr when they arrived in the Overline. The preceptor made restoring Exxa's memory his second priority; the first was assuring that no word of her condition, or her ability, was spoken outside his own household.

It was late afternoon, local time, when they arrived at Preceptor Parr's villa outside Lyander City. He had rooms assigned to them, and told them to bathe, sleep, eat, and wander about for the rest of the evening. He would be too busy to get back to them that evening, but the servants would see to their needs; they were used to communicating with guests of the villa in sign language. Delbit spent several hours fascinated by the vision screen he discovered taking up one wall of a common room. But he couldn't figure out the filing system of the vision disks, and didn't feel like asking anyone to explain it. Then he found Exxa and they sat in her room and they talked, and eventually they went to his room together, turned the light out, and went to bed.

* * * * * * *

He was falling...falling...falling into a vortex that had neither beginning nor end. He had always been falling, and would continue to fall forever. There was no up and no down, but only a steady and endless spin. And nebulous clouds that tugged at his face as he fell.

Somewhere there was another person.

A woman.

But gender did not matter yet. For there was no time, and therefore neither birth nor death.

Only the vortex.

And the growing globe in the center.

Growing larger and larger until its surface passed him, until it occupied all of time and space and gathered them into itself.

And then, with a suddenness that hurt, the ball shrank again, coalesced, hardened, took on form and shape, and caught fire, burning with a whiteness that encompassed the void.

He floated to the ground, for now there was a ground, had always been a ground, and the white ball in the sky was the sun. Names are so important.

And she floated to the ground some distance from him, and she stood, tall and terrible, clothed in her nakedness, and created the heavens and the earth. And he aided her. And they looked at what they had made, and it was good.

Somewhere, under the earth, he could sense evil growing. It smelled like laughter, and it looked like pain, and it felt like balls of red fire hurled into the air. But surely they had not created evil. Had they? In creating good, does one necessarily also create its antonym? He thought about it, and bright varicolored sparks filled the air in front of him.

And the woman stood before him, and she wore gossamer, and faery fire bound her long auburn hair. "You are me," she said, "and I am you, for I love you, my king."

"And I love you, my queen," he told her, "with the love that is all of life and makes all else possible."

"We are together in a dream," she said. "We are bound by dreams as others cannot even be bound by life. And yet I fear we may not be bound in life, so let us always share these dreams. We will always have these dreams, whatever else may come."

He was confused. "What can come, my queen," he asked her, "if we do not wish it? If we bid it stay away?"

"Life can come, my dear friend," she said, sadly. "And truth; and perhaps a mission, a task that cannot be denied."

"If you have such a mission, so be it," he said. "I shall be by your side."

She reached out and tangled his hair between her fingers. "It could be that we have separate missions," she said. "I would that I could stay here with you for all eternity, but it is not to be. I am afraid of tomorrow, of endless tomorrows, but I must face them. I must find out who I am, and what has happened to me, and why."

They floated together in silence for a while, and then dove deep, seeking the ruined silver palaces beneath the waves.

Deep in the earth, the evil grew.

They surfaced in a small pool in the inner courtyard of an ancient building. The flower garden, untended, had gone to glorious weed, and great globular flowers rested in the moonlight, waiting for the sun to tease them open. They played in the garden, and made love, and were happy.

The evil surfaced.

In the street the sound of tramping boots, as men marched six abreast past the wooden doors.

(Men?)

The Nimber Host marched by outside, as they lay hidden next to each other in the cold cellar. Neither men nor beasts, but foul-smelling creatures of an elder god, the Nimber were quick and bright and bad, and they worked well together their evil to perform.

The calla spies went forth, small flying things with one large eye and razor talons on one thin foot. They peered through windows, they peered through keyholes, they peered into cracks in the mind.

A crowd formed rapidly around the large man as he stood on the platform and spoke eternal wisdom. Delbit found himself at once in the crowd and alongside—and somehow part of—the large man. "Don't let it worry you, son," the man whispered. "I am large—I contain multitudes."

Delbit nodded from the crowd, watching as the man took a sip of water, and then spoke:

"We must form straight lines! We must duck and weave, if we are to remain upright. I offer you pencils, and a good time will be had by all."

The crowd cheered.

"Have you noticed that the ants are getting larger?" the man demanded.

They cheered.

"Butter knives are better knives! I offer you a peace of a sword!"

They stood up and cheered, carrying each other about on their shoulders.

"The secret is," the man intoned, leaning forward confidentially, "the Paraversal secret is—"

A hush fell over the audience. Delbit suppressed a sneeze.

"Delbit!"

He looked around. His princess was above him, suspended in a transparent gold ball.

"Goodbye, Delbit," she called.

"Wait!" He ran toward her, but the ball receded faster than he could run.

"The Golden Orb is taking me somewhere, Delbit," she called. "Wait for me."

"Forever!" he yelled. His feet were stuck in molasses, and he could not move. The ball dwindled and disappeared from sight. "Exxa!" he screamed.

He woke.

It was early morning. The bed next to him was empty. In something approaching a panic, he ran to the next door. Exxa's bed was also empty, except for her robe, tossed carelessly across the covers with the memory of her body still warm inside.

He turned to run down the hall, and suddenly realized that he had nothing on. Quickly he ran back to his own room, washed cursorily, and threw a layer of clothes about himself. Then he returned to the hall and tried to figure out which way to go.

A passing servant, with her arms full of bed linen, saw his confusion and pointed down the hall. She said a few words in a soft, melodious voice, indicated the second door on the left, and walked on.

Well, it was a place to start. Delbit went to the second door on the left and pulled—pushed—it open. Inside was the breakfast room, where Preceptor Parr was sitting at a round table putting jam on what looked like a square muffin. A very beautiful young woman was sitting next to him, but she wasn't Exxa, and Exxa was nowhere to be seen.

"What have you done with Exxa?" Delbit demanded.

"Good morning," Parr said, waving the muffin at him. "Sit down. What would you like to eat? My staff does interesting things with eggs. Not all of them edible."

The girl sitting next to Parr stifled a giggle by turning it into a cough.

Delbit dropped into a chair. Eggs didn't strike him as funny this morning. He couldn't decide whether to be angry or merely annoyed. He wasn't sure whether he should make a fuss about Exxa's disappearance or not. If she was in danger, he wanted to run to her side. But if she were merely getting her hair done or some such thing, he didn't want to look silly.

Parr nodded to him. "Let me introduce you to my good friend and personal secretary, Viola D'epp. Viola, this is Mr. Delbit Quint, who will be pleased to give you a chance to practice your English."

"Welcome to our villa, Mr. Quint," the woman said, smiling at him. "Preceptor Parr has asked me to take care of your needs while you are staying with us. We'll start with a suprahypnotic session after breakfast to get you started in learning Lesh."

A servant came in while Delbit was looking confused, placed a plate in front of him, and filled it with a mound of eggs.

"Lesh is the language of the Overline," Parr told him. "You will almost certainly spend enough time among us to make it desirable to learn to speak it."

"I'm very bad at languages," Delbit said.

"With our techniques that hardly matters," Viola told him. "Suprahypnotic induction is no respecter of inadequacy. You will learn the language despite yourself."

"Really?" Delbit looked impressed. "What a great way to learn. This must be a land of geniuses."

"Unfortunately it only works for linguistic skills, and a very few other things," Parr said. "And I do mean unfortunately."

"Where's Exxa?" Delbit asked, trying to look only mildly concerned.

"She is off getting her first session of suprahypnotic induction," Parr told him. "But in her case the object is a little different. I have two expert mentalists here, who will be working to remove the mindblock and restore her memory. With any luck, by the next time you see her, she won't be Exxa anymore."

"Oh," Delbit said. He picked up his fork and began shoveling egg into his mouth, looking down at his plate, hardly noticing the taste, or anything else. He had tried not to think about this. His Exxa, the girl he loved, and who loved him, would shortly be swallowed in the larger personality, with its great ocean of memories, that was about to be returned to her. Would there be any place for him alongside this new person?

Delbit felt a touch on his arm. He looked up. Viola had slid into the chair next to him and was intently studying his face. "It will be all right," she told him. "You'll see. You will have a whole new set of problems when your girl gets her memory back, and they may be very difficult ones. But her feelings for you will not change."

Delbit felt the blood rushing to his face. "How did you

know?" he said.

"I know," she replied. "I looked at you, and I knew."

"She knows," Parr said from across the table. "She always knows. I don't know how she does it. Science knows not how she does it. She looks at your face and she understands more about you than you yourself. It's because she cares. She can't help caring."

Delbit took her hand. "Thank you," he said.

"Eat your breakfast," she told him. "I believe you're about to live out an ancient Chinese curse."

"What's that?" he asked.

"'May you live in interesting times,'" she told him.

CHAPTER SEVENTEEN

Delbit came out of the suprahypnotic induction session with the distinct impression that his brain was itching. It wasn't a horribly uncomfortable feeling, except that he couldn't figure out how to scratch the itch. "It feels funny," he told Viola, as they walked back across the courtyard to Preceptor Parr's office-in-residence.

"I've always found it so," Viola agreed. "But suprahypnotism is a useful method for implanting language and both examining and removing memories."

"You mean, like what happened to Exxa?"

"Perhaps much like that, although Ensir Parr believes that another method was used. We should know shortly."

"That's true," Delbit said. Then he fell silent for a minute, musing on the possibilities. How much would the woman he called Exxa change when she remembered who she really was, when she regained the past life that was now shut off from her? And would she feel toward Delbit the way her abbreviated self had? Exxa was, in a way, newly made, and had known few men before Delbit. How could a woman with a newly regained life-time of experience, of knowing really interesting men, still care for a shoemaker's apprentice?

As much as he wished for Exxa's recovery, Delbit feared what it might mean to him.

"This way," Viola said. "We'll go in the side door. The preceptor said to treat you like one of the household, and not a guest."

"Is that good or bad?" Delbit asked. "After all, some of the members of this household are slaves."

Viola laughed. "That's true," she said, pulling the door open. "But slavery is not so easily acquired on Overline as that. You must agree willingly to be a term-slave, and the conditions and ramifications must have been explained to you thoroughly beforehand. And then an interceder reexplains them, and questions you thoroughly to make sure you understand before you actually enter into service."

"Interceder?" Delbit asked.

"That's what they call the sort of judge that deals with offline and underline matters."

"But then, why would anybody agree to be a slave?" Delbit asked.

Viola considered. "Well, suppose you were from a strand where they practiced human sacrifice. And suppose you were it. And your heart was going to be torn out in the morn to satisfy the unnatural hunger of the alligator god. And somebody came to you in the middle of the night and said, 'I have an interesting offer for you that may substantially increase your life expectancy.' What would you do?"

"You mean if you said you weren't interested, he'd leave you there?" Delbit asked.

"Even so," she said. "Why not? You can't go around rescuing everyone in the Paraverse who's in trouble just because you're a good guy. There are far too many people in trouble at any given time to make that possible. You have to have some less altruistic motivation, and some limitations."

Delbit shook his head. "It still doesn't sound right. Do they really do that?"

Viola shrugged. "With the additional caveat that the only people recruited for term-slavery are already slaves in their home strands. And, usually, in less than ideal circumstances. Actually, it's a good deal for them. Besides, if they don't like it, they can always say no."

"Yes, but even if you are a slave—to leave your own home

and everything you ever knew to become a slave all over again somewhere else.... I don't know. Do many people accept?"

Viola smiled. "I suspect most do," she said. "And gladly. I did."

Delbit turned to her, and found his mouth was open. "You?" he asked.

"Even so," she said.

"But—" he said. "I thought—"

"I am especially favored," she told him. "And Ensir Parr is a good master even to the worst of his, ah, subjects."

"Well!" Delbit said.

"Although the situation does admit of problems that are not apparent to the casual observer," Viola told him. She took his hand. "Come, let us show the preceptor the results of your suprahypnotic treatment."

"That's right," he said. "When—ohmigod!"

"What?"

"We've been speaking Lesh."

"True. And your accent is excellent."

"I didn't even realize."

"You were distracted."

"I certainly was," he agreed.

Viola knocked on the oak-paneled door of Parr's office, then entered. Parr looked up from his desk and pushed aside the keyboard he was using. A hole in the side of his desk promptly opened and swallowed it. As the monitor screen slid into the desktop, Parr stood up and stretched. "Well, Mr. Quint," he said, "how does your new language fit?"

"Fit," Delbit said. "Yes, that's a good way to put it. It itches a little, like a new shirt, but aside from that it fits fine, Ensir Parr."

"I'm glad," Parr said. "There are a small number of people, something like two percent, for whom the super-hypnotic techniques do not work. Nobody knows why. Had you been one of those unfortunates, your life on Overline would have been very circumscribed."

"I have two questions," Delbit said. "The first is, how is Exxa, and the second is, just what is my status here?"

"Exxa is fine," Parr said. "Although we won't know for sure for several hours, she seems to be in the process of being cured. Whoever did this to her knew exactly what he was doing. But we can be grateful that he also was very careful not to hurt her in any way. It's going to be very interesting to find out why.

"As to the second question, what do you mean, your status?"

"Well, you have slaves, and freemen, and nobles, and probably a few other classes that I don't know about yet. The soldiers, for example. They're mercenaries, aren't they? And they're not citizens?"

"That's right," Parr said. "The class structure of the Overline is very complex, because it has grown layer by layer without removing the previous layers before the new ones are applied. Every attempt to regularize it has been bitterly resisted by somebody, and so it just goes on getting more complex.

"But as for you, young Mr. Delbit, you and Exxa are special cases. For one thing, I have given the word of the Preceptory that you will be looked after and taken care of. And we don't forget such things, nor do we take them lightly. For another thing, Exxa is certainly going to be of great value to us, and we require her willing cooperation. And from the looks of it, she would not take it well if we mistreated you. So it is to our own self-interest to treat you well. And we of the Overline are masters at attending to our own self-interest."

"There is a trace of bitterness in your words, Preceptor Parr," Viola said. "And Delbit is going to get the wrong idea." She turned to Delbit. "The preceptor is merely exercising an old grudge. But I think the beast gets quite enough exercise as it is without parading it before friends. There is a favored category for those who have been of special service to the Overline, which adequately describes you and Exxa."

"The Overline treats well those whom it has to treat well," Parr agreed. "You need have no concerns as to how we will treat either you or your lady friend."

Partly mollified, and partly puzzled by undercurrents that

he didn't understand, and that no one seemed interested in explaining to him, Delbit went off to wait until Exxa was done with her treatment. It was much later in the day when a servant came into his room and laid out a suit of clothes on his bed. "The preceptor would like to see you," the man said. "He suggests that you change your attire for the occasion, and has selected this suit himself. It should fit, sir."

"What occasion?" Delbit asked, eyeing the purple suit jacket with its wide lapels with apprehension.

"He didn't say, sir," the servant said.

Delbit dressed, and half an hour later the servant came to get him and escorted him to Ensir Parr's library. The room was quite large and full of bookshelves, as a library should be. The shelves lined the walls and jutted out from one wall, filling half the room, and they were full of books, disks, and other forms of media storage. An array of skylights provided natural light for the room, which was supplemented by overhead fixtures and reading lamps, positioned beside a mélange of styles of chairs and desks that filled what of the room wasn't full of books. It was an ideal room for anyone who liked to read.

Parr sat in a comfortable chair behind a small leather-topped desk. To his left was a very long couch that ran the length of the room several feet in front of the bookshelf-filled wall.

"Ah, Delbit," Parr said, looking up from his desk. "Come in. Sit down, please. This is Observer Jefer Semel. We await the arrival of the woman you knew as Exxa."

The observer, a tall, slender man with thinning sandy hair and the bemused expression of one who has seen much of life and is amused at its absurdities, got up from the couch, gave a half-bow, and sat back down.

Delbit suddenly felt as though he had been kicked in the stomach. This was it. She was cured. And he was—well, he'd find out in a moment. He went to the other end of the couch and sat down. "What happened to her to make her lose her memory?" he asked. "Who is she really?"

"We will all find out shortly," Parr told him. "I didn't want to interview her without an observer present, and I thought that she would be reassured by your presence. Thus our little group."

Delbit looked around the room. "I thought you wanted to keep this a secret for the time being," he said.

"I do," Parr said. "Observer Semel won't tell anyone unless requested to do so. He is here to watch and record what takes place, so that my version of the event can be verified if that ever becomes necessary. Until that time, our secrets are as safe with him as they would be with a priest on your strand. If I remember your strand correctly. It is priests that keep secrets—not so?"

"Some priests," Delbit said.

"Well, all observers keep their observations to themselves unless requested by the initiating party. And the disks of record are scrambled so that nobody else can read them without the key. Is that so, Observer Semel?"

The observer nodded. "Even so," he said. "It is our function."

"And you are recording this?" Delbit asked.

"There are four cameras dispersed about the room," Semel said, "not counting the one in the shoulder of my jacket. There will be a very good record of this, I assure you."

"Ah!" Delbit said. He might have the language, he realized, but it would take a while before he understood the technology. What sort of camera could one hide in the shoulder of a jacket?

The door opened and a man in a blue smock darted into the room. "We are ready, Ensir," he said. "The girl has responded well. She has been with your, ah, servant Viola for the past half hour, who has prepared her for the questioning. Although, in truth, the personality that emerged needs little preparation. You can see her now."

Parr nodded. "Very good, Dr. Wichec. Please send her in."

The man bobbed his head once or twice and then darted out of the room. A minute later the door opened again, and Delbit stopped breathing. He felt his heart lodge somewhere around his throat.

Viola entered first, and behind her came the girl-woman who had been Exxa. She wore a simple white dress that clung to her body from shoulder to hips and then flowed to her ankles, and her hair hung loose behind her; but she was—different. She moved with grace and assurance, and radiated confidence and purpose. And she was beautiful—breathtakingly, hauntingly beautiful. What the difference was, Delbit couldn't have said. But a universe of difference there was between the girl who had gone in to get her memory restored and this woman who had come out.

"Ensirs," Viola said, stepping aside for her companion, "allow me to present our guest: Lady Sabina Josephine Mary Edith Stephanie von Falkynberg, daughter of the Duke of Falkynberg and hereditary Princess of the Golden Orb."

Delbit swallowed.

Lady Sabina curtsied low, a well-learned gesture that was simple, and graceful, and altogether natural. "Preceptor Parr," she said, "and Delbit—my dear Delbit—and I don't believe I know this gentleman."

"Allow me to present Ensir Jefer Semel, my lady—or is it Princess?" Parr said.

"My lady here," she said. "Princess in one place only, and that is far from here, and it may be that I shall never see it again. And my friends call me Sabina."

"Welcome to Overline, Lady Sabina," Parr said. "And welcome back to your own mind. Are you prepared and willing to talk about what happened to you?"

"I know not what happened to me," Sabina said, "although my memory is returned to me. I will tell you as much of it as you wish to know, or as I am able to relate."

"Very good," Parr said. "Thank you. Please sit down."

He gestured to a chair across the desk from him, but instead she crossed the room and sat next to Delbit on the couch. "Ask your questions," she said, slipping her hand into his.

Delbit took her hand and pressed it, afraid to speak.

Parr smiled. "Let us start with the simple ones," he said. "Who is Sabina Josephine Mary Edith Stephanie von Falkynberg, hereditary Princess of the Golden Orb, and where is she from?"

Sabina smiled. "My father is Graf Edgar von Falkynberg," she told him. "We live in Schloss Baum, in Falkynberg, in Austria, and my father is duke over an area which is made up of a hodgepodge of counties, some not physically connected, which make up the Duchy of Falkynberg. We also have a residence in London, where we are for four months of the year, since the Emperor of Greater Austria is also the King of England. My father is the foreign minister in the present government, and Emperor Richard depends on him."

"And—?" Parr said.

Sabina looked at him. "I know what you want to know," she said, "and I shall tell you. But give me a moment. All of my life I have been taught that this is the one thing I must never talk about. Not to anyone. Not for any reason. Not to my doctor, not to my lover, not to my confessor, had I a confessor. But since I see clearly that I will need your help, I must tell you about it. Just give me a moment."

"As long as is required," Parr said. "And I assure you that this is our secret. It will not go beyond this room except to my immediate staff, whom I have in the past trusted with my life. Even so I would not trust them with this, but it is going to be essential."

"So be it," Sabina said.

"I have forgotten my duties as a host," Perceptor Parr said, touching a button on his desk. "Drom," he said to the squat servitor who answered, "a bottle of the Epstein-Green '86 Sauvignon Blanc and five glasses."

Drom bowed and disappeared.

"You want to know how I do what I do," Sabina said. "That I cannot tell you, for I do not know. We have tried experimenting, and have established a few facts, but very few. It is difficult to research something that you cannot discuss, and few of us choose to take up a life of science, so we are not equipped to find the answers."

"Who is 'us'?" Parr asked.

"We, the Falkynbergs, are members of the Twelve Families,

which is one of the nine groups that make up the Sedge."

"Sedge?" Parr said.

"The Sedge," Princess Sabina said, "is what we call that select group of people who possess the secret and the ability to flip at will through the Paraverse. Incidentally, our two peoples must have intersected in the past, since we, also, use the word 'Paraverse.'"

"Interesting," Parr said.

"The Sedge is also used to describe that group of strands that we influence."

"Like most words," Parr said, "it picks up meanings as it rolls along. Who are the Twelve Families, and the eight other groups?"

"The other groups are Hesperson, the Circle, the Greensleeves, the Lost Tribe, the Children of Change, the Flitters, Pandora, and the Friends of the Bee. We don't know much about the Friends of the Bee." She turned to Delbit. "It's good to see you, friend. You haven't said anything since I reappeared. Are you afraid I've forgotten you as I remembered everything else?"

"I was," Delbit admitted. "Something like that. But you're holding my hand, and all's right with the world."

"Yes," she agreed. "That's so." She turned back to Parr. "The Twelve Families occupy about half a hundred strands on both sides of Elb, usually at some level of nobility or other on what-ever strand the particular family lives. We help each other out, and share information."

"What is an Elb?" Delbit asked.

"Elb is a strand, deserted of humans, that has somehow twisted itself amid those occupied strands upon which we dwell. We use Elb as a retreat, and each of the families has its own estate somewhere on it. Our estate is known as Calla. It is an island in the Atlantic that on occupied strands is called England. But we now usually abide in Castle Nimber, on the West Continent, for my father is acting as the Guardian of Elb since the true Guardian disappeared twenty years ago. That is why I am the Princess of the Golden Orb."

"I see," Parr said.

"Elb is, in a sense, the focus of our power, and our true home. It is the one place where we don't have to be acting, because everyone there is one of us. It's also a sort of focus point, because for some reason you have to go through Elb to get from one side of the Sedge to the other. We sometimes refer to the East Sedge and West Sedge, for that reason. My father's job as Guardian is to keep Elb safe for the Twelve Families, and for the other Sedge-flippers."

"Are there threats against Elb?" Parr asked.

"There have been. Because of its central position, and because a flipper must go through Elb to pass from East Sedge to West Sedge, it is a very important place. Like the canal through the Isthmus of Suez on my strand."

"And because it is a lovely and unspoiled world, there are many who would like to spoil it," Viola said.

"Why were the Friends of the Bee trying to kill you?" Parr asked. "If those were indeed bee-people back at the jail."

"They were," Sabina said. "As to what they want with me, I have no idea. Their motives are obscure; their ways are secretive; their habits are unknown."

"We will have to find out," Parr said. "It would seem that there are two groups concerned with your welfare, one of which wants you alive but out of the way, and the other of which wants you dead, and has somehow communicated that want to the bee-people."

"Cheery," Sabina said.

"What is this Golden Orb that you are princess of?" Parr asked.

"It's a small bauble that looks like an egg on a stick," she told him. "The egg is about eight inches around, and the stick about two feet long. I've always thought it was incredibly ugly. Its practical value, as my father has pointed out, is that it is stuffed with precious gems. It contains an immense fortune in portable wealth, in case we ever have to flee fast from wherever we are.

"Its symbolic value, within the Sedge, is very powerful. Our nobility is not based on ownership of land, unlike the hereditary nobility of the flats. All our titles within the Sedge nobility are based on objects or symbols, which symbolize our place within the Twelve Families."

"Flats?" Delbit asked.

"Flatlanders," Sabina explained. "Those unable to move throughout the Paraverse, condemned to live their lives on but one strand."

"Tell me about what you call flipping," Parr said.

"I can't describe it," she said. "I can teach it by example. I hold your hand and take you through with me, and you sort of feel what it's like. But that's very dangerous."

"How so?" Parr asked.

"Most people, something over nine out of ten, come through dead. We don't know what kills them. It's as though they've stopped working. Sometimes they can be revived by instant intensive medical attention, if we've come through to a hospital. And sometimes not."

"Migod," Delbit said.

Sabina squeezed his hand. "Yes," she said. "But I didn't know. We were lucky."

"What happened to you?" Parr asked. "How did you end up in a mental hospital with no memory?"

"I don't know," she said. "I've tried to piece together my last memories before I, ah, woke up with none, and it's all a haze. I was preparing to leave for London. I was at Madame Madeleine's in Wallenstein—she is my dressmaker. It's impossible to arrive in London without a complete wardrobe, even though the first thing one does is replace it entirely with the latest London fashions. She was called out of the fitting room, and two strange women entered. Suddenly they grabbed me, and one of them put something over my face. And that's it. That's the last thing I remember."

"Well," Parr said. "We'll have to do something about that, won't we?"

"Can you help me?" Princess Sabina asked. "Help me find

out what happened—and help me undo whatever evil has been done in my absence. For I'm sure someone was plotting evil. Else why would they do this?"

"This in itself was evil, Princess," Parr pointed out. "It is against Overline policy to interfere in the internal matters of other strands. But in this case, an exception shall be made."

"I'm so glad," she said. "I need friends at this moment."

"We'll have to discuss the politics of the Sedge, and examine the various possibilities," Parr said. "And I want to go over your dreams with you, with some professional help."

"My dreams?"

"Yes. I think they might give us some interesting information. But we'll start with the premise that whatever is happening, a few more weeks won't matter. This will give us a chance to learn from each other, and move intelligently instead of striking blindly into the infinite."

"I hope that's so," Sabina said. "I mean, that a few more weeks won't matter. I am worried about my father, and I'm sure he's worried about me. I can't imagine what sort of plot is going on, and my very ignorance frightens me. The Sedge is a very political group, and assassination is an occasional, if extreme, political device. It never works, and never leads to anything good, but people sometimes forget that."

"As soon as we determine just where the Sedge lies," Parr said, "I'll have automated perusers sent out. With any luck, we'll have pictures of your father riding to hounds, or whatever Sedge noblemen do, before the week is out."

"I hope so," Sabina said. "I do hope so."

CHAPTER EIGHTEEN

"I want to go," Delbit said. "I might be useful." The words sounded silly to him, as he could not imagine what possible use he could be, but he wanted to go on this expedition more than anything he had ever wanted.

"You should stay here," Preceptor Parr told him. "You have already done quite enough for us, for Sabina, and for yourself. The only place you should go is to school. There is much that you don't know. If you are to be of use to yourself, or others, you must learn."

"Learn what?"

"Everything possible," Parr said. "Knowledge is indivisible. Concentrate on those things that interest you, and that will keep you busy for a lifetime. Even the extended lifetime you may acquire if you stay in Overline."

"I want to learn," Delbit said. "Honest I do. The person I want to be is much smarter than the person I am. And I'll begin as soon as we get back."

Preceptor Parr looked crossly at him. "The gods are on your side in this one," he said. "Or possibly not—it depends on what happens. But you can go. I, unfortunately, cannot go. And as it is still the better part of valor to keep this whole business as deeply under the rose as it can crawl, I wish to use no outside help for as long as possible. I am sending you and Viola along to accompany Sabina. You are to protect her, to follow her directions as much as possible, and, mainly, to keep me informed. If I have to help, I can do it more intelligently if I know what's going on."

Delbit managed to look surprised. "Viola!" he said.

Parr laughed. "Delbit!" he said. "Why the one more than the other? I work with the material at hand. She, also, wants to go. She is as quick on her feet as you—quicker, perhaps. She is trained in the martial arts, and you are not. She is much more experienced in the ways of the Paraverse. And besides, I have a secret, hidden reason, based upon arcane Overline law, for wanting her to go."

"Yes, but I thought she was your—ah—"

"Secretary? Companion? Lover? Slave? She is all of these. The Paraverse is strange, and life compounds the strangeness. There is a saying here that the ways of preceptors are dark and twisted, but one who follows them is sure to arrive. Let us hope that there is merit in the saying. Viola chooses to go with you. She is fond of the Princess Sabina Stephanie, and would help her achieve her goal. I choose to let her—no, to encourage her to do so."

"Why?" Delbit asked.

"She would not be pleasant to live with if I refused her," Parr said. "Let that reason suffice."

"Whatever you say, Preceptor," Delbit said.

"That's right," Parr agreed. "I trust you have spent the past weeks familiarizing yourself with the customs on Sabina's strand, and have learned German."

"I have."

"Good. You'll leave tomorrow. Get outfitted with clothes and weapons this afternoon."

Delbit spent the afternoon trying on the latest in London fashions as worn in Sabina's home strand. Then a tall, stocky, completely bald man named Lisso, who was Preceptor Parr's private armorer, showed him the various weapons that were built into the garments, and how to achieve results with them without blowing his own limbs off.

"Any questions, young sir?" Lisso asked, slapping the last deadly tool back into place under the lapel of his jacket.

"Yes," Delbit said. "Why does Preceptor Parr need his own private armorer? And"—he gestured around the room—"enough weapons to supply an army?"

"You exaggerate, young sir," Lisso said. "There are barely enough arms and equipment here for a good company of infantry. As to why the preceptor keeps it, and me, about the place, well now, you'd have to ask him that."

"Of course," Delbit said. "Thank you for your advice and assistance. For the first time in my life, I feel positively dangerous."

"Well, let's try to make sure that you remain more a danger to your enemies than to yourself," Lisso said. "Try to remember what I told you, and practice every chance you get. A trained reaction may save your life. Ask Miss Viola—she knows."

"She practices with this stuff?"

"She is an expert with personal weaponry, as well as unarmed combat. It is her fancy."

Delbit shook his head. "I do not understand the Overline."

"Nor do I," Lisso agreed. "But I am not paid to, so I don't worry about it."

Delbit did not see Sabina or Viola for the rest of the day. After a dinner eaten alone, he went back to his room and tried to sleep. For a long time the attempt was unsuccessful, but finally he slept.

A servant woke him early the next morning, and he took a long, hot shower before getting into the suit that had been so carefully crafted for him, packing into the one suitcase he was allowed everything he wanted to take, and going down the hall to breakfast.

Preceptor Parr was there already, with Viola, and it was no more than ten minutes before Sabina joined them. When they had finished their breakfasts and were on their second cups of coffee, Parr pushed his chair back and looked around the table. "I think it's time for a council of war," he said.

Viola leaned forward. "We are about to hear Preceptor Parr's counsel of war," she said, smiling. "And it should be well worth listening to. War is his avocation."

Parr looked amused. "I do study war, it is true," he said. "My excuse is that only by knowing the workings of war can we prevent or minimize the damage of war. But my real reason is that I find it fascinating."

"It must be something in the bones of men," Sabina said, sipping her coffee, "that causes so many of them to find death and destruction fascinating. Which is why we have so much death and destruction."

Parr turned his smile on her. "In the Middle Ages," he told her, "after a battle, when the uninjured troops had left the field, the local peasant women used to come out to the scene with heavy staves, so they could beat the helpless wounded to death and take their clothes."

"Nobody's perfect," she replied.

"My interest in war is not because of the gore and suffering," Parr said. "Personally, I abhor pain, either the inflicting or the receiving. But I find war endlessly fascinating, because it is the one place where human beings give the best they can. The goad of eminent death and the destruction of loved ones is very powerful. You see incredible bravery, and intelligence, altruism, and cooperation, and all the good human traits working at their highest in the middle of the tragedy of war. Of course, you also see incredible cowardice, and stupidity, and selfishness; and even that is worthy of note."

"I thought you liked the strategy and tactics, and all that stuff that gives grown men an excuse to play with toy soldiers," Viola said.

"That too," Parr admitted. "Which brings the conversation around to your strategy on this little mission."

"This first trip is to be for information gathering only," Viola said. "We will find out for sure who kidnapped Sabina, and why, and then return here to regroup and plan our next step."

"So say you now," Parr said. "But the unexpected has a way of popping up at strange times, which is why it remains unexpected. Some contingency plans might be in order."

Viola turned to Sabina. "Tell the preceptor your thoughts on this," she said.

Sabina nodded. "Viola and I have been discussing the possibilities," she said. "It has to have been someone from the Twelve Families that kidnapped me."

"I had already concluded as much," Parr said.

"Why?" Delbit asked.

"For two reasons," Sabina told him. "First, only someone close to me would know where I was going that morning. I assume that my abductors seduced one of the household servants into betraying me, but even that shows a certain amount of intimacy. The second reason is the extreme care they took with my person—removing my memories, when it would have been so much easier and faster to merely remove my life."

"And yet another reason," Parr said. "Your dreams."

"Those horrible dreams? What can be learned from them?"

"There are certain recurring themes. Nimber, for example."

"That's so. Castle Nimber is the fortress of the Guardian of Elb."

"And Calla?"

"My home on Elb. That's true. I remember. Horrible things named Nimber and Calla were in all my dreams."

"The images were inserted there by whoever removed your memory," Parr told her. "Since the words had powerful positive associations for you, they tried to supply even more powerful negative associations."

"They would have been better leaving it alone," Viola said, "Since 'calla' and 'nimber' are not words that come up often in normal conversation. But evil people can't help overdoing things."

"True," Parr agreed. "Many villains are caught by their unnecessary excesses. That might be a way to hunt for this one. Unfortunately, I have nothing more concrete to add to the suggestion, but you three are very clever and will certainly make something more of it."

Delbit grinned. "That seems to be your idea of strategy,

Ensir," he said. "Don't plan anything, just wait around until someone else makes a mistake."

Parr turned to glare at Delbit, and then returned his gaze to Sabina. "Are you ready to go?" he asked. "Is there anything you need?"

"I believe we are ready to go," Viola said.

"I can think of nothing I need," Princess Sabina said. "I thank you, Preceptor Parr, for your kindness and your assistance. You have invoked a debt on the von Falkynbergs, and neither I nor my father will ever forget. Someday you may have to call on us for a service. If so, we will be there."

"Ridiculous," Parr said, looking embarrassed. "I am pleased to have been able to help you, but it was all part of my job."

"Nonetheless," said Sabina Josephine Mary Edith Stephanie von Falkynberg, Countess of Falkynberg and hereditary Princess of the Golden Orb.

CHAPTER NINETEEN

Much as she wanted to see her father, Sabina decided on a roundabout way to arrive back in the Sedge. Whoever had kidnapped her must know by now that she was missing from the home for the bewildered in which he had left her, and would be watching her home. It would be prudent to find out what was happening before she stepped back into the middle of it.

They went on an established transporter link to Fourth-Level Campbell-Smith-Area New York, and took an atmosphere-hopper to Berlin. Delbit stared out the window as the rocket plane pierced the clouds, his sense of wonder combating his sense of complete panic. He spent the rest of the trip staring down at Earth as it turned beneath the craft, his sense of wonder winning the battle until the plane entered the atmosphere again, and Earth approached with frightening speed. He kept his eyes closed while the plane landed.

They left the airport in a waiting car, and the OSS driver took them to a field close to the city. Less than three hours after they left the Overline they were closing the door on the small transporter that would take them into the Sedge.

They took off the raincoats that had concealed their Sedge-area hiking costumes and rolled them up and stuffed them into their bags. "This machinery has a certain advantage," Sabina said, stowing her bag in a corner of the small luggage rack. "It's nice to be able to travel about the Paraverse and take with you more than just what you can carry in your hands or on your back."

"Is there a limit to how much you can take with you when you blip?" Delbit asked her. "I mean, could you put a piano on your back?"

"I couldn't," Sabina said. "Even if I could lift it in the first place. There are those who could, I believe. The limit seems to have something to do with mass."

"What happens if you try to take too much through with you?" Viola asked.

"Either you don't go, or you do go, leaving all the stuff behind."

"Why were you losing your clothes when you blipped before, if you can take stuff through with you?" Delbit asked.

"That's one of the things they did to me," Sabina said. "Whoever got inside my mind. First they made me forget how to blip at all, and then, in case by some accident I did anyway, they put a little kicker in my unconscious mind so I would leave my clothes behind. It was supposed to discourage me, I suppose."

"Perhaps it was just to make you easier to find," Viola suggested.

"There is that," Sabina said. "The doctor on Overline was most annoyed when he found the hypnotic command, or whatever it was. He said they really shouldn't have tried anything like that, it was gilding the lily. Apparently it's what enabled my unconscious mind to blip me away from the mental hospital even when my conscious mind had forgotten how."

"That's the sort of thing Castimere was talking about," Viola said. "An unnecessary excess."

"Castimere?" Sabina asked. "Oh, yes, Ensir Parr. For some reason I don't think of him as having a first name."

"Hold on," Viola said, and she flipped a switch.

Again Delbit felt the stomach-turning sensation of moving about the Paraverse.

Handguns ready, they opened the door.

The transporter was resting on a slight slope on the well-manicured lawn of what was obviously a vast private estate. The manor house, a large, ornate four-story chateau, was visible perhaps a mile away, atop a low hill. It was late afternoon. There was no one in sight.

"Well?" Viola said.

Sabina went outside and took a deep breath, and then another. Then she sort of felt the air with her fingers held in front of her. "We're close," she said. "Really close. But I can't be sure. I have never arrived at a strand this way before."

"What do you want to do?" Viola asked.

"Wait! I have an idea," Sabina said. She took two steps forward and, with the merest pop, disappeared.

Thirty seconds later she was back, several steps farther away. "It feels almost right, but we're just a bit off," she said, returning to the transporter. "How well can you fine-tune this thing?"

"I have a very delicate touch," Viola assured her. "Get in and tell me which way."

"Just the way we were going. Two strands. Maybe three."

Sabina pulled the door closed behind her, and Viola touched the controls. This time Delbit didn't feel anything.

"Try this one," Viola said.

Sabina pushed the door open and peered out. They were on the same slope, with an identical lawn stretching out in front of them. There had been some sort of lawn party in progress when they appeared. There were now several dozen people in fancy costumes running away in all directions, and four or five lying flat on the ground with their hands over their heads. One man, in the uniform of a colonel of Hussars, was approaching the transporter cautiously, his saber drawn. "Do not run," the colonel yelled out over his shoulder in German. "It is not a monster, it is a small cottage!"

Sabina gingerly stepped outside. She looked around and palped the air once again with her fingers. "No," she said, coming back inside. "This isn't quite it. One or two more blips should do it."

"Okay. Close the door," Viola said.

"How can you tell?" Delbit asked.

"Tell what?"

"Which strand you're on."

"Oh." Sabina paused to think about it.

"Step outside and try this one," Viola said.

"I don't know exactly," Sabina told Delbit as she pushed open the door. "There are slight differences in feel to the different strands. I am only aware of them for a little while after I arrive."

They were on the same slope, with the same manicured lawn, but there was a line of trees much closer to them along one side, and the house on the distant hill looked somehow different. "This is it," Sabina announced. "Not my home strand, but one well into the Sedge. My Uncle Sigismund lives on this strand."

"What does he do?" Delbit asked.

"He is the King of Bavaria," she said.

Viola laughed. "A princess, a slave, and an articled apprentice are going to visit a king," she said. "A very grim fairy tale this is."

"You have an awful lot of freedom for a slave," Sabina said.

Viola nodded. "You always have a lot of what you don't want," she said.

Sabina patted her arm. "I find it hard to think of you as a slave," she said.

"I find it hard to think of anyone as a slave," Viola answered.

Sabina looked Viola in the eye, and then put a hand on each of her shoulders. "You are my friend," she said, "and I would help you, but there is nothing I can do. You could be free at any instant you choose. But you love him. And he wants more than anything to free you, to have you as an equal. But the instant you become an equal, he can no longer have you. Of such patterns are great tragedies written."

"Yes," Viola admitted. "And also comedies. Which, do you suppose, are we living? And will we ever know?"

Delbit looked from one to the other of them, and felt that he should say something. But nothing useful came to mind. He took the luggage from the rack and put it outside the door. Finally he said, "We'd better go," and stepped outside.

"Life is a series of random accidents," Sabina said, as she

followed Delbit through the door. "And comedy and tragedy are merely the same events as seen through different eyes."

Viola set a couple of switches and then joined the outside, closing the door behind her. About five seconds later, to the accompaniment of a soft whooshing sound, the transporter disappeared.

"What now?" Delbit asked.

"I don't fancy carrying these bags all the way to Berlin," Sabina said. "But I can probably make it as far as that house. Let us go and inquire of the owner whether he will assist us."

They were dressed as hikers on this strand, so no one would think it overly strange of them to appear suddenly out of the forest. Taking excursions into the woods was a common form of entertainment.

They shouldered their bags and hiked the mile to the manor house. It turned out to be empty except for servants, as the owner and his family were visiting the sea along the Piedmont Riviera.

Sabina, with a combination of charm, an ineffable air of authority, and several gold coins, bribed the major-domo to allow her to bribe the coachman to drive them the twelve kilometers into Berlin.

"What's the background on this strand?" Delbit asked as they bumped their way along the badly paved road into the city.

"We are in the Pan-German Empire," Sabina told him. "There was a great war in this strand, starting in 1906. By 1915, when it was over, *Das Grossdeutcher Reich* controlled almost all of Europe. And it still does. The French are allowed to have a police force, but not an army. The dozen or so kingdoms that make up the northern half of Italy are all under German or Austrian domination. England is once again very powerful because of her overseas provinces, but she was thirty years recovering from the war."

"And America?" Delbit asked.

"The U.S. of A. stayed uninvolved. After the war she turned her sights west, and used her bases in the Philippine Islands to develop her own empire in the Far East."

"Who had we better be?" Viola asked. "That is, if anyone asks us. Is anyone liable to ask us, by the way?"

"If we check into a hotel we will have to sign some name and some home address," Sabina said. "But they won't ask us for identification. At least, so I believe."

"What names should we sign?"

"I am Ursula van Spaek of the Grand Duchy of Vail, in Southern Africa. An identity, as it happens, that I have used before. I even have an account in a Berlin bank in that name. You are my cousins Hetty and Dirk. You have never been in such a city before, and are enchanted by everything you see."

"As I probably shall be," Viola said.

The coachman took them to the Kaiserhof on Wilhelm-Dritte-Strasse, where the hotel flunkies took over and glided them through the check-in process and into a suite of rooms on the third floor on a stream of obsequiousness.

They had dinner brought up to the rooms: a saddle of lamb, stuffed guinea hens, poached North Sea salmon—an amount of food that seemed to Delbit sufficient for a platoon of hungry men, but that the hotel seemed to consider normal for two slender young women and an only slightly overweight young man. They then discovered that they couldn't discuss anything of importance while eating, because three waiters hovered behind them, seeing to their every gustatory need, and effectively if unwittingly stifling conversation.

When the dinner was over, the waiters cleared out along with the dirty-dish detritus, although they insisted on leaving some food behind in covered dishes because the Vailans had eaten so little they would surely get hungry later.

"It is now"—Delbit glanced up at the dial of the great-grandfather clock that dominated one wall—"almost ten-thirty. Is there anything we can do tonight, or should we get some sleep and continue in the morning?"

"The night is just beginning for the nobility," Sabina said. "This is when they go out to play." She went over to the ornate porcelain telephone on its ornate inlaid table against one wall. "Let's see if my royal uncle is in Berlin now."

"Don't identify yourself," Viola warned her.

"With dear, chubby Uncle Sigismund?" Sabina asked. "Well, perhaps you're right. Until we know more."

She picked up the handset. "Put me through to the residence of the King of Bavaria.... Hello...? May I speak to His Royal Highness's social secretary, please? This is the social secretary of the Grand Dutchess Titiana Petrovna.... Not available...? Well, to whom am I speaking...? Major whom...? Oh—Domo, I see. I'm sorry, the connection is poor. Well, could you tell me if His Royal Highness will be in town next week...? Here now? Thank you very much, you've been most helpful.... No, don't bother, I'll send a note.... Yes, thank you.

"Uncle Sigismund is in town now, although not in residence," Sabina said, hanging up the phone. "Which means almost certainly that he is at the Klementine."

"What's that?" Delbit asked.

"A private club frequented by actors and—to my uncle's delight—actresses of the musical stage. Berlin is famous for its musical stage. Let us go to the Klementine and have an audience with the King of Bavaria!"

They passed the club doorman without even causing a raised eyebrow, as Sabina had said they would. It was clearly the doorman's belief that a wealthy-looking young man accompanied by two beautiful young ladies belonged in the Klementine, and it was pointless discussing it.

"My uncle reigns upstairs," Sabina said, "in a small private room, surrounded by beauty and beverage. This way."

They went up a narrow staircase with thick carpeting and walls decorated with paintings of naked women in rural settings, then along a corridor with flocked wallpaper and gas-mantled sconces. Sabina turned the handle on a maple door with gold trim and pulled it open slightly. The sound of giggling emanated from within. She opened the door wide.

The room inside was about fifteen feet wide by twenty feet

long. Running around the walls was a continuous life-size mural depicting pornographic scenes from Greek and Roman mythology. There were six or seven low couches arranged around a circular table containing bowls of fruit and bottles of wine and brandy. Each couch had its own small table holding a glass and a plate. On one of the couches farthest from the door reclined a portly man with gray hair, muttonchop whiskers, and a red toga. Surrounding him were a bevy of attractive, scantily clad young ladies, what there was of their dress carrying out the Roman theme.

"Good evening, Uncle Sigismund," Princess Sabina said, stepping into the room. Delbit and Viola came in behind her and Delbit closed the door.

The chubby monarch sat up, splashing some red wine on his toga in the process. His eyes grew wide. "Sabina Stephanie!" he said.

"Good to see you again, Uncle," she said.

King Sigismund turned to the pretty ladies surrounding him and shooed them out of the room. "Go, go, go," he said, pushing the air with his fat palms. "Go downstairs. I have to talk to this, ah, young lady. I'll call you back shortly. Now go, that's a good girl."

When the last of them had departed the room and closed the door behind her, he turned back to Sabina. "I had nothing to do with it!" he screeched, raising his hands in horror. "You must believe me."

CHAPTER TWENTY

"Tell me all about it, Uncle," Sabina said, settling on one of the couches. "And don't try anything funny. My friends here are armed to the teeth."

"Child!" King Sigismund said, hugging his arms across his chest defensively. "You don't have to threaten me. I dandled you on my knee when you were a baby."

"And when I grew up, you had me kidnapped," she replied.

"Me? I don't know who told you such a thing, but you have been grievously misinformed. It wasn't me. You should know that. How could I do such a thing? I, who love you? I didn't know about it until after. Baron Vayst had you kidnapped. I was against it from the start. I'm so glad that you're all right. We were so worried when you disappeared from the sanitarium. We were afraid to tell your father."

"What does the Black Baron want with me?" Sabina demanded.

The king shrugged. "How should I know?" he asked plaintively. "All this political intrigue is beyond me."

Sabina turned to Delbit. "Shoot off his toe," she said.

"What?" the king demanded, looking horrified as Delbit drew his beamer. "What did you say, Sabina my dear? You wouldn't do a thing like that. You couldn't."

"His right big toe," Sabina specified. Delbit aimed carefully.

"You're joking!" Sigismund insisted, waving his right foot wildly from side to side.

"And then his knee," Sabina said. "With any luck, you won't

have to go any higher."

"No—wait!" King Sigismund screeched. He dropped his foot to the couch. "I'm too old and too fat to play such games."

Sabina leaned forward and spoke into her uncle's ear. "I love you like an uncle," she told him. "But I have been mistreated and pushed around very badly for the past few months, and I want to know just what is going on. And you are going to tell me."

"How did you find out I was involved?" the king asked.

"You told me," Sabina said, leaning back. "I just came up here to ask your help."

Sigismund shook his head. "I always had a big mouth," he said. "That's how the rest of me got so big. I suppose I'd better help you. I haven't liked any of this very much anyway. But, you know, I really am as non-political as possible. I bend like a weed in the prevailing wind. I don't see why all this intrigue is necessary anyway, you know."

"Neither do I, Uncle," Sabina said, sitting on the couch next to him. "Tell me all about it."

"Baron Vayst came to see me some months ago. He said he had been talking to others of the Sedge nobility, and that we had a decision to make. He said that we natural leaders of the Sedge had a responsibility to look after our own interests and those of our followers." Sigismund paused and looked appealingly to Sabina. When she didn't respond, he continued, "According to the baron, your father was unduly eager to take over the position of Guardian of Elb when the true Guardian disappeared twenty years ago. He wondered why this would be."

"Yes, and why would this be, according to Vayst?"

"I am forgetting my hospitality!" the chubby king said suddenly, clapping his hands together. "Who are your friends? What would they like to drink?"

"My friends are nemesis and revenge, and they drink blood," Sabina said.

"Ah, my, but you have your father's gift with words," King Sigismund told her. "And truly you have made your point. I was mistaken."

"This is Captain Quint, and this the lady Viola D'epp," Sabina said. "They are indeed my friends, here representing the powerful group of strand-changers from beyond the Sedge that rescued me."

"I would doubt your story," King Sigismund said mildly, "except for the clear fact that the weapon that lad is waving in my direction was not manufactured on this strand, or any strand in the Sedge. Although I have no trouble recognizing its intent. And there is something definitely offstrand in the way he is glowering at me. Put that away, Captain Quint, my lad. It might go off by accident, you know. I don't trust such things. Never use them myself. And you have nothing to fear from me. No reason to wave a deadly weapon about. Have some brandy—or wine. No? I thought not—overly serious people never seem to want to drink. Well, there is tea in the pitcher over there. Iced tea. Some of the girls prefer it."

"Baron Vayst—" Sabina said.

"Ah, yes. It has something to do with the Golden Orb. Apparently the baron has discovered that the Orb possesses certain—ah—powers. Or so he claims. He says that your father schemed to get hold of it. And that we had to stop him, in our own interest."

"So you had me kidnapped. I suppose you offered to trade me for the Orb."

King Sigismund nodded, looking unhappy. "Yes," he said. "The baron was afraid your father would have too much power once he learned how to work the Orb."

"And you believed that? Uncle Siggie, I'm ashamed of you!"

"Well, it made sense," the king said. "I mean, after all, your father did take over as Guardian of Elb."

"It was the true Guardian's will," Sabina said. "You know that. It was written down and verified and everything years before he disappeared. And I was made Princess of the Golden Orb by the Guardian on my second birthday, which was two years before he disappeared. And my father had no idea that he was chosen until after the disappearance."

"So you say. So he says. But how do we know that?"

"What could possibly make you think otherwise?"

"Baron Vayst."

"That man is so twisted that he can't walk in a straight line. You know that. At the dinner table he doesn't say 'Pass the butter,' he says 'Look over there.'"

"That's so," King Sigismund said. "But he is so plausible when he talks to one."

"Well, one had better learn to stay uninvolved," Sabina said. "I'll tell my father not to do anything too nasty to you. Does he know who is involved?"

"No," Sigismund said. "The missive was unsigned."

"Has he replied?"

"Yes. He wants proof that you are all right before he will negotiate any further."

"Good for my father. Proof that you were unable to give him, of course, since you had no idea where I was."

"That is so."

The door was suddenly flung open and half a dozen men burst into the room. They were arrayed in a variety of flamboyant costumes and brandished a variety of ornate weapons. Two of them, dressed in blue double-breasted suits with identical red piping on all the seams, were waving massive silver revolvers that looked as though they were meant to be held by hands bigger than the human race had evolved; three dressed as footmen had staves of various lengths; one in a black dinner jacket had a sword-cane, the sword part in one hand and the cane in the other; and two in military garb drenched with gold braid waved bared sabers in front of them.

King Sigismund jumped to his feet, clearly unsure whether these new arrivals were monarchists or anarchists. "What is this?" he yelled. "What's going on here?"

The group stopped, frozen, inside the door, looking as though they were posing for a portrait to be called The Hunt Is Called Inside. One of the blue-suited pair, who was the apparent leader of the group, said, "Your Highness—"

"Yes, yes," His Highness said. "Well?"

"The, ah, girls said that some strangers had burst into the room here, and you had sent them away. The girls, that is. They became concerned."

"How nice of them," the king said. "And it is good of you to care enough to burst in on me without knocking, brandishing that silly assortment of deadly paraphernalia. I do appreciate it, really I do. And I'm sure that my niece, the Countess of Falkynberg, and her friends appreciate it as much as I do."

"Oh," the man said. "We are very sorry, Your Highness. We wouldn't...." He began backing through the door, jamming himself against the men behind him, who hadn't started to move yet.

"Leave!" His Highness said. "Just leave. Write your apology and put it in my box downstairs. For now, just leave!"

"Of course, Your Highness." Like a cork being pulled from a bottle, the disparate group popped back out the door and slammed it behind them.

"Well!" King Sigismund said, plopping back down on his couch. "What is this club coming to?"

"It was good of you not to, er, make any confusing comments to those gentlemen regarding our presence here," Delbit said, sitting down and wiping the sweat off his brow with his handkerchief.

"I," the king said, tapping himself on his chest, "have changed sides. I truly have. I don't know what came over me. I must have been mesmerized by the baron." He pushed himself to his feet once again. "Let us all hold hands and pass through to the duke, your father's, strand. I will tell him everything, and seek his advice."

"Fine," Sabina said. "Go and change into your traveling clothes—I assume you don't want to wander around Berlin on either my strand or yours dressed in a toga—and we will wait here for you."

King Sigismund stared down at his bulk. "It is a handsome

toga," he said, "but I suppose you're right. I shall return." He tiptoed around the table and stalked from the room with amazing grace for one of his bulk.

"I can't do that, you know," Viola said. "I hope you haven't forgotten. You and Delbit can pass from strand to strand without machinery, but I can't."

Sabina turned to her. "I haven't," she said, "and you can."

"I can? What do you mean? How do you know?"

"I was going to tell you later. I noticed when we held hands. I get a different feeling from the flats." She turned to Delbit. "Perhaps that's how I knew it was all right to take you through with me that time. Perhaps on some level I remembered."

"So that's one of your Sedge traveler's abilities?" Viola asked. "Why didn't you mention it before? And why, in that case, did we bother taking the transporter?"

"First of all, it's my ability, not a general one. As far as I know, nobody else can do it. I think it has something to do with the Golden Orb, which really does have unusual powers that we don't understand. It seems to work on its holder on some deep level to increase Paraverse-traveling abilities of several sorts. Since I am the only one who has been holding it for the past twenty years, I am the only one it has acted on."

"What is it really," Delbit asked, "and where does it come from?"

"Perhaps the Guardian knew," Sabina told him, "but if so he didn't tell anyone before he disappeared. It is not the work of any culture or race on any strand that we know of."

"It would seem that this Baron Vayst has some idea of its worth," Viola said.

"Yes. We'll have to find out about that."

The king returned, wearing a fur cape over pantaloons and a puffy shirt. "Well, here I am," he said, "ready for any hardship. I have told the myrmidons that I am leaving, so they won't wonder what happened to me."

"About taking the transporter," Sabina said, "it was much faster, and let us take our luggage. Besides, we were so far away in the Paraverse. It has dials and things to just go from one strand to another far away. I would have had to do it in much smaller steps, and it might have taken days."

"Oh," Viola said.

"What is a transporter?" King Sigismund asked.

"I'll explain later," Sabina said. "Let's go."

"Shall we all hold hands?" the king said. "I will hold Fraulein D'epp's hand, and yours, my dear niece. Then we'll be boy-girl-boy-girl."

"Should someone go through first, cautiously, and make sure the room is empty on the other strand?" Sabina asked.

"This is my private room on that strand, too," the king said. "But perhaps you're right." He held his breath and crossed his eyes, and disappeared. Twenty seconds later he was back. "All clear," he said. "And I've turned the lights on."

Sabina patted him on the back. "Uncle, you're a prince," she told him.

"I'm a king," he said. "Take my hand. You too, my dear."

They held hands. Sabina closed her eyes and the king squinted.

The room shifted. The couches and table disappeared. The room was now empty, except for a large four-poster bed in the far corner and a couple of dressers against the wall. The ceiling above the bed was mirrored.

"Uncle!" Sabina said, looking up at the mirrored ceiling.

"Niece!" Sigismund said. "Let us go downstairs."

"Isn't whoever is here going to be surprised to see us?"

"I own this house on this strand," Sigismund said. "And the servants believe that I have enemies and use secret entrances to come in and out. I'm sure they spend a lot of time when they should be dusting the silver looking for the secret entrances."

They started down the hall.

From somewhere below them came the sounds of running feet and a series of loud thumps, as though large pieces of furniture were being overturned.

"I'd better see what's happening," King Sigismund said.

"You people wait here—and keep out of sight until I get back!" He tiptoed down the stairs, and about thirty seconds later came racing back up. "The Friends of the Bee!" he panted. "There's a swarm of them downstairs. They seem to be attacking the house, for some unaccountable reason. The footmen have thrown up a barricade across the hall using two sofas and the big china cabinet—and that St. Pierre soup service was in the family for over a hundred years—but it won't stop them for long. I must remember to give whichever footmen survive this a bonus."

"The reason is me," Sabina said. "They are after me. I hate to think what they want."

"Back to the room," King Sigismund said. "And thence back across the time stream to the club."

They retreated to the room and closed the door. Then they once again held hands, and the Paraverse shifted.

"It always makes me hungry," the king said, taking an apple from the table.

"Everything always makes you hungry," Sabina told him.

"True."

"Maybe we'd better go," Delbit said.

"Maybe you're right," Sabina agreed. "We'll get a carriage."

"I'll see to it," the king said. "Follow me."

Several loud noises, followed by the sharp crack of a high-caliber handgun, sounded from somewhere below them, and a man screamed.

"Oh, no!" Sabina said.

The downstairs gun exploded several more times, and another one joined in. Now the sounds of objects hitting each other were simultaneous with a variety of yelling and screaming.

"Stay here," Delbit said sharply. "Let me check." He ran forward to the staircase and rapidly tiptoed down. At the landing he dropped to the floor and peered cautiously around the corner and down the next flight.

Men and women in various stages of dishabille were running about from door to door, screaming at each other as they pulled their clothes on. In the lobby four men in the blue suits of the

Klementine staff were hiding behind various articles of furniture, coolly shooting at seven or eight men all in black, who were grouped behind an upturned piano and returning the gunfire with beams of crackling light. A door farther down the hall was suddenly kicked open, and two of the black-clad horde appeared in the doorway and began firing in support of their comrades.

Several men had come out of various upstairs rooms, and were crouching on the stairway behind Delbit. "Anarchists!" one of them declared, aiming a small, silvered pistol over Delbit's shoulder. "The revolution has finally come!"

"But why would it begin here?" another asked, clutching his cavalry saber firmly in his hand and peering down the stairs.

"Excuse me, gentlemen," Delbit said. "I must see to the ladies." He pushed his way by them back up the stairs and returned to the king's room.

"Well?" King Sigismund asked, looking petulant. "More bees?"

"Yes," Delbit said.

"I thought so." The king turned to Sabina. "They must really want you, my dear. And they have our exits blocked. This house exists only on these two strands, and I don't fancy dropping two or three stories to the ground on some other strand. I suppose if they close in, we'll have to chance it."

Viola took a spherical object that looked like a black tennis ball out of her handbag and spent a minute whispering into it. Then she tossed it into the air in front of her and, with a soft pop, it disappeared.

"What was that?" the king asked. "The ball went and you stayed. A good trick."

"A complex mechanism," Viola told him, "that is going to bring us help. I assume we do need help?"

There was the sound of shooting on the staircase.

"Any assistance will be gratefully accepted," King Sigismund said.

"I could try to sneak downstairs and blip to another strand," Sabina said. "It's me they're after. They'll leave you alone."

"No, thanks," Delbit said. "I venture we're all in this together."

The king looked at Delbit as though he were about to say something, but then he changed his mind.

"We'd better barricade the door," Viola said. "The arrival of help will not be immediate."

They dragged three couches over to the door and piled them one on top of another, wedging them together as firmly as possible.

"Now what?" King Sigismund asked. "I am better at strategy then tactics."

"Now we find separate objects to hide behind, so we're not all bunched up together," Viola told him, "and we shoot anything that tries to come through that door until we know it's friendly."

"I have a small pistol that will not be of much use," King Sigismund said, pulling an automatic smaller than his palm from a pocket of his fur cape. "Were it not that all gentlemen go armed in this strand, I would not even have this. I'm not even sure it's loaded." He squeezed the trigger, and the gun went off with a loud burp, and bits of plaster flaked off the wall. "It is loaded," he said, looking startled.

"That is a high-velocity, hollow-point slug," Viola said, examining the damaged spot on the wall. "You will seriously annoy anyone you hit with that, despite its small size."

"Really?" the king said, looking at his gun with new interest. "And I always thought it was a toy."

CHAPTER TWENTY-ONE

It took ten minutes for the fighting to reach the door to their room. By then the exterior defenders were clearly in retreat, and the Friends of the Bee held sway in the outside hall. They began methodically pounding on the door until they had pushed it open a few inches. A black-clad arm was thrust through the opening, and it began prying at the piled-up couches. Viola blasted the arm with quick shot, and it was withdrawn. The noises stopped.

"Going to go discuss it, probably, and work out a plan," Sabina said when Delbit wondered aloud where they had gone. "These bees are very methodical."

"You there inside the room!" a high-pitched voice called from the hallway. "We want the princess. We are to restore her to her friends. She will not be harmed. You will not be harmed. Otherwise, we must use violence, which we would deeply regret. Throw down your weapons!"

There was a pause. Finally King Sigismund stood up. "Nuts!" he yelled, in as loud and as deep a voice as he could manage.

They all looked at him, and he shrugged. "I read it somewhere, on another strand," he said. "It seemed appropriate."

The Friends of the Bee outside spent some time muttering among themselves, and then one of them called, "It is you who are nuts!" and several shots were fired in through the crack in the door.

"Don't fire unless you actually see a target," Viola said. "We don't have all that much ammunition."

"How much does one of these beamers hold?" Delbit asked.

"About fifty charges," Viola said. "And I have several extra bulbs in my bag. But still, that's not many against a determined foe. And these black bugs seem to be determined."

"What about the police?" Viola asked.

"They're probably outside the building already," King Sigismund told her. "But they won't attempt to come in. The Berlin police are, after all, unarmed on this strand. They will wait until later today when they can get a high court order to draw weapons before they storm the house. At which time we'd best keep out of their way, since they'll shoot anything that moves."

There was an explosion from the hall, and the top of the door blew in, scattering debris around the room. The couches stacked below moved an inch, but they still held.

"I have always believed that solid furniture is a good investment," King Sigismund said.

"Come on, you sons of bees," Viola yelled. "One of you stick your head through the door. Come on!"

A hand appeared briefly in the doorway and tossed in a black cylinder, which rolled to the center of the room.

"Gas!" Delbit yelled.

A black-clad figure appeared in the doorway long enough to fire three shots with his beamer, and then he was gone.

Sabina darted out from behind her couch and grabbed the cylinder off the floor. She stood up and disappeared.

Five seconds later she reappeared in the center of the room without the cylinder. She took two steps toward Delbit, and then collapsed on the floor.

Delbit ran out and picked her up, half-carrying and half-dragging her to the protection of his upturned couch. "The gas got her," he cried, cradling her in his arms. "What can I do?"

Viola blasted several shots out the door to discourage the bees, and ran across the room to Delbit's couch. "She's all right," she said after checking Sabina's pulse and bending over to listen to her breathing. "She'll wake up shortly. In the meantime—"

King Sigismund's pistol cracked three shots off, and they

heard a scream from beyond the door and then a muttered curse to an unknown god.

For five long minutes nothing further happened. Then, with a series of three quick, sharp explosions, a section of the wall to the left of the door disintegrated, blasting splintered wood over the room. When the dust cleared, three black-clad bees began blasting deadly beams of energy into the room from behind an upturned dining table. One of the curtains behind Delbit caught fire and burned with a black smoke.

Slowly the bees pushed the heavy table forward, and two more bees appeared in the hole behind them. Another pair ducked behind the piled-up couches in front of the door and shot steadily and methodically into the room.

"This is it!" Sabina whispered. "They're getting ready to move in!"

A light blinked on Viola's bracelet.

"Drop to the floor!" she yelled, pulling Delbit down. The king flattened himself behind his couch without question.

There was a high-pitched whine, and a section of the far wall dissolved. Men in blue body armor with strange-looking handguns poured through the hole in a well-orchestrated rush, surrounding the black bees and firing selectively to disarm when they could. In a few moments the battle was over, with six bees wounded, three dead, and four captured stunned but unharmed. Several others, perhaps as many as a dozen, blipped into nothingness rather than be captured.

King Sigismund got up from behind his couch, dusted himself off, and went over to inspect the prisoners. "I could have sworn...," he said, peering at each one closely. Then, with a muttered exclamation, he reached forward and ripped one of their faces off, revealing a pasty-white face beneath the rubber mask. "I thought I recognized that voice!" he said.

"Baron Vayst!" Sabina said.

"Even so."

The baron spat at King Sigismund and twisted around, trying to break free of the trooper holding him.

Sigismund slapped Baron Vayst hard across the face. "He was about to disappear," he told the astonished trooper holding the baron, "and I had to distract him. If he took you through with him, you might not survive the trip. Tie his hands and feet securely. That should discourage him. Or make him easy to retrieve if he does choose to blip away."

Preceptor Parr peeled off his blue armor. "It looks like you people have been having fun," he said. "What has been going on here?"

* * * * * * *

Two days later they were sitting in the Purple Room in Schloss Baum, the castle of the Dukes of Falkynberg, talking to a very relieved Duke Edgar.

"It is clear what happened," the duke said. A slender man with a short salt-and-pepper beard trimmed straight across at the bottom, he paced back and forth across the rug. "I have been remiss. I thought the title Guardian of Elb was a mere formality, and that the duties were meaningless. Obviously others thought otherwise. The baron was convinced of this strongly enough to kidnap my daughter and enlist the aid of the Friends of the Bee. Although how he managed that is a question in itself, since they won't associate with anyone else."

"Perhaps he has always been a member," King Sigismund suggested.

"And you—" the duke said, waving a finger at Sigismund.

The king raised his pudgy hands in front of him. "I know, I know. I, also, have been remiss. I believed when I should have doubted. I have learned a great lesson."

"We shall have to find out about this," Duke Edgar said. "Perhaps we should start by attempting to discover what really happened to the Guardian of Elb. There are secrets within secrets here, that become visible now that we have peeled back the edge." He turned to Preceptor Parr and Viola, who were sitting together to the side of the room. "How I can thank you, I don't know. Tell me what I can do."

"I think we shall be able to help each other quite a bit over the coming years," Preceptor Castimere Parr told the duke. "It will be for the future to see who remains in whose debt."

"Well said," Duke Edgar agreed. He turned to Delbit. "And you, sir—it seems I owe you everything. And therefore, anything I possess is yours. Name it."

Delbit looked at Sabina, who was sitting several feet away. She got up and came over to take his hand. "Whatever you want," she said to him softly.

Delbit stood up. "Thank you, your grace," he said. He squeezed Sabina's hand. "I don't think I'm ready to have the only thing I might ask you for. I am returning to the Overline with Preceptor Parr, who has promised to do something about my lack of education. When I have figured out just what I want to be, and have taken some steps toward attaining it, I will remind you of your offer. Until then, I only hope to remain a welcome guest in your house whenever I can manage to come by this way."

"A welcome guest in any of my houses, I assure you," the duke said. "You show more wisdom than most, and you speak well."

Delbit looked embarrassed. "Your daughter and I had a long talk about this," he said. "I think most of the words are hers."

What Sabina had said to Delbit was: "I think I love you, and I think I would go anywhere you ask and do anything you wish. But I think that would fade, and in a very few years I would no longer respect you. If you want to go off and become the person I could respect for all of time, I will be here waiting." The most difficult thing Delbit had ever done in his life was agree, even though he knew she was right.

"I have never had reason to doubt my daughter's wisdom," Duke Edgar said.

Later that afternoon Castimere Parr and Viola D'epp walked together down a garden path. "Kiss me," Parr said.

Viola looked at him. "Yes, master," she responded. Taking

his face in her hands, she kissed him; and he held her perhaps a bit more tightly than usual.

"That is the last command I shall ever give you," he told her when she released his mouth from hers.

"What do you mean?" she asked.

He took a folded paper from inside his jacket. "With the greatest pleasure," he said, handing it to her.

She opened it. "Citizen?" she said. "What does this mean? What is Grand Council order two sixty-three dash eighty-two?"

"I just handed a similar document to Quint," the preceptor told her. "It means you are a citizen of the Overline. It means you are a free citizen of the Overline."

"How can it be?"

"That special provision I mentioned," Parr said. "GCO two sixty-three dash eighty-two. A special citizenship quota for people from another strand who perform a useful service for the Overline, putting their own lives at risk beyond the call of duty. It's usually used for the mercenaries, but nothing in the regulation says it is so restricted."

"Then I'm free?"

"As a bird."

"You are clever."

"It's my one redeeming feature."

"I am no longer a slave?"

"Citizens of the Overline cannot enslave other citizens of the Overline."

Viola let go of his hand. "I can do whatever I want?"

"Within certain limits."

"I don't have to make love to you anymore?"

Parr looked at her and shook his head slightly. "No, you don't have to."

"Good," she said. "Let's make love."

"Willingly," he said, taking her in his arms.

ABOUT THE AUTHOR

MICHAEL KURLAND is the recipient of two Edgar scrolls and was nominated for an American Book Award for his first Moriarty novel, *The Infernal Device*. Among his other works are *Death by Gaslight*, *Ten Little Wizards*, *A Study in Sorcery*, *The Unicorn Girl*, and *Star Griffin*. His most recent work of nonfiction, an idiosyncratic history of Forensic Science called *Irrefutable Evidence*, has enjoyed a European vogue. The latest Moriarty novel, *Who Thinks Evil*, will be released shortly to great acclaim. His works have been translated into Chinese, Czech, Danish, French, German, Hungarian, Italian, Japanese, Polish, Portuguese, Russian, Spanish, Swedish, and some alphabet full of little pothooks and curlicues.

Mr. Kurland presently lives in a Secular Humanist Hermitage in a secluded bay north of San Francisco, California, where he kills and skins his own vegetables. His website is michaelkurland.com. Missives sent to mjkurl@gmail.com will reach him.

www.ingramcontent.com/pod-product-compliance
Lightning Source LLC
Chambersburg PA
CBHW021243260626
47155CB00004BA/1282